Scratch Planet

David Waters

Shipshapery by Thalia Proctor. No doubt still making friends,
meeting penguins and reading books in a much better place. A marvel
of a person. A marvel of a friend.
Miss you x.

Scratch Planet
Copyright 2022 by David Waters
ISBN: 9798809118392. (paperback)

Sounds harsh, but I'm pretty easy going, so feel free to contact me at
mywispatok@gmail.com

General book cover design by mdashiqur3 (Fiverr)

Character art on front cover by **Giovanna Perez** - check out
www.behance.net/GiovannaPerezC and **Instagram** (strange_introverse Strange Tales
From Rendavan)

This book is dedicated to Buggy and Fourforty and Chisel and Scuba who are most definitely real . . . kind of . . . maybe . . . well, as real as any of us . . .

But, whether real or fictional, love the characters in your life every day, because every day gets shorter and shorter.

Chapter One

Sinewy strands tangled in his frantic fingers. Roots! He changed direction – towards the roots – *upwards*. In his head, the counter went back down to zero. He started again, focusing, counting each scratch he made. One, two, three . . . six . . . ten . . . twenty . . . loose soil and tiny clumps of grass dropped onto his face. He pushed hard with his right hand and broke through into cool, fresh air. A stream of it filtered into his cramped tunnel. The boy sucked in some delicious deep breaths. Almost there. He pulled his hand back inside and stared through the gap. The night sky gave a sinister wink. *Come out if you dare.*

Squeezing his head through first, he wriggled free like a caterpillar emerging from a chrysalis. Born again. His first thought was for his family. Their house . . . *his* house . . . crushed. It wasn't the only one. The whole street had been levelled . . . the road, the pavement, shattered. No one could have survived that. And yet, as he gazed around, he didn't feel sad, he didn't feel a sense of loss. In fact, quite the reverse, he felt . . . *in good spirits*. There had to be survivors. Not everyone could have been caught inside buildings.

He scanned his murky surroundings for movement. At the base of the hillside, something caught his eye. A shadowy silhouette emerged from behind a hedgerow. He recognised the gait. 'Buggy . . . HEY, BUGGY!' No response. Too far away. The boy got to his feet and began stumbling down the slope. He called out again, 'Buggy! Hey, Bug! You OK? What happened? Another sinkhole? A quake? You seen anyone else?'

Buggy turned and raised a finger to his lips. He pointed towards a construction site portaloo. It was pretty much the only thing left standing amongst the rubble. A continuous muffled drone carried over the silence. It was coming from inside. The two boys crept forwards. An arm's length from the door, they paused. With a nod from his friend, Buggy reached for the latch.

There was a sudden metallic screech as the door burst open. An old woman shot out, holding a small leather-bound bible in front of her like a shield. She screamed as she moved, 'Get thee behind me, Satan!'

Buggy reeled backwards, cradling the hand that had been smashed by the opening door. 'JESUS CHRIST, MRS MAGNER!'

The old woman froze, her eyes wide and wild. She turned her face towards Buggy, tilting her head slightly. 'Don't you blaspheme! He was here!' She drew the bible to her chest. The silver embossed cross glinted in the moonlight. 'You, young Simeone . . . Simeoney . . . what is it they call you?'

'Buggy.'

'That's right. I remember you. He came in the night. Did you hear him, Bugger, you and your friend?'

Buggy bent over, hands on knees, taking a moment to recover. 'It's Buggy, Mrs Magner. People call me Buggy. And this is my friend . . . erm . . . ' he paused, 'my friend . . . Muddy. Muddy, this is Mrs Magner. She delivers leaflets for the church.' He leaned towards his friend and lowered his voice, 'She's a bit . . . cuckoo, only remembers nicknames. So, I made one up for you.'

'What? Fourteen years and that's the best you could come up with?'

'Have you seen yourself recently?'

'Muddy,' interrupted Mrs Magner. She gave a slight introductory nod of her head.

'Mrs Magner,' acknowledged Muddy. He tried not to stare at the old lady's left eye. It was almost white, like a thick fog had drifted across her eyeball.

'He was here in the night.'

'Who was here?'

'Satan.'

'Oh, right, of course.' Muddy looked to Buggy for help. All he got was a slight frown and shake of the head. *Don't upset her.* 'Where was Satan, Mrs Magner?'

The old lady had a quick look around. 'I hid in there, praying.'

'In the portaloo?'

Mrs Magner nodded slowly. '*The . . . beast . . . knocked . . . at . . . my . . . door.*'

Muddy tried to think of a sensible response but drew a blank. He fired a *you know her, you deal with her* look at Buggy.

Buggy did his best to step up to the plate. He moved to the old lady's side, put a comforting hand on her shoulder. 'Don't worry, Mrs Magner. Satan . . . erm . . . well, it's a portaloo, he probably, you know . . . just needed a dump.'

Mrs Magner grabbed both boys with a strength that belied her wiry frame. 'I will send wild beasts among you,' she hissed, 'which shall rob you of your children, and destroy your cattle, and make you few in number; and your highways shall be desolate. And I will draw out a sword after you; and your land will be desolate, and your cities waste . . .' She went silent. And her silence was magnified a thousandfold. Nothing broke it. No traffic, no TVs, no radios . . . nothing. The three of them stood like that for an age, absorbing the devastation around them. As suddenly as she had grabbed them, Mrs Magner let them go. 'There! Look there!' The old lady stumbled away through the darkness. 'An angel!'

Muddy gave Buggy a gentle shove. 'He probably just needed a *dump*?'

'Just trying to put her mind at ease.'

'And an image of Lucifer laying down a log in her sanctuary is going to do that, is it?'

'Works for me,' shrugged Buggy. 'Mrs Magner! Come back! We should stay together!' he shouted.

The old lady disappeared from view. Both boys set off in pursuit.

Muddy reached the house first. It was wrecked but hadn't been completely flattened like the others. Even in the gloom, Mrs Magner's footprints were clearly visible in the dust outside. They circled around a pile of bricks and led into what used to be a kitchen. From there, the trail went along a hallway and over a fallen lounge door. Inside the lounge, a peculiar stand-off was taking place. Mrs Magner was in the centre of the room, patting her bible and staring at a small girl. The small girl was in the corner of the room, patting her toy dog and staring at Mrs Magner.

The girl looked about five years old. She was covered in dust and bits of debris but the mop of blonde hair on her head seemed to glow in the darkness. Her big blue eyes were like saucers, bloodshot and moist. They were surrounded by circles of clean skin, where she had rubbed the tears with bunched fists. It served to make her eyes look even bigger. Her face was dry now. She had no tears left.

'Angel,' announced Mrs Magner.

'Is that her name?' whispered Muddy.

Mrs Magner said nothing.

Buggy moved forwards for a better view. 'Well, I guess it's her name now.'

The room fell silent.

'I know,' said Muddy, 'let's all stand here staring at the small, frightened child. That should really comfort her after everything that's happened.' He nudged past Mrs Magner and crouched by the girl's side. 'Hi, I'm . . . well, I guess I'm

Muddy. That's my mate Buggy, and that . . .' Muddy struggled to find a suitable description, 'that's Mrs Magner. Is this yours?' He reached towards the girl's toy dog and patted it. The dog had a collar around its neck. The collar had six bands of tiny lights around it. When the collar moved, the lights flickered. The girl looked at the lights and seemed to relax a little, so Muddy continued to pat the toy. 'He's a lovely little dog. I bet you look after him really well. And we're going to look after you really well too. So, there's no need to be afraid anymore. Does he have a name, your dog?'

The girl looked up at Muddy then looked back at the lights without answering.

'No? Well, luckily I've got a great imagination and that means I'm good at making up names.' Muddy paused. 'I think I'll call your little dog . . . err, Little Dog, if that's OK?' He lifted the toy's head. 'Is that OK with you little dog? Hmmm? If I call you Little Dog from now on?' He stooped and put his ear to the toy dog's mouth. 'Pardon? Yes? Oh, that's great. Thanks, Little Dog.' Muddy looked up at the girl's face. She was frowning. Not an angry or fearful frown, but a curious frown, as though she was trying to work out if the boy in front of her really had spoken to her toy dog. 'And what about you?' asked Muddy. 'Looks like we'll be calling you Angel unless you'd like to tell us your real name?'

The girl sniffed. Then picked her nose. Then turned away.

'Alright, well, Angel, you and Little Dog stay here for a moment. Me and Buggy are going to have a look around this house . . . what's left of it. Mrs Magner will stay with you.' As soon as the words left his mouth, he realised how utterly uncomforting they were. He might as well have said, *me and my mate are going to leg it now and leave you alone with the mad old witch, OK?* He ruffled the girl's hair. 'Call us if you need us though.'

Only one bedroom in the entire house was in decent shape. It was missing a wall, but it had a sturdy roof and two useable beds. The boys rescued two mattresses from rubble in the other rooms before fetching Angel and Mrs Magner.

'There's no power anywhere. It's getting a bit lighter out, but it's still too dangerous to go wandering around. We should stay here for a few hours and get some sleep. This room is safe,' assured Muddy. 'Angel, you and Little Dog can have that bed.' He pointed to the bed in the corner, furthest away from the open wall. 'Mrs Magner, that one's yours. Me and Buggy will take the mattresses.'

Muddy dragged his mattress next to Angel's bed and sat with his back up against the wall.

Buggy positioned his by the stairs. He sat and looked out through the open space. 'No sinkhole could have caused all this.'

'Oh, I know what caused it,' said Mrs Magner with unnerving certainty. She lay flat on her bed. 'All in whose nostrils *was* the breath of life, of all that *was* in the dry land, died. And every living substance was destroyed which was upon the ground, both man, and cattle, and the creeping things, and the fowl of the heaven, and they were destroyed.' She drew the bible from her pocket and clasped it to her chest with both hands. She looked like a corpse that had been laid to rest.

Muddy tutted. 'Well, there's a lovely bedtime story for the kids. Thank you, Mrs Magner. Really cheered us all up, that.'

Buggy glanced over, silently mouthed the question, *what's she on about?*

'She's basically saying that everyone in the whole wide world is dead.'

'Oh.' Buggy thought for a moment. 'Well, we're not dead.'

Mrs Magner chuckled and closed her eyes.

'Precisely,' agreed Muddy. 'A good point well made, mate. Listen, maybe each of us should say what we remember from last night. Then we can try to piece together exactly what happened.'

And so, they sat, ready to share their thoughts – two boys, an old lady and a young Angel. And not one of them spoke a single word.

Angel was the first to fall asleep.

Chapter Two

Muddy was woken by a hand pressing down on his mouth.

'Come and have a look at this,' whispered Buggy. He gave a quick nod towards Angel and Mrs Magner. They were both still fast asleep. 'Let's not wake them.'

Muddy eased himself off the mattress. He ached. His fingertips stung. 'Why you up already?' he mumbled.

'Couldn't sleep. Mrs Magner was snoring like a hog. I mean *really* bad. Wouldn't be surprised if it was her snoring that wrecked the village.'

'So where are we going?'

'Out.'

The boys picked their way through the ruins, past the now fallen portaloo, and headed up the hill. Muddy pointed at the hole in the ground where he'd emerged from his premature grave.

'I was close,' said Buggy. He pointed to a small pit a few feet to the left. 'I tried to dig you out.'

'Wouldn't have expected anything less,' said Muddy. 'I'd have haunted you for the rest of your life if you hadn't.'

'Wouldn't have expected anything less,' replied Buggy.

They laughed and walked on.

'You think we were lucky?' asked Muddy.

'Why? Because we happened to be messing around inside the caves when all this happened?'

'Yeah.'

'Erm . . .' Buggy let out a sigh and gave a simple shrug.

'Great answer. Well thought out.' The smile dropped from Muddy's face. He pushed his hands into his pockets and kicked a small boulder, sending it rolling down the hillside. 'This doesn't feel right. When I escaped from the ground last night, I didn't even feel sad,' he confessed. 'I looked around, saw all this, and . . . and thought my family . . . your family . . . gone. But for some reason I just didn't feel sad, like, it didn't feel as if they were . . . '

'Dead,' finished Buggy.

'Yeah.'

'Well check this out.' Buggy stopped at the tree line. He pointed to the far left. 'Over there, a massive sinkhole has opened up on the edge of the village. But here's the crazy thing. Look at the crushed roads and houses.'

Muddy gave the area the once over. 'It's almost neat, like perfect lines of destruction.'

'Or tracks,' offered Buggy. 'The fields, gardens, trees . . . they're virtually untouched. And you know what you just said, about not feeling sad, because it didn't feel as though anyone was dead? Well, I went searching this morning . . .'

'And?'

'No bodies, *anywhere*.'

'They could just be buried.'

'All of them? Thousands of people, all buried out of sight? No. No chance. I know for a fact there were at least a dozen people out on this hill. I saw them before we went into the caves. That was just seconds before the quake started.'

Muddy shook his head. 'So . . . what's happened to everyone?'

'I don't know,' replied Buggy, 'but I'll tell you something else, something even more weird . . . '

'Go on.'

'You might not have noticed, but I haven't come across even *one single*—' Buggy's heart skipped a beat as Mrs Magner stepped out from behind a tree. 'Holy cr—'

'Don't you swear!' warned the old lady.

'Where did you come from!' exclaimed Buggy. 'I nearly sh—'

'Don't you swear!' repeated Mrs Magner.

Buggy bit his tongue. 'Where's Angel?'

'Still asleep.' Mrs Magner moved between the two boys. She squeezed on her bible, as though absorbing the word of the Lord through osmosis. 'And lo, there was a great quake, and the sun became black as sackcloth of hair, and the moon became as blood. And the stars of heaven fell unto the ground, for the great day of his wrath is come; and who shall be able to stand?'

Buggy stared at her. She was starting to get on his nerves. Her words were just religious ramblings. He should ignore them. But he couldn't. They were making him feel uneasy. 'Mrs Magner, please, talk . . . normally, will you?'

Mrs Magner squeezed down harder still on her precious bible and stared at the boys, one eye dull, one eye bright, both eyes tired . . . haunted. 'You're too young. It's not right. It can't be right . . . not right at all.'

'Too young for what? What's not—'

'RUN!'

The three of them turned in unison as a teenage girl came tearing through the trees towards them. 'RUN!' she repeated. 'This way, NOW!'

'Why?' shouted Muddy as she zipped past.

The girl had a quick glance back over her shoulder but kept on running. 'CAN YOU NOT FEEL IT?'

Muddy concentrated. No. He couldn't feel "it". Then the bottom of his jeans shuddered ever so slightly. 'Another quake! Can you run, Mrs Mag . . . ' he cut his question short. Mrs Magner was already halfway down the slope, following the girl. He turned to Buggy. 'Leg it!'

'Angel!' shouted Buggy, 'she's still in the house. It won't stand up to another quake.'

Muddy changed direction. 'We'll have to be quick!'

The boys sprinted down the hillside, over the piles of bricks and across the shattered roads. As they reached the doorway to the house, Muddy slowed up. 'You get Angel, I'll watch where that girl goes.'

Buggy came out a few moments later carrying Angel over his shoulder like a fireman.

'You OK carrying her like that?' asked Muddy.

'Light as a feather,' lied Buggy.

Side by side, the boys took up a slow jog. Muddy led. 'The girl took Mrs Magner up towards our old school. They went out of sight where the park joins the playing field.'

Buggy nodded. Around them the vibrations grew steadily more violent. He was breathing hard. 'You thinking . . . what . . . I'm thinking?' he asked.

'That you're already knackered, and you need to get down the gym and sort yourself out?'

'Unusually . . . heavy feather. You know . . . what . . . I mean.'

'Yeah,' said Muddy. 'The girl. She's gone underground.'

Buggy smiled. 'We . . . got . . . week's detention . . . going in there. Those were. . . the days.'

'Pass Angel to me,' said Muddy, realising his friend really was starting to struggle. 'I'll take her for a while. We'll do it like a relay.'

Every hundred metres or so, Angel was passed from one to the other. She clung to her carrier like a limpet. As they neared the school field, loose rubble and trembling ground made the footing treacherous.

'Over here! HURRY!' It was the girl. She was holding the metal cover to the school's underground storage unit open.

Buggy was forced to slow down as he reached the entrance. The child draped across his shoulder was squirming and fussing. 'What's wrong with Angel?'

Muddy looked at her. She'd started crying but didn't look hurt. 'Nothing,' he said. 'She's just scared.'

Angel's crying immediately turned to wailing. She added pointing to the performance.

'Wait!' shouted Muddy. He turned around, scanned the route they'd taken. The sparkle of tiny white lights caught his eye. 'It's Little Dog . . . she's dropped Little Dog.'

'Tough.' Buggy kept on walking.

'You take her inside. I'll go back for Little Dog. It's all she's got.' Muddy ran for the toy, falling twice before he reached it. In the distance he saw the house they'd slept in crumble to the ground. The vibrations worsened. By the time he got back to the underground entrance, he was on all fours with Little Dog's ear clamped in his mouth. The girl was still there, holding the metal access flap open. She grabbed his arm and pulled him inside.

'Worth risking yourn life for a stuffed plaything?' she asked, her voice shuddering with the quake.

Mouth still full of toy, Muddy nodded. 'Uh huh.'

'Follow the tunnel. There is a storage room at the very end. The others are in there.'

Muddy looked along the passageway. Soil was falling from the ceiling like brown rain. He hesitated. 'I'm not sure I can go,' he said. 'I've already been buried alive once.'

The girl glared at him. 'Move now or you will not be buried alive, you will be buried dead.'

When Muddy still didn't budge, she gave his shoulder a reassuring squeeze. 'Go. Trust me. We will all be safe in there. And we will not have to stay long.'

Muddy yanked his jacket over his head to shield himself from the falling clumps of soil. Halfway down the passageway, he glanced back. The girl was still at the door. It looked like she was trying to bolt it shut. What good would that do in a quake?

When he entered the room, Muddy went straight over to Angel. He gave Little Dog to her. The effect was immediate. As soon as Little Dog's collar sparkled, Angel calmed down. Her arms quietly embraced the toy. Her eyes quietly embraced the dimly lit space.

'Hey,' Buggy stood up to greet his friend. 'It sounded horrendous out there.'

'Trust me, it looked worse than it sounded.'

'Great,' said Buggy, 'and where's the girl?'

'On her way, I think.'

'She's . . . unusual.'

'What do you mean, *unusual?* We don't even know her.'

'Ooooh,' Buggy jumped all over the defensive reply, 'you lurve her.'

'And you love Mrs Magner,' snapped Muddy.

There was a moment of silence. Then both boys laughed. 'You went too far then,' said Buggy. 'But seriously, come on . . . you've seen what she's wearing, right? A black wetsuit! And you don't think she's unusual?'

'She might have been swimming or surfing.'

'In the woods!' Buggy tapped on his friend's head. 'Err, hello? She's a weirdo. Fit though,' he added, just as the girl came in from the corridor.

'Who is fit?' she asked.

'Erm, you know,' said Buggy, 'we err . . . we were just saying how Mrs Magner is very fit . . . for her age . . . athletic. Didn't you see how fast she sprinted down the hill after you?'

'No.' The girl crouched against the wall. Talking didn't seem to be on her agenda.

Muddy went over and sat next to her. 'What's going on out there?'

'A plague,' piped up Mrs Magner.

Muddy ignored her. He turned back to the girl. 'Really, what is it?'

The girl shrugged. 'Why are you asking me? The old woman might be correct for all I know.'

'You told me we'd be safe in here, as though you knew for sure.'

'And we will be.'

'Mmmm.' Mrs Magner nodded in agreement. 'There shall no evil befall thee, neither shall any plague come nigh thy dwelling.'

'See?' said the girl. 'The old lady . . . knoweth.'

'The old lady spouteth rubbish,' whispered Muddy. He leaned back and rested his head against the wall. 'So, have you got a name?'

'Have you?' snapped the girl.

'Blimey, you're a bit prickly. Well, as it happens, we appear to be going by nicknames right now. Easier to remember for Mrs Magner. I'm Muddy. That's Buggy and that's Angel . . . oh, and you've met Little Dog, of course.'

The girl nodded. She looked up at Buggy. He was restless, pacing to and fro. 'How did you get that appellation?'

'How did I get that what?'

The girl paused. 'That . . . nickname, "Buggy".'

Her question had its desired effect. Buggy came to a stop. 'You really want to know?'

She nodded.

Angel let out a little giggle. 'Bug . . . Bug . . . Bug . . . Bug . . . Bug eeeee.' She giggled again.

'You too?' smiled Buggy. 'Alright then.' He folded his arms and leaned against the wall. 'Well, I was fascinated by insects when I was a baby. Used to crawl around the garden pointing at them. I didn't know the different species, so I just used to call everything "bug". It was my first word. Before "mamma" or "dada" even. When I was three, I made a toy car in the shape of a bug using two skateboards, some cereal packets and about a bucketful of glue. Mum and Dad liked it so much they drilled some hooks into the garage wall and hung it there. I didn't like that. I wanted it to be outside with the other bugs. But I had to wait until I was five years old before I was tall enough to unhook it.' Buggy pointed at Muddy. 'He helped me lift it off the wall, and we carried it to the top of the drive. I had this theory you see, I was confident, at the time . . . bear in mind I was only five . . . that if I sat in my bug car and he pushed hard enough, it would sprout wings and fly. So, I sat in it. And he pushed me. *Hard*.'

Muddy grinned. 'I've always been very thorough.'

'And so, me and my bug car did fly,' continued Buggy, 'down the driveway and straight into the iron garage post. Then me and the piece of bug car that was embedded in my shin flew to hospital.' He lifted the bottom of his trouser leg.

'See? The main scar looks like a bug body and the thin scars left by the stitches look like bug legs.'

The girl raised an eyebrow in acknowledgement. 'And you?' she said, turning to Muddy. 'How did you get yourn nickname?'

'I got covered in mud. Last night.'

The girl stayed attentive. After the impressive bug story, she was obviously expecting more.

'That's all I've got,' shrugged Muddy.

'Oh. OK.' The girl stood and walked over to some shelving on the wall. 'I prefer yourn story,' she said, glancing back at Muddy. 'It is straightforward and to the point.'

Behind the girl's back Buggy mouthed *I prefer your story* at his friend. Then he blew a few silent kisses. Muddy rolled his eyes and flicked him the V.

The girl lifted three sleek backpacks from the middle shelf. They were made from the same black material as her wetsuit. She put one on. The material appeared to merge with her clothing, following the contours of her body. This made the backpack hardly noticeable. She handed one to Buggy, then one to Muddy. 'Time to move,' she said. 'You should leave the old woman behind.'

Buggy snorted a laugh. 'That's not a bad idea! I knew I'd end up liking you.' But when the girl remained straight-faced, it dawned on him that she wasn't joking. He shook his head, as though trying to dislodge the disbelief. 'What?'

'The little girl too. Leave them both.'

'I think I speak for everyone when I say you can stick that idea up your—'

'Don't you swear!' warned Mrs Magner.

Buggy bit his tongue for the second time that day, but his patience with the old lady was wearing thin.

Angel shuffled towards the corner of the room.

'Mrs Magner,' said Buggy, 'are you even listening to what this girl is saying? She is talking absolute—'

'Don't swear!' The old lady cut in again. 'No. No. You control yourself, young man. If you feel a bad word coming out, substitute it for another one . . . you substitute it for . . .' Her good eye flicked around the room, quickly scanning the shelves . . . books . . . boxes . . . sports equipment . . . nets . . . bags . . . bats . . . boxing gloves . . . empty bottles of . . . 'Pop!' she blurted. 'You substitute it with "pop".'

Buggy shook his head. 'I am surrounded by—'

'Don't you swear!' Mrs Magner's jaw went rigid. A bit of spittle hung from her bottom lip, boinging like a bungee rope.

Angel wriggled tight to the wall and covered Little Dog's ears.

'Bug,' Muddy called out. 'We all need to stay calm, mate. Everyone's a bit tense, not just you.'

'"A bit TENSE"? I don't think I'm getting tense! I think I'm going completely nuts! One minute me and you are messing about in the caves like we've done since we were five years old, the next minute the whole world is smashed to smithereens! Now it's like no one else ever existed.' He pointed at the girl. 'This girl runs out of the woods in *scuba* gear shouting "follow me" like some kind of crazy—'

'DON'T YOU SWEAR!' shouted Mrs Magner.

'STOP TELLING ME NOT TO SWEAR! IT'S *YOU* SHE WANTS TO LEAVE BEHIND YOU . . . YOU . . . POPPING SENILE OLD POP!'

'SEE!' screamed Mrs Magner. 'YOU CAN DO IT IF YOU TRY!'

'ENOUGH!' Muddy stepped in between the two of them. 'Listen, this girl just saved our skins, no question,' he looked at Buggy, ' . . . right?'

Buggy gave a reluctant nod.

'OK. Good.' Muddy turned back to the girl. 'But he's right, we're not going anywhere without Angel and Mrs Magner. You *are* crazy if you think we'd leave them behind.'

The girl looked agitated, like she wanted to argue but didn't have the time. 'Bring them then. Do not say I did not try to warn you when this decision comes back to bite you in the . . . ' she glanced at Mrs Magner, 'pop.' Jamming her shoulder up against a large grey cabinet, the girl pushed. The cabinet slid along the ground. There was a tunnel cut into the wall behind it. 'This way,' she said.

Muddy ushered Angel and Mrs Magner forward. The old lady nodded and patted his hand in silent thanks.

Buggy hung back until everyone except Muddy was out of earshot. 'What are we doing?'

'She saved us from the second quake.'

'If it *was* a quake . . . '

'What do you mean?'

'All the time the ground was shaking, I could hear something else in the background. Something distant. It sounded . . . mechanical.'

Muddy nodded. 'I heard it too. When I went back for Little Dog.' He shook his head. 'This is just . . . insane.'

'And I keep thinking about the view from the hillside,' added Buggy. 'The pavements and houses crushed and churned up evenly. I mean . . . what are the chances of a quake doing that? It's almost as if they'd been . . . I don't know . . . ploughed, or something.'

'Maybe we're still in shock from last night?' offered Muddy. 'You don't usually lose your temper like that. We're not thinking straight . . . we could be hallucinating even?'

Buggy shook his head. 'Hallucinating or not, there's something very wrong about that girl. Her clothes, her accent . . . and were you listening to what she just said? She wanted to leave a little old lady and a young child behind. And do you know what . . . she *meant* it. And we're just going to follow her?'

'I don't think we have a choice. She seems . . .' Muddy patted the backpacks and pointed to the tunnel, 'prepared.'

Chapter Three

It was getting hot. The morning sun had risen fast and fierce. It set a green carpet of dew sparkling at their feet. The group had fallen into a line – the girl leading, Mrs Magner and Angel next, then the two boys bringing up the rear. Muddy was trying not to look at the girl. She'd caught him staring at her twice now. He fixed his gaze on Mrs Magner and Angel instead. Why had the girl wanted to leave them behind? Did she think they wouldn't be able to keep up? One too old, one too young? But they were doing OK. And the two of them seemed to have formed a bit of a bond. Perhaps a joint sense of defiance had brought them together? One of Angel's hands was clamped to the old lady's. Her other hand was clamped to Little Dog. She was dipping him up and down, letting his legs and tail brush against the tall grass. It was like a scene from a family picnic. So normal. So abnormal.

'How long have we been walking? We haven't seen another soul.'

Buggy's question snapped Muddy from his trance. 'I can't tell. Not even sure where we are. She's been keeping to the countryside. Haven't seen any landmarks. Anyway, you're the best at geography.'

'Not when there's nothing visible above the trees. And we haven't been travelling in a straight line. I guess if our village is anything to go by, all landmarks have been flattened,' replied Buggy. 'So . . . no landmarks . . . and no people. Mrs Magner was right. The whole world *is* dead.' He took out his handkerchief and blew his nose. The quakes hadn't destroyed hayfever. 'Why would she deliberately keep to the countryside?'

Muddy shrugged. 'Safer maybe? Why don't you ask her?'

'Can't.'

'Why not?'

'Don't know her name. She never told us.'

'Oh yeah,' nodded Muddy. 'Maybe it's time she got her nickname then?'

'Well . . . what about "Mrs Muddy", since you love her and everything?'

Muddy laughed. 'You nob.'

'Whoa! Hold on! You can't say things like that!' Buggy wagged a reprimanding finger. 'You have to use "pop" from now on, remember?'

'Apologies. You popping nob.'

'Better,' acknowledged Buggy. 'Look at this. What do you think it is?' He held up a tiny canister that he'd pulled from his backpack. It had a nose-sized dent in the top with a button next to it. He gave the button a cautious squeeze. A puff of air slapped his face.

'What are you doing!' hissed Muddy. 'You can't just mess about with this stuff. It could be anything!'

'There's no smell,' replied Buggy. Almost immediately, a grin spread across his face, and he snorted out a little laugh. 'It might help my asthma.'

'Yeah, sure,' nodded Muddy, 'the random item you pulled out of the random backpack given to you by the random girl is perfect for your asthma.'

Buggy gave the canister another little squirt. He smiled again.

'Why are you smiling like an idiot?'

'No,' coughed Buggy. His smile widened. He pressed the nozzle again.

Muddy manoeuvred his friend into the trees, out of sight of the others. 'Answering that question by saying "no" doesn't even make sense!' He snatched the canister away. 'You have no idea what's in this!' He looked at the surface of the canister closely. There was no writing on it. No clue as to its contents. He looked back up at Buggy. His shoulders were shaking with the effort of holding back a laugh. Muddy raised the nozzle to his own nose, gave the canister a little squirt. Sniffed. Buggy was right. There was no odour. He gave it a longer press in case he'd missed something. 'No,' he said.

'No,' repeated Buggy. That simple word seemed to tip him over the edge. He couldn't hold back the laughter any longer. Between guffaws, he sucked just enough air into his lungs to allow him to speak. 'Scuba!' he managed. 'We . . . should call . . . her . . . Scuba!'

Muddy chuckled. He squirted the canister a few more times. 'And this must be her oxygen tank for the forests and trees that she swims through!' he added, before creasing up himself.

The girl had backtracked as soon as she'd noticed the boys were missing. She moved through the trees and stood, watching, silent, incredulous. The boys were in hysterics. Tears were rolling down their cheeks. They could hardly breathe. They looked as though they were about to do themselves an injury.

Buggy was the first to notice her. He pointed. 'We . . . just . . . named you!'

Muddy pointed too. Pointing was suddenly the funniest thing he'd ever done. 'Scuu . . . ba!' he squeaked. The boys doubled over, clutching their sides. They grabbed each other for balance and roared again. It was no good. Standing was far too hard. They slowly fell to their knees and melted to the ground in fits. 'Look,' howled Muddy. He began to mime a front crawl. 'Remember when we first saw her . . . swimming . . . through the . . . woods!' His voice rose higher with each word. He was only just able to squeeze them out. Both boys went apoplectic. Buggy began doing the breaststroke, which somehow started him moving slightly backwards along the ground. That destroyed any control that may have remained in Muddy.

'I'm . . . sinking!' shouted Buggy. He had no idea if anyone could hear him. He could hardly hear himself.

The girl just stood and watched. She was unsure of what to do. She'd never come across people behaving in such a manner. 'Mine scratchgas sample!' she snarled, noticing the now-empty canister. Rage flared inside her. But under the circumstances, what could she do? Certainly not what she *wanted* to do. She hauled the boys off the ground, accepted her nickname and said nothing more. The less they knew, the better. It would all be over soon.

It was a long time before the boys came to their senses. Longer still before the girl spoke to them. 'I can hear water. Is there a river nearby?'

'Could be,' answered Muddy. 'But . . . Scuba . . . ' He sensed Buggy wincing beside him, but he didn't know what else to call the girl. And she didn't seem to mind her new name. '. . . I don't exactly know where we are any more.'

Scuba pointed to a bowl-shaped dip in the in the ground. It had some sawn tree trunks arranged inside it like benches. 'Rest there for a while.'

Muddy thought he should try to clear the air. 'Listen, I'm sorry about the arguing in the school storeroom earlier . . . and the . . . other . . . laughy thing.'

Scuba gave a dismissive shake of her head. 'Understandable. It is wearing off. Now I am going to have a quick look around. There are snacks in yourn backpacks. Eat some. They will help,' she added as she walked away.

Muddy waited for her to go out of sight. He dropped his backpack next to Buggy. 'Look after this. Need the loo. Back in a bit.'

'Wait, what's "wearing off"?' asked Buggy.

'Eh?'

'She just said "it" is wearing off.'

'I don't know. The shouty arguey atmosphere maybe. Gotta go.'

Scuba had already disappeared among the trees, but her footfalls had squashed the sparkle from the grass. Muddy followed the dark patches of green. Spying hadn't crossed his mind. He just wanted to meet up with the girl and talk, away from the others. But something in his head screamed caution. Without even realising, he began stepping more and more carefully over the twig covered ground. He heard the river before he spotted Scuba. She was standing on a large rock in a horse-shoe shaped clearing. Muddy stopped. This was close enough. A row of saplings provided him with cover. He eased the top branches down for a clear line of sight. On top of the rock, Scuba looked like a wind-up figurine. Long-limbed and lithe, she was motionless, as though waiting for someone to turn the key and set her spinning. An itchy nose broke the pose. In one fluid movement, she scratched it, slipped her backpack off and turned slightly, into the sun. Her deep brown eyes twinkled. Then, like two black butterflies landing on a precious flower, her eyelashes fluttered and closed. Muddy's gaze was drawn to a tiny brown mole. It sat to the left of the girl's lips like a full stop. It was the only blemish on otherwise flawless skin. It made her even more captivating.

The full stop rose slightly. A smile. She looked peaceful, untroubled – simply enjoying the sensation of warm sun on her face. Her two jet-black plaits wobbled in the breeze. They were thick and rope-like, sticking out from her head at first, then curving in towards the base of her neck. Their tips had been tied off in the shape of a cross.

Scuba's eyes flashed open. Muddy thought he'd been spotted, but the girl turned away and jumped down from her rock plinth. She strolled to the river's edge, paused. Her hands must have been dirty, but instead of washing them, she just wiped them down the sides of her wetsuit. She moved forwards. A series of delicate sploshes reached Muddy's ears. His heart began to thud against his ribcage. His legs gave way under him, forcing him to crouch down and hold onto the trunk of the nearest sapling. He felt like he was about to vomit. *The girl was walking on the water.* Each step left nothing more than a delicate, ever-expanding ring on the river's surface. Halfway across, she stopped and raised her arms to the heavens. A perfect hoop, golden and bright, materialised above her head. Muddy wanted to get up and run, but his legs wouldn't allow it. They were cemented to the spot. Even when the girl began walking back to shore, his legs continued to betray him.

Thinking quickly, Muddy undid his bootlaces. He waited. When the girl brushed past the saplings, he looked up. 'Oh, hey, there you are,' he said. His mouth was dry, his voice hoarse. 'I was just following some footprints, didn't know it was you. Nearly fell over these.' He pointed to his laces and tried to keep his hands from shaking as he re-tied them.

Scuba stared down at him – long enough to make him feel extremely uncomfortable. She spoke slowly, firmly, 'Relax. It is me. Do not be afraid.'

Scuba left. Muddy stayed put. He gazed at the floor, trying to get his head straight, waiting for some strength to return to his legs. When he finally stood, he found Mrs Magner right up in his face. 'What is *wrong* with you, Mrs Magner! Why do you keep creeping up on people?'

The old lady leaned close. Her whispered words brushed across his neck like an icy breeze. 'But when they saw him walking upon the sea, they supposed it had been a spirit and cried out. And immediately he talked with them, and saith unto them. Be of good cheer. It is I. Be not afraid.'

Chapter Four

'You're as white as a sheet! What happened in those woods?' Buggy added a nudge, nudge, wink, wink for good measure.

Muddy didn't say a word. He couldn't get the image of Scuba walking on water out of his mind. Since she'd appeared she'd kept them all safe. She wasn't scared. She wasn't confused. It was as though she was on a mission . . . sent to guide them. And the ring that had appeared above her head? It looked like . . . like a *halo*. Muddy came to a very uncomfortable conclusion. He stared at Scuba, then at Angel. Was it too late to be swapping nicknames around?

'Hey,' hissed Buggy, suddenly more concerned. 'Really, what's the matter?'

'I think I know what's happened,' said Muddy.

Buggy shuffled uneasily. He waited until no one was paying attention, then moved closer to his friend. 'Go on?'

Muddy looked him right in the eye. 'It's not the whole world that's dead. It's just us.'

Buggy opened his mouth as though he was about to speak. He frowned. Closed his mouth. Then he opened it again. 'What do you mean?'

'I can't put it any plainer than that.'

'So . . . you think we're going to die?'

'Listen to me. *We . . . are . . . already . . . dead*. That's why we haven't seen anyone. It's why there are no bodies anywhere. Everyone else is still alive and going about their daily business while we're stuck here in . . . dead . . . land or whatever it is.' Aware that his voice was rising, Muddy stared back at the ground. 'Oh, and Scuba's an angel,' he added.

There was a moment of complete silence.

'Sorry,' said Buggy, 'being dead is obviously affecting my hearing. Scuba's a what?'

'*Scuba . . . is . . . an . . . angel*. She just walked on water. And she's got a halo. I saw it.'

'No no no. That's it.' Buggy shook his head. 'Enough is enough. We've got a mute little girl who does nothing but stare at her sparkly toy dog, Mrs Magner who's . . . who's just *wrong*, and now you're telling me that the nutter in the wetsuit is an angel. No. That's it. I'm not staying with this lot anymore.'

Buggy slapped his hands on his knees. Muddy grabbed hold of his backpack and pulled hard, preventing him from rising. 'You want to run away from an angel? That's your plan?'

Buggy thought for a moment. 'Yeah.'

'And just how do you think you're going to survive?'

'Survive? According to you, we're already dead.' Buggy tapped his backpack all the same.

'Ooooh, right, you see, I thought you were being crazy suggesting running from an angel, but now I realise that you want to run from an angel *and* steal from her? Well, that's OK, then. Great plan, moron.'

'You coming?'

Muddy sighed. He'd known Buggy all his life. And he knew his friend was usually content to go with the flow. It was unusual for him to make such an impulsive decision. But this whole situation was unusual. 'Of course I'm coming,' he said, 'but give me a minute first.' He got up, walked over to Mrs Magner, sat next to her. A few moments later he shouted over to Scuba. 'Hey, Scuba, me and Buggy are going for a quick look around. See if we can pinpoint exactly where we are. Back in a sec.'

Scuba didn't seem overly concerned. 'Be back in five minutes. We need to push on.'

'Sure.'

The boys used the time well, putting as much distance as they could between themselves and the camp. It wasn't long before flashes of grey came into view between the thinning trees. Knowing they were close to a town relaxed them a little. Neither boy had spoken up to that point.

'What did you say to Mrs Magner?' asked Buggy.

'I asked her if she wanted to come with us. She didn't. She said she'd look after Angel. So, then I asked her how they say "you", "your" and "yours" in the bible.'

'Err, why?'

'Because I wanted to know. And she told me they use "thee" or "thou" and "thy" and "thine".'

'Great. So?'

'So . . . I'm not sure,' shrugged Muddy. 'But Scuba kept saying "yourn". I mean, who says that? At first, I figured it must be, you know, religious angel-speak or something. Mrs Magner squashed that theory. Anyway, I also told her we'd be back for her and Angel, as soon as we've worked out what's going on.'

Buggy shook his head. 'Just think about it. What are you saying? Obviously, Scuba's no angel. She wanted to abandon an old lady and a child back in the storeroom, remember?'

'The same old lady and child that you just abandoned, you mean?'

Buggy looked at the floor. 'It's different,' he mumbled. 'Anyway, if Scuba's not an angel . . . what is she? And more importantly, what are we?'

'Alive maybe?' Muddy reached out and pinched his friend's forearm, hard.

'Ow! You . . . pop.'

'Exactly,' smiled Muddy. 'You wouldn't have felt that if we were dead! I was wrong before!'

The boys came to a stop. The town in front of them was deserted. Only about half of it was still standing. The other half was completely flattened, just like their village.

'You remember on the hill yesterday,' said Buggy, 'I was about to tell you something, just before Scuba appeared.'

'Yeah.'

'Well, I'd been out looking for bodies while you were all asleep. And I didn't find any. The thing is, I didn't find anything. *Anything.* I started out thinking, if I'm looking for dead bodies I follow the buzzing of the flies, right? Well, there was no buzzing . . . there were no flies.'

Muddy signalled for quiet. 'You're right. Not just flies. No animal noises at all. No birds. No insects. Nothing.' He pointed to a plume of dust and ash, rising in the distance. 'But there's *definitely* something here.'

A tiny vibration tickled the soles of their feet. The two boys looked at each other.

'We're not running from this one,' said Muddy. 'Come on.'

They moved through the empty streets, hugging the walls, checking around each corner before continuing. As they neared the dividing line between the standing and the shattered, the vibrations grew stronger, and the air grew warmer. The boys peered out from behind the final house. The sound of crunching concrete merged with a deep, ferocious roar. A red glow pulsed across the horizon, illuminating the base of the dust cloud they'd spotted from the woods. *Something* had to be causing it. As they stood and watched, the red glow thickened. The roar grew louder. That could only mean one thing: the *something* was creeping towards them.

'Do not go any further!'

The boys turned around. It was Scuba.

'Stay with me,' she shouted. 'You have no idea what is going on.'

'Are you an angel?' asked Buggy.

'Are you a moron?' came the angry response.

'Yes, he's a moron,' shouted Muddy. He turned to Buggy. 'What did you go and ask her that for?'

'Hang on! You're the one who said she was an angel!'

'Well . . . yeah, but you didn't have to just come right out and say it like that.'

Scuba walked up to them. Mrs Magner and Angel were in tow.

Buggy wanted confirmation. 'So, we're not dead then?'

'No, you are not dead. But linger here for approximately three minutes more and you might be.'

A bank of hot air blew over them, drying their eyes. They all gave a synchronised blink. Streams of molten metal appeared over the horizon. The flowing, glowing liquid bubbled past, filtering into a single ploughed channel just metres from where they stood. It curled and hissed its way to an enormous sinkhole and cascaded over the edge, disappearing into darkness.

Mrs Magner stepped past Scuba, agitated, focused. 'For a fire is kindled in my anger, and shall burn unto the lowest hell, and shall consume the ground with her increase, and set on fire the foundations. They shall be devoured with burning heat, and with bitter destruction: I will also send the teeth of beasts upon them, with the poison of serpents of the dust.'

Mesmerised by the hellish waterfall, everyone stared into the void as Mrs Magner spoke . . . everyone except Buggy. His eyes hadn't shifted from the horizon. He took two shaky steps back, gently thumped Muddy. He pointed. 'What . . . is . . . that?'

A monstrous machine loomed through the ash. Even from such a great distance the group were swallowed by the shadow it cast. Its wheels alone were hundreds of metres high, and equally as wide. Spiked and ridged metal tread smashed through brick as though it was eggshell. Buildings turned to dust in apparent slow motion as the machine rolled forward, steady, relentless. A beam of bright light, coming from the centre of the machine, swept to and fro as it advanced. Most astonishing of all was the source of the red river; housed on the main body of the machine were two colossal serpents, metallic scales glinting. Their heads twisted from side to side as their mouths spewed brutal jets of flame onto the crushed material beneath the wheels. Anything that didn't melt was instantly incinerated.

Muddy turned to the only person not in shock. 'Scuba, what's going on? What are they doing?'

'Destroying anything that is man-made.'

'Why?'

'Because yourn planet is a scratch pla—' Scuba suddenly shoved Muddy aside. 'NO! Buggy! NO!'

No one had noticed him move. And now Buggy was out in the open, too far away to be stopped. He was heading for the beam of light. Was the machine searching for survivors?

Buggy must have thought so. He was running towards it shouting, waving his arms, 'Hey! Stop! Stop! Help us!' The beam sought him out and held steady on his position. He looked so tiny. The circle of light shrank, focused in on him. It turned to strobe lighting, flickering fast and bright.

And Buggy was gone.

'Buggy!' Muddy broke cover and began racing towards the spot where his friend had disappeared. He crashed to the ground as Scuba leapt on top of him. She held him tight and raised her arm. A dome of light, the same colour as her halo, enveloped them both. The spotlight from the machine passed over without stopping. From inside the shield Scuba shouted, 'If it scans you . . . it will move you.'

Muddy stared through the shivering dome, captivated by the gargantuan wheels. The machine kept on coming.

'Can you hear me?' Scuba squeezed his shoulder. 'Can you hear me?' she repeated.

Muddy nodded.

'Do as I say. Do it quickly. Take off yourn clothes.'

'Take off my wh—'

'DO IT NOW!' shouted Scuba.

Turning his back to her, Muddy obeyed without further hesitation. Circumstance seemed to demand it. When he was naked, Scuba reached for his hand. She flattened his palm and then produced a cube of black material, no bigger than a dice, from inside her own suit. A tiny black needle protruded from the centre of one of its sides. Scuba jabbed it into his palm. 'Make a fist. Squeeze it tight.'

Muddy winced. Then he squeezed the cube as though his life depended on it. He felt it soften in his grip. Black liquid began oozing through the gaps in his fingers. But instead of dripping to the floor, the liquid coiled up his arm and spread to cover his entire body. It was a suit. Just like Scuba's.

Scuba reached up and poked the centre of the dome. It disintegrated with a crackle. It had protected them from the machine's light. It had also protected them from the noise. With the shield gone, the sound of destruction was ear-splitting. Scuba pulled Muddy to his feet. A deft flick of her wrist and a tiny pea-sized sphere appeared in her fingers. She shouted through the din as she pushed the goo-covered ball into Muddy's suit, 'Wherever you end up, either blend in or do not get seen!'

'What are you talkin' ab—' Muddy's suit stiffened violently, stealing his breath. He felt faint . . . then *fizzy* . . . then nothing.

Chapter Five

Muddy opened his eyes as soon as he felt the suit relax. He wished he hadn't. He felt the material clear away from his face, but then fragments of it began to elongate from his collar and slither back across his cheeks. He twisted and shook, pawing at his neck to try and block the thin black needles. Silence reigned as the material oozed into each ear cavity. There was a moment of intense pain . . . a hiss, jumbled echoes . . . and a distant whir settled in his head. Blackness spilled into his eyes, momentarily blinding him. More pain. As his vision cleared, so the pain began to subside. In the top corner of his right eye, almost imperceptible, was a tiny circle. Its tone deepened and faded. It looked like a tiny snake chasing its tail. It moved in perfect time to the spectral whirring that had settled in his head.

Muddy tried to take in his surroundings. He was on his back. It was cold. The suit seemed to recognise that. It compensated almost immediately, generating warmth. He was lying in some kind of white powder. More of it was falling from a dusky sky. He reached up, plucked one of the white flakes from the air and brought it close to study it, but as he did so, it turned to liquid. Another landed on his lips like an icy kiss. It too, melted away. He dabbed his tongue onto it. Water! It had turned to water! Shouts and squeals floated through the air. But these were happy shouts and squeals. Not people running from giant crushing machines. Perhaps he wasn't in danger anymore? He sat up. He certainly wasn't next to Scuba anymore. Muddy looked around. His stomach did somersaults as realisation dawned . . . he wasn't even on his own *planet* anymore. Across from him stood black metal railings. Beyond them, a church. Things here were familiar, yet very different. Children were playing in the yard. *Children.* Running between the benches. Scooping up the white powder. Squashing it into a ball shape then throwing it at each other. The white balls exploded on backs and heads and arms, triggering howls of laughter. Muddy found himself smiling too. Their joy was infectious. He squashed a handful of the cold powder. It was amazing. All the individual specks stuck together in a clump that he could mould and shape.

Radio crackle drew his attention away from the churchyard. There was a woman at the top of the street. An adult. The light from the streetlamps fell across her shoulder as she walked. Three small silver numbers glinted. A four, another four and a zero.

'Go ahead. Over.'

'Fourforty delta mike, we've had reports of a disturbance at the church on St Martins . . . over.'

'Yes yes. I'm at the location now. Just kids throwing snowballs. I'll get them to move on.'

'Received. Over.'

Muddy felt his pulse quicken. He could understand the words. People here spoke the same language as him. So, these things were *snow* balls. More laughter from the children as they saw the woman approaching. They scattered . . . their happy squeals disappearing with them down the side streets. The woman made a U-turn and jumped over the church railings. Muddy didn't know what to do. She was heading straight for him. Scuba's words came back to him . . . *blend in or do not be seen*. Well, he'd definitely been seen. That left blending in. Doing what he'd seen others do. He squeezed the ready-made powder ball in his hand. He took aim. And threw. It was a great shot. It hit the woman right in the face, knocking her hat to the floor. Muddy laughed, partly because that's what he'd seen the children do, partly because it was actually quite funny. He waited for the woman to respond likewise . . . and waited some more.

He didn't hear laughter; he heard the words "you little", followed by some unfamiliar words that he couldn't quite catch. The woman grabbed him by the arm. 'That, young man, is assault. You're coming with me. The residents here have had enough of you lot and your antisocial behaviour.'

'I'm sorry,' said Muddy. 'I thought . . . I thought it would be funny.'

'You thought wrong.'

Muddy asked the very next question that sprang to mind. 'What planet are you on?'

'Oh, you think now is the time for cheek?' Fourforty shook her head. 'Here's some free advice. You have the right to remain silent. I think it best you exercise that right.'

Muddy exercised it. All the way to a police station. When they entered, Fourforty went up to a man at the front counter. 'Sergeant, I've got this youth on Assault Constable and Breach of the Peace. Possessions include one backpack.' She looked for the zip. 'How do you open this thing?'

Muddy shrugged. 'I'm not sure.'

Fourforty put the whole backpack into a thick plastic bag. She sealed it and handed it to the Sergeant. 'See what I'm up against? Asked me what planet I was on when I told him he was coming back to the station!'

The Sergeant nodded, hiding a grin. 'Kids today, heh? No respect. I'll book him in. Take him to cell five . . . see if the attitude improves.'

Vibrations shot up Muddy's legs as the cell door crashed shut. It unnerved him. Reminded him of the quakes. He slumped onto a plain blue mattress. Things felt different now. His head felt . . . clearer. But with clarity came pain, and not physical pain this time. One after the other, all the losses began to hit him. His parents. His home. His hope. It was almost impossible to take in. Through the blur of tears, the snake continued to chase its tail . . . only now it was much, much smaller.

In the front office of the Police Station the Sergeant finished up his report. 'I think that's probably long enough for your boy, officer. Thanks for dealing with that. You can get back to your own ground now.'

Fourforty smiled. 'You're too soft, Sarge, it's only been ten minutes.' She strolled over to the cell. 'Hopefully this little experience will make him think twice in future. I'll get some details and send him off with words of advice.'

Standard procedure dictated that she slide the wicket across to ensure the boy was clear of the door. She did it slowly to prolong his detention. Then the officer's actions became more urgent. She fumbled for the keys and rushed in. Her prisoner wasn't just clear of the door, he was clear of the cell. Fourforty scanned the sparse surroundings. 'Sarge! The boy . . . the boy's gone!'

Chapter Six

Scuba was on him before he'd had chance to pull himself together. She didn't say a word, just held him down, put a finger to his lips and signalled for him to look to his left. He found it difficult to contain himself. A second ago he'd been locked in a cell on a different planet. Now he was back home with Scuba. He looked where she had pointed. He saw a creature . . . more of a machine than a creature . . . made up of saucer-shaped metal discs, a crackling purple mist acting like a flexible link between the separate pieces. It moved slowly, carefully. Three leg-like extensions, three arms spread equidistant around the body, one head. The head extended upwards on the purple mist, scanning the edge of the forest with a sheet of red light. When it moved into the trees, Scuba slipped off her backpack, opened it and pulled out two rings. She placed one on the middle finger of each hand, tapped them together. A burst of light zipped between them. 'Wait here. Do not move. Do not make a sound.' She dropped her backpack next to Muddy and headed off.

Scuba's backpack began to keel over. Muddy found himself willing it to go all the way. It did. It fell, open end towards him. He looked to the trees. No Scuba. He looked at the backpack. Glanced at the treeline again. Back to the backpack. He reached out . . . helped a few things accidentally fall from the opening. A folded cloth flopped onto the grass. It was dirty, old, stained with reddish brown blotches. All around the edges were glyphs and numbers, the same pattern repeated again and again. There was some kind of writing in the centre: childlike, scruffy. A flash of black in Muddy's eyes and the jumble of unfamiliar lines and strokes became readable . . . *MAY- YANIA, Tinta. Little sister. They have taken your life. And they think me dead. They will think again. I am weak. I am worn. I will be reborn. This promise begins with your blood and ends with mine or theirs. MAY-YANIA, Tinta. Little sister. I will be your sorrow. I will be your tomorrow. My name is MAY-YAN* . . . There was no more to read. The base of the cloth had been burnt away. Muddy felt guilty, like he'd intruded on something deeply personal. He quickly refolded the cloth and stuffed it back into Scuba's backpack.

Only one other thing had *almost* fallen out. The corner of a clear pouch was poking from the backpack. Muddy pulled it. It plopped onto the grass. Four pea-sized beads sat inside it. They were beautiful. Frosted green crystals with tiny pinpricks of light twinkling inside them. Muddy opened the pouch. He took out a bead. It was smooth to the touch, except for a line of tiny ridges running around its middle. He moved it closer to study it.

'Find anything interesting?'

It was Scuba. She was standing over him.

'No. . . I mean sorry, these beads fell out when you went after that thing.'

'Well, now you can add this one to them.' Scuba tossed a bead to him. This one was purple. It was covered in an oily gloop. '"Planetary Integrated Placement". Known as PIPs. They hold transport location details. I can find out where the user has been and modify it so that I can go to those places too.'

'And this PIP is from that robot thing? You killed it?'

Scuba frowned and squatted down. 'Sure, if you think a robot can be alive in the first place.' She used her thumb and forefinger to force Muddy's eyes wide open. 'I used a PIP to get you out of here earlier. But I did not have time to vet it. I see yourn suit has initiated full audio and visual translation. That is a new feature. I do not think many, if any, languages have been uploaded.' Scuba cupped Muddy's face in her hands. 'You have been crying,' she whispered. 'It is OK. This is normal. The scratchgas has worn off.' Her thumbs traced the tracks of his tears.

Muddy pulled away and shot a glance around. 'Where's Buggy?'

'I have not located him yet.' Scuba gave a little shake of her head. 'I set a return timer on yourn PIP. I had to wait for you. How many thumps did you feel in transit?'

'What if that robot got him?'

'It was a survey scout. Harmless. But we cannot afford to be spotted.'

'What's a scratch plammm—' A palm went over Muddy's mouth.

'I am not here as a personal tutor,' snarled Scuba. 'If yourn friend had not run out into the open, I would have been rid of you by now. Tell me where the PIP took you.'

Muddy stared at her. She seemed more volatile than before. He wondered if she'd seen him mess with more than the PIPs in her bag. 'Well, I'm sorry,' he said, 'but Buggy did run out into the open, so you're stuck with us. And we're stuck with you. And like it or not, I have questions. When we saw that giant crushing machine, you called my planet a scratch planet.'

'*Where . . . did . . . the . . . PIP . . . take . . . you?*'

'*What . . . is . . . a . . . scratch . . . planet?*'

They stared at each other. Neither one prepared to budge.

Scuba's jaw clenched. She stood up, pulled Muddy to his feet. 'You believe yourn eyes, correct?'

Muddy nodded.

'Then look around. You are alone. Everyone else on this planet is gone. Yourn family, yourn friends, yourn strangers. This planet, like many others, is just a nursery . . . a showroom. It was full of stock. Two days ago, a gas was released into the atmosphere to . . . *numb* . . . all life mentally. It makes the stock unaware of the displacement.' She looked at Muddy. 'The gas that you inhaled would have made yourn emotions fluctuate.

I am guessing yourn real thoughts and feelings will have only recently returned?'

Muddy thought back to the police cell. 'You guess right,' he said.

Scuba continued with her explanation. 'When the rental period ends, or the entire stock of a planet is being sold or re-housed, the planet is referred to as a "scratch planet". The surface is relayed, anything man-made destroyed, all substances returned to theirn natural form, any missing materials replaced.'

'They start from scratch.'

'Exactly.'

'But . . . stock?'

'Stock. Everything. Any life form that the environment has been designed to support. You included. You are just a product . . . owned. You can be displayed or grown on virtually any planet that has a breathable atmosphere, sufficient heat and liquid water. You were designed and bred with desirable characteristics, intelligent enough to evolve, form social structure and so forth.'

'If all the stock has been moved, why are me, Buggy, Angel and Mrs Magner still here?'

'Because some stock on yourn planet was recently taken off the endangered species list. A few of you can be hunted. That is why I am here. Now tell me where the PIP took you?'

'Hang on! Hunted! You can't just slip that little gem in and expect to move straight on!'

Scuba smiled. 'I did not mean that *I* was here to hunt you.' The smile dropped from her face. 'You would already be dead if that were the case. No. You are safe enough. Now tell me, where did the PIP take you?'

'Another . . . place . . . planet . . . I don't know. Another planet. I met a woman, some kind of law enforcement. She wouldn't tell me what the planet was.' Muddy shook his head. '*Hunted?* Hunted by who?'

'You touched items on that planet, correct?'

'Yeah, lots of things, some amazing cold, white powder called snow. It was sticky . . . but not sticky if you know what I mean. It turns to water if you warm it up. *Hunted?* By who?'

'Sit.' Scuba pulled Muddy to the ground and sat cross-legged in front of him. She tapped some sections of his suit. Miniscule lights flickered all over it. The lights began to merge, travelling up to his shoulders then down his arms. Scuba cupped her hands and touched Muddy's wrists with her thumbs. She waited. Light skipped between them, forming a small ball in Scuba's cupped hands. She sighed. Impatient. Bored. Muddy figured she must have done stuff like this a million times. 'These suits are so slow,' said Scuba. 'They need an upgrade.'

Muddy gawped as the ball of light began to float and spin. The colour of the sphere changed from grey to brown to green, then most of its surface rippled with a deep blue. White, wispy clouds appeared around it, twisting and twirling.

'Right,' said Scuba, 'you were on a planet called Earth . . . analysis shows possible scratchgas in the atmosphere. That cannot be right. It is not marked as a scratch planet. I need to run further analysis on that.'

'Scuba.' Muddy didn't get a response. 'Scuba.'

'What!'

'HUNTED ... BY ... WHO?'

Scuba clapped her hands and the planet disappeared. 'I told you to leave the old lady and the girl behind. You would not listen. They are not human. They are cyborganics. A species for hire. There are many different types. They usually work in pairs. One is the hunter, the other just a location beacon. The beacon is always in a form that is seen as cute or of no threat, so it can get in close.'

'What? You mean like a ... like a child?'

'Yes.'

Muddy pictured Angel and shook his head. 'No. Not Angel. And Mrs Magner can't be a cyborganic. We've known her for years.'

'Cyborganics integrate themselves into the target society. They look like them, grow like them, act like them. They are obsessive by nature, suited to areas such as religion or medicine. It gives them focus. That focus is needed to occupy them for an indefinite period. You see, as a tactic, some will self-delete all knowledge of who they really are. It is the perfect cover. Not even they know theirn true identity or purpose. Only exposure to scratchgas triggers that. When released into the atmosphere, scratchgas is absorbed into theirn organic bodies and signals the nanotechnology within them. It reboots them if you like, making them self-aware. Then they go about the assignment. They hunt theirn targets. They kill theirn targets. Make no mistake, when Mrs Magner remembers what she is, she will hunt you, she will kill you and she will deliver yourn corpses to whoever hired her.' Scuba paused. 'And by now she must be close to remembering.'

Chapter Seven

Buggy reached for the nearest tree and vomited. Again. Being moved by that . . . whatever it was . . . had left him nauseous and dizzy. It was dark. He was in thick woodland. That's all he knew. He rifled through the backpack that Scuba had given him. Nothing in there felt like a torch. Except that empty canister. His fingers touched a thin strip of material. There was a single small round lump in its centre. He drew it out, held it close. He could just make out a small cross on the material, possibly red, it was difficult to tell. Medicine. It had to be. When that machine had moved him, it hadn't cared about whether or not he would get injured. He'd landed right on his backside in a pile of stones. Hindsight was telling him that maybe it hadn't been a good idea to run towards the light. Buggy gripped his right buttock. Winced. "Behind-sight" was telling him that it *definitely* hadn't been a good idea. He popped the tablet out of the wrapper and into his mouth. It tasted awful. Medicine for sure. Even though nothing felt broken, a bolt of pain surged across his backside with each step that he took. Buggy felt compelled to take advantage of being alone. 'MY . . . ARSE . . . KILLS!' he shouted. It seemed to help.

'Don't you swear.'

Buggy froze. Had he really heard that? It was feeble. Almost a whisper. From his left-hand side. He turned towards it. Headed through the darkness. Silence reigned again. Maybe it had been wind blowing through the branches? He toyed with the idea of shouting "arse" repeatedly as he walked along, like an expletive sonar system. Instead, he just stopped still and concentrated. Beyond the wind and his own breathing, he could hear something else, a dull . . . crackle . . . something burning . . . gentle, not like the flames from those metal serpents. He moved closer to the sound. A soft orange glow oozed through the thick undergrowth. The glow led him to the edge of a clearing. On the far side, near a small fire, sat Mrs Magner. He could only see her side on. She looked ill. She was right up against a tree, facing it, scratching at the trunk. He could hear her whispering and muttering, poking at the flickering shadows as they danced across the bark. Buggy watched her for a while. She must have been transported by that machine too. No wonder she was so upset. What would a woman of God make of such an awful experience? Buggy felt bad for getting angry at her before. She'd frustrated him, but he'd known her a long time and she was a good, kind person. And she was a familiar face. For that alone, he was grateful. He stepped into the clearing slowly, so as not to startle her. Right next to him, curled in a ball at the base of a tree, lay Angel. Buggy knelt by her side and gently stroked her head. Even in her sleep, she was squashing Little Dog to her chest like she would die without him. Buggy patted the toy too. As he did so, he noticed something by Angel's feet that disturbed him. A discarded bible. He picked it up and walked over to Mrs Magner. In the dim glow from the fire she looked gaunt, tired. She rocked forwards and backwards, not paying attention to anything except the shadows and the bark. Her sleeves had fallen up her arms, revealing a myriad of scars.

'Mrs Magner, are you OK?'

The old lady went still. Utterly and absolutely. She brought her arms back to her side, pulled down her sleeves. She stayed quiet. Didn't even turn towards him.

'Mrs Magner. It's me, Buggy.'

The old lady shuffled around. 'Don't wake it,' she hissed.

'Don't wake what?'

'Hmmm,' Mrs Magner waved away her own remarks. 'And in the end who will if I don't?' She looked up at Buggy, her eyes moist. She nodded to herself. 'Darkness makes things different, doesn't it? The mind. Thoughts. The things you feel . . . ' She nodded again. 'Hmmm. Just don't wake it.'

'Mrs Magner, you're not making—' Buggy checked himself. 'You look tired. Here . . . ' He fumbled around in his backpack, found a food bar and handed it over to her. Mrs Magner took one quick, tiny bite, folded the rest in the wrapper and stashed it away inside her dress. 'And I found this over by Angel,' said Buggy. He handed the bible to her. The old lady stared at it for a moment. She reached out tentatively. As soon as her fingers touched the black cover, she pulled away as though scolded. The bible fell to the ground with a thud. Buggy didn't know what to do. Seeing Mrs Magner like this made his heart ache. He felt helpless. He was no doctor. He was no psychiatrist. Swallowing down the lump in his throat, he did the only thing he could think of. He sat. He took Mrs Magner's hand in his. He picked the bible up, let it fall open. And he began to read to her by firelight. 'For thou art my lamp, O Lord, and the Lord will lighten my darkness. For by thee I have run through a troop, by my God have I leaped over a wall. As for God, his way is perfect, the word of the Lord is tried, he is a buckler to all them that trust in him. For who is God, save the Lord? And who is a rock, save our God? God is my strength and power, and he maketh my way perfect.' Buggy glanced up at Mrs Magner. As crazy as it seemed, the words of the bible were affecting her. She had straightened, she was nodding as he spoke, her good eye sparkled. She looked focused. Buggy continued. 'He maketh my feet like hinds' feet, and setteth me upon high places. He teacheth my hands to war, so that a bow of steel is broken by mine arms. Thou hast also given me the shield of thy salvation, and thy gentleness hath made me great. Thou has enlarged my steps under me, so that my feet did not slip. I have—'

'No more!' Quick as a flash, Mrs Magner knocked the bible from Buggy's hand. 'No more. No more now.' She slipped her hand from his grip, picked the bible up and passed it back to him. 'She *will* come for you.'

Mrs Magner turned away from Buggy and crept on all fours towards Angel. Slowly. Softly.

'What? You mean Scuba?' said Buggy. 'Us, Mrs Magner,' he comforted, 'she'll come for *us*.'

'Yes . . . us,' acknowledged Mrs Magner, curling up next to Angel. She stared at the sleeping child, reached out and stroked her hair. 'She'll come for *us*.'

Chapter Eight

'Shame, it is getting light. You are always easier to locate in the dark, you humans.'

'"You humans"?' laughed Muddy. 'Come on, you're human too.'

'Of sorts,' conceded Scuba.

'Meaning?'

'Meaning . . . human origins but evolved in minutely different ways. Minutely significant. Mine home planet is massive compared to yourn. Ten times its size. It has fluctuating gravities. The majority of the surface is covered in a vast ocean. We have three suns. Four moons. It is a planet that puts enormous stresses on the body. That is why ourn scientists developed the skinsuit. It compensates for the changes in gravity, atmosphere and . . . whatnot. We merge with it at birth, become . . . conjoined.'

Muddy frowned. 'A skinsuit?'

'Yes, this black one. It is both a synthetic and biological lifeform . . . intelligent . . . multifunctional . . . essentially a second layer of living skin – made from microscopic scales of raphenia, a material unique to ourn planet which uses a synthetic bacterium to merge and combine with blood and DNA.'

Muddy pointed at Scuba's suit. 'That one? That black one right there?'

Scuba nodded.

'What . . . you mean that one, the black one, the black one that's exactly like *this* black one?' He pointed to the black material that was now covering his own body.

'Yes. The one you have is from mine sister. When a family member dies, the second skin seeks out the next of kin for re-distribution. I re-distributed it to you. That is why the needle went into yourn palm. The skinsuit needed yourn blood.'

Muddy thought about that for a moment. Then he let out a low groan that grew slowly louder. 'I'm wearing a dead person! Get it off! Get it off me! It's your sister! She's on me! She was a girl. Your sister was a girl, right?'

'They usually are.'

Muddy pulled at the black material, trying to wipe it away. 'Well, I'm not a girl. What if I turn into a girl?!'

Scuba watched on, unimpressed. 'It may improve you.'

'And you said when a family member dies! What did she die of? What if I catch it!'

'You cannot catch what she died of. She was murdered. By a Dreddax butcher. The day mine planet became a scratch planet.'

Muddy stopped in his tracks. The cloth from Scuba's backpack. Its story became horribly clear to him. 'Your sister . . . I . . . I'm sorry. I was being . . . thoughtless,' he said.

'If you think I am going to be hurt by such things, you are very much mistaken. And if you think I value *yourn* opinion enough to be hurt by it, you are twice mistaken.' Scuba carried on walking.

'Well, I'm sorry anyway,' repeated Muddy, secretly glad that Scuba had moved ahead of him. She wouldn't have seen his involuntary shiver. Wearing her dead sister was going to take some getting used to.

'Forget it. What happened to mine people is why I do what I do.'

'You haven't actually told me what it is that you do.'

'Mayhap that is because I have never had to tell anyone before. You should have been relocated by now. *That* is what I do. Relocate the hunted. Mine job is to track and retrieve. Mine team deal with the relocation.'

'Team?'

'Mineself and the four other survivors from mine planet. We became . . . proactive . . . when ourn population was wiped out. You see, we are unique in the worlds and this skinsuit affords us many benefits. It not only helps to maintain us, it facilitates fast interplanetary travel with its ability to integrate gravitational wave distortion, dark matter and quantum mechanics. It protects us during that travel. It instantaneously adapts to varying environments . . . many, many things. So, we decided to make the best use of it by rescuing other life forms that were being hunted. We decided to make a difference.'

'And what about the ones not being hunted? You think it's OK to let them be moved around like pets?'

'Well . . . they are pets. They just do not know it. It is how the worlds work. And you have no understanding of it. You are human, so you believe the worlds revolve around you and you alone. Yourn race is arrogant, selfish, insular, destructive . . .'

'Alright, alright! Enough with the compliments. Why bother rescuing us if we're that bad?'

'Because stupidity is yourn main problem, not malice. There are worse species.'

'And are there more habitable planets, as well as that Earth one?'

Scuba nodded and gave a sarcastic little wave.

'Oh, yeah, I meant besides your planet too.' Muddy kicked himself. He wasn't being a good advert for the non-stupidity of humans.

'There are,' confirmed Scuba.

'You know, Earth felt familiar somehow . . . the people, the buildings and things.'

Scuba nodded, unsurprised. 'Of course. You have the same origins. You were all bred on a single planet. Then you caught on. Humans became a craze among the higher beings. You have a very short lifespan, compared to theirn, and they find it amusing to watch you from afar, see how you get on with the trials and tribulations of those short lives. Suitable planets they own receive modifications and yourn species is bought from scratch planets to stock them. Humans are all over the multiverse because of this. When any sentient stock, human or otherwise, is transported to a new owner, the majority of theirn biological memory is deleted. Theirn brains are defragmented, if you like. It prevents anxiety and trauma, so they remain unaware of the move, unaware of any "past life". But, to address yourn observation, there is some regulated . . . slippage, hence continuity in language, belief systems, myths and whatnot in separate populations, separate worlds.'

'Is that why you think it's OK to move people? Just because their memories are deleted?'

'Stock is moved unharmed, and the stock has no idea. It just continues to live its life freely. However, to set beings aside to be hunted for sport is offensive. That, I can do something about – stock relocation I cannot.'

'Everything seems very black and white with you.'

'Wasting time on the shading costs more lives than it saves.'

'What about Mrs Magner and Angel. You just wanted to leave them behind. Just like that. You're not even sure they are what you say they are.'

'I stand sure enough.'

Muddy shook his head. 'So apart from only seeing in black and white and having no heart, how else are *you* different?'

'Better sense of smell amongst other things.' Scuba stopped walking, she pointed in the general direction of a dense section of forest. 'Can you smell that?'

'You're not going to ask me to pull your finger, are you?'

'What?'

'Nothing,' shrugged Muddy, 'just something Buggy does now and again.'

'Over there.' Scuba pointed to a thin wisp of smoke snaking through the trees ahead of them. 'Stay behind me.'

Scuba moved towards the source of the smoke slowly and methodically, checking all around as she walked. Progress was way too slow for Muddy's liking. He tried to move past her, but she pushed him back. He tried again without success. His third attempt elicited a slightly different response. As he moved towards her, Scuba made a fist and gave him a gentle push in the centre of his chest. The next thing he knew, he was on his back, staring up at her.

'Do as I say when I say it,' said Scuba. She continued towards the smoke.

Muddy lay there for a few moments, bewildered. She'd only given him a tiny push, but it felt like he'd been smashed by a sledgehammer. It had knocked him right off his feet. He stood and followed at a respectful distance . . . until he caught sight of Buggy, lying face down on the ground up ahead. 'Bug!' he shouted as he ran.

Buggy stirred. 'Hey!' he said. He rose from the floor. 'That thing, that machine, the moving me business . . . it made me really tired. I didn't know where you were . . . where I was.' Buggy rubbed his eyes, greeted his smiling friend and continued babbling. 'It was crazy. I was with you lot and then I . . . I don't know. I found Mrs Magner and Angel and we . . . .' Buggy went quiet. He took a couple of steps back. Eyed his friend up and down. 'You taken up ballet since I last saw you?'

'I don't want to talk about it,' snapped Muddy.

Buggy eyed Scuba up and down too. She was standing over Mrs Magner and Angel. 'So, you decided to get matching clothes,' said Buggy. 'You're a proper couple now. Nice one.'

'Shut your face.'

'I'll shut my face if you tell me why your girlfriend looks like she's going to murder Mrs Magner and Angel in their sleep.'

'Yeah, erm . . . I need to fill you in on a few . . . '

Before he could get into the details, Scuba turned to them both. 'A simple cut,' she said, 'and I can prove that she is a cyborganic. The nanobots in hern bloodstream will not be visible, but they will be drawn to a strong magnetic field.'

Mrs Magner's eyes shot open. She scrambled backwards. 'And the blood shall be to you for a token upon the houses where ye are: and when I see the blood, I will pass over you, and the plague shall not be upon you to destroy you, when I smite the land.'

The sudden outburst woke Angel. She pressed Little Dog to her chest and scurried to Mrs Magner's side.

'Scuba!' shouted Buggy, stepping in front of her. 'What do you think you're doing? Haven't we all been through enough?'

'Enough? Thanks to you and yourn stupidity, this situation is now a shambles. And I am the one who must unclutter this shambles.' Scuba turned away. She paused as she passed Muddy. 'The way you ran over when you saw yourn friend face down on the ground, you thought she had already done for him. Do not try and tell me contrary,' she snarled.

'You have no idea what I thought, or what I think,' replied Muddy. He looked at Mrs Magner clutching her bible, Angel clutching Little Dog. He saw no cyborganic. He saw no cyborganic beacon. He saw no evil. He looked back at Scuba. 'You should have a bit more . . . faith. We're all having a bad time. Not just you.'

'Fine,' said Scuba. 'I will say not a thing more. You know what will happen.'

'What will happen?' asked Buggy.

'Nothing,' said Muddy. 'Nothing will happen.'

'I thought you and he were friends,' said Scuba. 'Tell him what you know. Do it now. There will only be time for a few questions.'

Muddy sighed. He looked at Buggy, nodded towards a spot out of earshot of Mrs Magner and Angel.

Throughout the whispered update, Buggy kept his eyes fixed on Scuba. She didn't join them until Muddy had almost finished and she didn't say a word until he was completely done.

'There are superior life forms that enjoy watching other species' cultures develop from afar. It entertains them,' she added.

'And who thinks they own us?' asked Buggy,

'It is difficult to explain.' Scuba took a moment. 'OK, well, you are a carbon-based life form. Physical, with a tiny mental capacity.' She made a point of holding Buggy's gaze. '*Very* tiny. Yourn species has been selected and genetically engineered over millions of years by specialists. Specialists employed by a life form that is . . . let us just say more mental than physical. In theirn natural form, they would not be visible to yourn human eyes. You will only see the giant mechanical bodies they inhabit when they leave theirn home planet. Those metal bodies enable them to interact on other, more physical, worlds.'

'That crushing machine?'

'Exactly. Amorphi controlled. And they have a class system. Only the lower classes go off-planet in those Amorphium shells. Clean up and gardening duties, you might say.'

'Is that their name, "The Amorphi"?'

Scuba nodded.

'And you say your job is to get us back to our families?'

'Yes.'

'Maybe we should let Mrs Magner and Angel listen to this,' said Buggy.

'They have no interest.' There was a sudden edge to Scuba's voice. 'Or did yourn friend not explain that part?'

'He explained it. Doesn't mean I believe it.'

Muddy jumped in. 'What I don't understand is this: when we spoke before you said people's memories are erased when they are relocated.'

'Correct.'

'So, if you do get us back to our families, wherever they are, they won't remember us?'

'No, they will not. But *you* will not remember you either. Yourn previous life memories will be wiped, yourn biological brains defragmented, but you will be reintegrated into the same family unit afresh. You will be healthy. You will be content.'

'But we won't remember ourselves . . . each other . . . any of this?'

'You may not understand it, but it is for the best. Enough questions.' Scuba turned away and headed off.

Buggy shrugged. 'Well . . . I still have no idea what's going on. But I guess anything's better than this . . . right?'

Muddy didn't answer. 'Mrs Magner, Angel, it's time to go,' he said.

Chapter Nine

'*Stop!*' It was an urgent whisper.

The group crouched behind Scuba.

'Something is amiss. We should not be able to view mine team so easily.'

Muddy looked down the slope. Four people were clearly visible, sitting on the ground with their backs to a hoop of light. He'd seen a hoop just like it not long ago, above Scuba's head when she'd walked on water. Only the hoop at the base of the slope was bigger, much bigger.

Scuba pressed sections of the black material on her forearm. A tiny light fizzed from the top of her suit to the bottom. As it did so, the material began to mirror the colours and appearance of the surrounding foliage. 'Everyone wait here,' she said. 'Do not move a muscle.'

Scuba lay on her stomach and snaked down the hill. As she drew near her team, she paused. '*Ney-ute ba'la'du.*' No response. She moved closer, called out again. Still nothing. Circling her team, she edged close enough to touch one of them. She reached out, gently nudged the body. It fell sideways onto the grass, lifeless. She didn't need to touch the others to know they were the same. Scuba stood, her suit crackling as it went back to black. 'Follow mine exact path,' she shouted. 'Under no circumstances deviate from it.'

By the time Muddy reached her, she had laid the four bodies side by side.

'Your team?'

'These four, yes. That one, no,' Scuba pointed to a separate body, half hidden by bracken.

'I'm sorry,' said Muddy.

Scuba said nothing. She went to work, patting the bodies down, searching the surrounding area.

Buggy went to the body in the bracken. The thing was dead. Even so, it still had the capacity to raise the hairs on the back of his neck. He stared down at it. Thin, metallic strips, maroon in colour, covered the slender torso. It was some kind of armour. The strips fitted so tightly; Buggy could count fifteen ribs each side. The creature was human shaped, but appeared stretched somehow, thin, but muscular. Its elbow joints had three small pyramid structures evenly spaced around it, three more side by side under its wrist. Grey tubes were threaded through the centre of each pyramid, like cables in a cable tidy. The barbed ends of each tube stuck through the pyramids on the underside of the creature's wrist. Black blood stained the ground. More dripped from a crack in the creature's mask. Buggy called Muddy over. 'Take a look at this.'

The boys stared at it some more.

'It's got five fingers and a thumb on each hand,' observed Buggy.

'Greedy,' muttered Muddy. 'Those cables look like flesh. Check out the barbs on the ends. You think they are part of its body?'

Buggy shrugged, 'Alien spaghetti?' he said. He looked around for Scuba. 'Hey, Scuba, this spaghetti thing, are there more?'

'Not in the immediate vicinity.'

'That's a yes then,' said Buggy. He heard Scuba huff.

'A race called the Dreddax work for the Amorphi,' she shouted. 'They facilitate the recycling of scratch planets. A separate tribe of Dreddax, known as Dreddax butchers, do not. They work for theirnselves, gathering intelligence, ascertaining the location of scratch planets. They sneak in, steal what they can or sometimes attack planets on theirn own. They operate outside of Amorphi protocols. You are standing over the body of a Dreddax butcher. They do not like what mine team have been doing. It affects . . . business.'

Buggy looked at the four bodies next to Scuba. Her team. Her ex-team. 'You must affect their business a lot,' he said. 'Why does it have a mask on?'

'Dreddax are amphibious, evolved to extract oxygen more efficiently through liquid. Theirn mask serves as a filter as well as armour. Lift it off if you like. There is a small release mechanism under the chin.'

It sounded like a challenge. Buggy looked at Muddy and shook his head. Muddy looked down at the body. He didn't want to take the thing's mask off either. And yet he felt compelled to. He crouched next to it. Reached out. As his fingertips followed the rim of the mask, they became slippery due to the creature's black blood. He found a tiny latch, put a little pressure on it. Nothing. Curled two fingers around it and pulled harder. Still nothing. He felt around the latch. Noticed a thin groove – tried pulling that, tried pushing up, up and right, up and . . . a violent hiss broke the silence, startling both boys. Buggy took a reflex step away. In a less glamorous move, Muddy rocked back on his heels, lost his balance and fell flat on his back. The visor from the creature's mask landed on his chest. He froze. When nothing bad happened, he lifted the visor and peered through it. Everything took on a yellow hue. He looked towards Buggy. Text began running across the bottom of the visor – it took a moment for his eyes to translate: *live human artefact collectable rare – value 5000mc.* Muddy homed in on Scuba next and noticed two things. Firstly, the text at the bottom of the visor changed – *priority target – capture incapacitated or animate.* Secondly, Scuba's eyes were filling with tears. It was the first time he'd seen her looking anything other than supremely confident. And it scared him more than the corpse at his feet. Muddy got up. 'Hold on to this for a sec.'

'Sure.' Buggy took the visor without even looking. He was still concentrating on the hairless head of the unmasked creature. A series of small holes arced across the top of its skull, each one filled with a membrane at different stages of closing.

It had two shiny black eyes that only seemed to consist of pupils. A line of smaller holes ran vertically between them, up the bridge of its nose, eventually joining with the holes across its forehead. It had lips, but its open mouth was more rounded than a human mouth. What horrified and captivated Buggy most were the rows of teeth that spiralled round and round into the darkness of its throat.

Muddy gave a little cough, just to let Scuba know he was coming. She had moved out of sight behind a tree. 'Hey,' he said.

She turned away, lifted her hand to her face as though she was scratching an itch.

'I can go if you want to be alone?' Muddy offered.

Scuba gave a noncommittal shrug.

'You told me before that you and your team were the only survivors on your planet,' said Muddy. He waited a moment. 'This isn't your fault. You know that . . . right?' he said.

Scuba leaned back against the tree and slid to a crouch, still looking at the floor. 'They did not even know where I was.'

'But Scuba, you had too much to deal with. You weren't expecting Angel and Mrs Magner to be here . . . me and Buggy didn't help by running off . . . and then the Amorphi machine moving Buggy . . . all these things. Your team couldn't possibly have expected you to keep updating them.'

'No,' said Scuba, 'you misunderstand. I mean . . . mine team did not even know I was on this planet. They have never let me go on a rescue. They said I was too young. So, I studied yourn planet in secret, learnt the language, the terrain. I came here in advance. I prepared the tunnel. I planted the backpacks. I monitored you and yourn friend so I would recognise you when the time came. I was going to rescue you . . . bring you back for extraction . . . prove mineself.'

Muddy didn't quite know what to say. This girl had used him and Buggy as test subjects. Just to see if she could do it. That could have ended badly. In fact, it had ended badly. And yet . . . if she *hadn't* been there . . .

He knelt down beside her. 'Listen to me – that changes nothing. Despite everything that's happened, you got us here. Your team would have been proud. You make me feel . . . *safe*.'

Scuba looked straight up at him. 'I can still get you back to yourn families,' she said, a little steel nestling back in her eyes. 'I have searched the bodies. The datapod that held the information regarding yourn parents' new location was destroyed during the attack as per protocol. But there will be a hard copy on mine home planet. We can go there fir—'

Scuba's words were drowned out by a sudden loud screeching. She leapt to her feet.

Muddy automatically ducked. 'What's that?'

'Where are the cyborganics!' shouted Scuba. 'Where are they? They have tripped an alarm to bring the others!'

'OVER HERE!'

It was Buggy's voice.

'IT'S THIS DEAD DREDDAX THING!' he shouted. 'MRS MAGNER AND ANGEL WERE BY IT AND IT JUST . . . WENT OFF!'

Scuba ran over, grabbed Mrs Magner. 'What did you touch! WHAT DID YOU TOUCH!'

Mrs Magner began to tremble. Her head shook, ever so slightly at first then more definite. 'No . . . no . . . ' she stammered. 'And who is he that will harm you, if ye be followers of that which is good?'

The alarm stopped.

'Scuba!' protested Buggy. 'No one deliberately set off an alarm. They were just standing here, next to me. They did nothing.'

Scuba gave Mrs Magner a shove and stepped back. 'We need to leave. Now! If we are lucky the other Dreddax butchers will be some distance away. They believe all the Quarasians on planet to be dead. They may treat this as a false alarm. We will go to mine home planet. YOU,' she said, pointing at Buggy, 'come with me.'

Scuba walked Buggy over to the four bodies of her teammates. The bodies had become encased in a hard, black shell. 'Now that mine team are unable to transport us, we will need to travel in a different way. You must bond with a skinsuit like Muddy's.'

'Got a skin already, thanks. Not sure I want . . . '

'Take off yourn clothes,' said Scuba.

'Erm, seriously, I'm flattered and everything,' said Buggy, 'but I wouldn't want to step on my friend's—'

'There is no time for idiocy or coyness. Do it and do it right now.'

Buggy looked over at Muddy. Muddy gave him the nod.

After a quick look around, Buggy pointed to a patch of shrubs. 'You mind if I go behind this b—'

'Just hurry,' snapped Scuba.

'You mind if I finish a sentence bef—'

'Go! And hold out yourn hand when you are ready.' Scuba knelt at the base of the first body and pressed sections of the casing. A small black cube rose through the material. Muddy recognised it, the cube with the needle. A recycled skinsuit.

'It's cold in here,' said Buggy, his hand protruding from the foliage.

Scuba walked over and jabbed the needle into his palm. 'Now squeeze it.' She turned away and walked back to the bodies. Kneeling at the base of the next black shell, she pressed the same sections as before, in the same order. Another cube appeared.

'What are you doing?' asked Muddy as Scuba went to work on the third.

'I am extracting the raphenia cubes from the remaining bodies so that I can destroy them. The skinsuit will die with its owner. I must protect ourn technology.'

'But . . . ' Muddy held his breath for a moment. This wasn't going to go down too well. ' . . . if we are all travelling . . . then we *all* need a skinsuit. Mrs Magner and Angel need one too.'

Scuba erupted. 'You think I am going to give a cyborganic and its beacon a skinsuit! I am here to *save* you, not hand you to mine enemies on a plate and give them access to ourn technology into the bargain!'

'*You* don't have to do it.'

'That is not what I meant. Yourn idea is abhorrent. You have no idea what cyborganics have done to species in many other worlds.'

'Mrs Magner and Angel aren't cyborganics. And I'm not leaving them behind.' Muddy edged towards the two cubes that Scuba had already extracted.

'Touch those cubes and I will . . . ' Scuba's suit crackled as she clenched her fist.

Muddy reached out, slowly. 'Scuba, not everything is as black and white as you'd like it to be.'

The girl roared with frustration. Muddy flinched, thinking he was about to end up on his back for a second time. Instead, Scuba stormed over to the Dreddax corpse and kicked the armour off its chest. 'Not everything is black and white you say? Fine!' she shouted, plunging her hand deep into its ribcage. She pulled out a PIP. 'We will soon see where messing about with shading gets you!'

Rather than get involved in the argument, Buggy had decided to keep an eye on Mrs Magner. At the suggestion of her and Angel getting skinsuits, she'd started to shake. It made him think back to the previous night, when he'd seen her by the firelight – the scars all over her arms – how quickly she'd tried to cover them up. The thought of disrobing for a skinsuit must have horrified her. And yet, if they were all going to get out of here, she would have to have one of her own. He turned to Muddy. 'Give me the two cubes. I'll see to Angel and Mrs Magner,' he said.

'You luuurve her,' smirked Muddy, as he threw them over.

Buggy caught them with an amused snort and shake of his head. He walked back over to the old lady. 'It's OK, Mrs Magner,' he comforted. 'You don't need to worry.' He leaned next to her and lowered his voice. 'And your scars are nothing to be embarrassed about. Remember I saw them last night by the fire?'

Mrs Magner lowered her head. She nodded.

'Good,' said Buggy. 'Stand behind that tree and just reach out with your hand when you're ready. No one will see you.'

Mrs Magner passed Buggy her bible. She stood still for a moment, then nodded again and moved out of sight. After a bit of rustling, a bare arm extended from behind the tree. Buggy couldn't help but look at the scarring again – the scars were old, long healed, but there was a uniformity to them that he hadn't noticed by the firelight, rows of small, diagonal incisions all around the full length of her arm. 'This may hurt a tiny bit,' warned Buggy. He jabbed the needle into her palm. The old lady didn't react. 'Now close your fist and squeeze it tight.'

When Buggy had squeezed his cube, the liquid had spread rapidly. But, with Mrs Magner, he noticed that the black liquid seemed to be struggling. It took an age to ooze through her fingers. Then it edged up her arm, bit by bit . . . as though it were dipping its toes into water, testing the temperature as it went. Was the material rejecting the old lady? Was Scuba right? Could Mrs Magner be a cyborganic? Buggy glanced back to make sure no one else was watching.

When she re-emerged from behind the tree, Mrs Magner looked strangely more religious. She had put her tatty dress back on, over the top of the skinsuit. Her silver cross shone brightly against the black background.

Relieved to see that the skinsuit had worked, Buggy gave the old lady her bible. 'OK, Angel,' he said, turning to the young girl, 'your turn.'

Scuba was in the process of dragging the third shell to the golden hoop. Muddy watched as she appeared to pull threads of gold from one side of the hoop's edge to the other. The pattern multiplied by itself, creating an effect like netting. Scuba said a few words over the black shell and pushed it. As soon as it touched the netting it got sucked in, warping and disintegrating – like sand getting pulled through the centre of an hourglass, only this happened in the blink of an eye. 'You want me and Buggy to bring over the last one?' asked Muddy.

'No,' replied Scuba. 'That last one still needs the raphenia cube extracting. I must do that before transporting it.'

'OK, what can we do instead?' asked Muddy.

'Prepare for travel. In yourn backpack and Buggy's backpack there is a specialist master PIP. I also have one. These are the only kind of PIPs that allow travel to mine home planet. Since we only have three, you, Buggy and I will go first. Then I will take yourn PIPs and come back alone so that Angel and Mrs Magner can use them. The PIP is in a sealed strip. Take it out and place it into this part of yourn skinsuit.' Scuba pointed to the centre of her chest. 'The PIP is in the packaging with the little cross on.'

'Erm, yeah,' piped up Buggy. 'Slight problem . . . I thought the little red x meant medicine.'

Scuba shook her head. 'Speak sense.'

'I ate it.'

'You did *what?*'

'I was ill.'

'In the head?' snarled Scuba.

'It cured my nausea.'

'You bring on mine nausea.'

'Well, try eating one of those little balls.'

Scuba dismissed Buggy with an impatient wave of her hand. She turned instead to Muddy. 'Then just the two of us will return to mine planet. There should be a master PIP in storage. I will come back for Buggy and then those two.'

'I don't mean to make things worse,' said Muddy, 'but my backpack is still on that planet, Earth. The law enforcement officer took it from me.' He leaned forward and whispered in Scuba's ear, 'Besides, you wouldn't have come back for Mrs Magner and Angel. And like I said before, we aren't go—'

'Too late!' cut in Scuba. 'No one is going anywhere now. The butchers are back.'

Chapter Ten

A low hum filled the air.

'Haven't you got any weapons?' asked Buggy.

'We do not carry weapons,' replied Scuba. 'We are a peaceful race. We onl—'

'Behind you!'

Scuba turned around at Buggy's shout. Her skinsuit reacted instantly, spreading to cover her hands, head and face. The Dreddax butcher in front of her raised an arm. Each slithering strand attached to its elbow began spinning independently, pulsing black and red. Scuba ran straight at the creature. Leaping high, she aimed a quick, powerful kick at the extended arm. The red pulses glowed more brightly at the point of impact. As the butcher adjusted its balance, Scuba aimed a punch at the centre of its chest. Again she leapt, getting two punches off in the exact same spot. The creature rocked back slightly. Its arms went limp by its sides, but the living tubes unclipped themselves from the holders beneath its wrists. They began stretching out, like snakes searching for prey. Scuba got in close, ducked and weaved, jumped and punched, again and again, until each punch sent a puff of black mist shooting into the air. The tubes that had managed to curl around her body loosened. She dropped to her knees . . . and leapt again. This time she aimed a vicious blow at the point of the creature's chin. Its mask shattered with an explosive hiss. The Dreddax butcher slumped to the floor. The black and red pulses faded until only black remained.

There followed a moment of stunned silence. Buggy just stared at Scuba.

'What?' she said.

'Can you teach us how to be that . . . peaceful?'

'No, but I can show you how to use the skinsuit shield to protect yournselves.' Scuba looked over at Muddy. 'Mine sister's skinsuit has muscle memory for fighting. It will help you if you are a natural fighter. Do you know how to fight, Muddy?'

'Well . . . '

'Do not dally.'

'Couldn't fight my way out of a wet paper bag,' he said.

Scuba frowned. 'Very well. You will do the same as Buggy. Shield yournself but push the Dreddax butchers away from me if I become outnumbered. Stand side by side. It will be more effective. Stay away from theirn tube attachments, the ends are barbed and can inject a poison. At distance the tubes discharge the red pulses – tiny, high velocity projectiles made from a substance similar to molten lava. The projectiles are not theirn first offensive choice as they have limited . . . ammunition. But under no circumstances lower yourn shields.'

'What about Mrs Magner and Angel?'

Scuba ignored the question. 'Observe closely. This is how you activate, hold and direct yourn large shield.'

Both boys copied Scuba's actions. Buggy glanced over at Mrs Magner and mouthed the word "watch". Mrs Magner held Angel close.

When she was satisfied that the boys could raise their shields, Scuba ended the lesson. 'When the time comes, stay behind me. Keep yourn shields activated and facing the enemy.'

More humming from the direction of the tree line. Scuba knelt down by the remaining shell. There was no time to extract the raphenia cube. No time to drag the shell to the hoop for instant transportation. She pressed different sections on its base. A countdown appeared on the black surface. It crackled and camouflaged itself with the surroundings. 'This one will have to transport itself,' said Scuba. 'I will extract the raphenia on mine home planet.' She stood and turned towards the tree line.

'One thing,' said Muddy.

'Go on?'

'What's your definition of outnumbered?'

'If four or more come at me at once,' replied Scuba as she led them out into the open field. 'And even then, only if I am surrounded. If they are all ahead of me, don't concern yournselves.' Scuba stopped walking and nudged the boys left and right. 'Stand here and here. Stay alert. Dreddax butchers are already on planet, more may transport direct. They will appear as if from thin air, mayhap right next to you.'

Muddy scanned the edge of the forest. He could see tiny red pulses in the shadows. He could hear the hum. He looked back to see how far away from Mrs Magner and Angel they were. 'Scu . . . ' Muddy went quiet. Scuba was no longer next to him. That particular space was suddenly empty. 'Bug! Where did she go!'

'Eh?'

'Where the . . . *pop* is Scuba!'

'Don't know,' said Buggy, staring towards the trees, 'I was watching for Dreddax spaghetti. What are we supposed to do now?'

Muddy shrugged and put up his shield. Buggy did the same.

In the darkness of the forest, three yellow visors turned left, turned right, then eased back to centre, settling on the two boys. Three Dreddax butchers stepped out into the open.

'She's stuck us in the middle of this field like sitting ducks! And she's legged it,' whispered Buggy. 'It's because we wouldn't leave Mrs Magner and Angel. I bet you.'

'No,' said Muddy. 'She wouldn't do that.' Again, he looked around for Scuba, across the open field, along the tree line, back towards the golden ring. No sign.

The three Dreddax butchers began their approach.

'She definitely wouldn't have just gone. No way. She just wouldn't do that . . . ' Muddy looked at his friend, ' . . . I don't think.' The boys moved a step closer together.

Ahead of them, the Dreddax butcher in the centre of the group exploded in a spume of black. A shape – *a Scuba-sized shape* – clung to its back and dragged its lifeless body to the ground. Muddy felt an overwhelming sense of relief. Scuba had camouflaged her skinsuit. One down. Two to go. The other butchers were obviously having trouble keeping track of her, but they knew her rough position. Tiny, lightning bright projectiles ripped across the grass, crisscrossing the area around their fallen comrade. Scuba took a hit. A projectile thumped into her midriff. Her suit crackled back to black. She was OK, but now she was visible . . . and way too close to the Dreddax butchers. A barbed tube shot towards her – a direct hit. It thudded into Scuba's shoulder. The tube instantly retracted, disappearing back behind Dreddax armour. A moment later, that same Dreddax butcher held its arm high in the air. A small black disc materialised in its fingers.

'Walk backwards slowly!' shouted Scuba. 'Keep facing the front!' She jinked and rolled through the space between the two Dreddax, avoiding attempts to tag her with the black disc. Once through, Scuba darted across open ground, taking up a position behind the retreating boys.

'What's that disc?' asked Muddy.

'It caught me with a special barb. No poison. Took a sample to produce a DNA specific transporter. If it sticks that disc to me, I will be transported direct to the holding cells in theirn main ship. It appears I am currently worth more alive than dead.' Her eyes flicked between the boys. 'You two . . . not so much.' She smiled. 'So, keep yourn shields up. They will not be trying to tag you.'

Muddy found the smile unnerving. It made him think again about the cloth he'd found in her backpack. Maybe she was enjoying this revenge a little bit too much.

'Crouch down, hold yourn shields above yourn heads,' instructed Scuba.

The boys obeyed. As they crouched together, their shields blended to create a large, flat surface above them. Scuba used it as a springboard, running and jumping onto it. In mid-air she triggered her own shield. It came out as an extension of her arm – flat and razor thin. She scythed through the air and sliced the head clean off the Dreddax butcher to her left. As she landed, her shield re-shaped into a dome and deflected the projectiles fired by the final butcher.

'Scuba!' Muddy pointed to the edge of the forest. More yellow glows behind the tree line.

'Come to me!' she shouted. She ran back towards the golden ring. When the boys reached her, she domed her shield over them all. 'We cannot stay.'

'We've discussed this,' said Muddy. 'We're not leaving Mrs Magner and Angel behind.'

'Then you are responsible for whatever happens next.' Scuba turned to Buggy and pressed sections of his skinsuit. It changed to camouflage mode. 'Buggy, the Dreddax butcher that lay dead by mine team earlier, I extracted a tiny sphere from its body, its PIP, did you see from where?'

'Centre of the chest.'

Scuba nodded. 'Dreddax butchers work in units of three. Each unit has PIPs calibrated with identical information. The markings on the three Dreddax we just engaged tell me they are from the same unit. I want theirn PIPs. Mineself and Muddy will engage the remaining butcher and draw it away. I have already taken the PIP from the first one I killed. You must obtain the PIP from the body of the Dreddax butcher with the severed head. Join us back here, at the golden hoop.' Scuba pressed more sections of Buggy's skinsuit. It spread to cover his head and face. 'Go!'

When Buggy didn't move, Scuba gave him an encouraging shove. She turned to Muddy. 'Follow me. We must keep swapping places. The third Dreddax is ourn. It cannot be allowed to tag me with that transporter disc.'

'But we'll still only have *three* PIPs!'

'Shut yourn mouth for a moment and listen,' snapped Scuba. 'Mine home planet has strict security protocols. Each individual skinsuit requires a specialised master PIP, or the wearer will not be able to materialise on planet. Other planets do not have this security. We can attempt . . . I do not know the words . . . "piggyback transporting" to a non-secure planet already imprinted on the Dreddax PIPs. Two people, one PIP - as long as the two are in physical contact. You and yourn friend will have to carry the cyborganic and her beacon. So, we just need the PIPs from these three Dreddax butchers for it to work. But understand this – I have not had time to analyse or vet theirn PIPs. I have no idea where we will end up, or what we will find when we get there. If you still wish to take the cyborganic and its beacon, then we have no choice. It is a huge risk. And that risk is all on you.' With that said, Scuba moved off.

Buggy looked down at the severed head as he passed it. His heart pounded and he felt a little dizzy. The visor on the helmet was still flickering yellow. Black blood gushed onto the ground from the neck. He was so fixated on the head, he almost stumbled over the creature's body. He steeled himself. Trying not to look at the gaping wound between the shoulders, he stood astride the body and focused on the centre of the chest. There was a small circular plate, where the metal strips of armour converged. That was where Scuba had punched. Behind that plate he would find the PIP. Buggy clenched his fist. His first punch was pathetic. He looked back towards Muddy and Scuba. They were backing towards the golden hoop, weaving around each other as they went. With the black skinsuits covering their entire bodies, he couldn't tell them apart. That third Dreddax butcher was right on top of them. Buggy looked towards the tree line. More butchers had started to emerge. There wasn't much time. He looked down at the chest plate and clenched his fist again. His skinsuit crackled. It seemed to respond to his intent. He crashed his fist down. A glob of black blood spurted from the creature's open neck. Buggy felt vomit rise in his own neck. He swallowed hard. Punched harder. The right arm of the Dreddax twitched and bounced up off the ground. The barbed tubes on its elbows flicked upwards, stabbing at Buggy's skinsuit. His camouflage disappeared. Buggy looked at his arm. Thankfully the barb had not pierced the material, but it had left a row of small diagonal slash marks. He'd seen that same pattern before, repeated many times. Buggy glanced back at Mrs Magner. There was no time to dwell on it. The hum of advancing Dreddax made him refocus. They were close. And he was visible. Buggy began punching again, frantic now. Finally, the metal plate pinged off. He thrust his hand into the hole and felt for the pea-sized sphere.

'Now!' shouted Scuba. She took an extra step, moving within reach of her target. Seeing its opportunity, the Dreddax butcher lunged forward, reaching out with the black transporter disc. Scuba ducked and curled downwards. Her arm had been constantly linked through Muddy's and the momentum pulled him over her back in one fluid motion. The transporter disc stuck to Muddy's thigh. He held his breath. Even though Scuba had told him the disc wouldn't work on him, her plan had still made him nervous. Until now. With some relief, he tore the disc off his skinsuit and threw it to the ground. Muddy held his shield in front of him and rammed the Dreddax butcher with all the strength he could muster. The creature was forced backwards . . . and Scuba was waiting. With her camouflage working again, she'd huddled at the butcher's heel. The butcher fell over her. She was on it in a flash, aiming a powerful kick at the base of its mask.

Buggy reached them just as Scuba was extracting the third and final gooey PIP. He handed his PIP over to her.

'Good work. We have the three. Pick a number, one through five.'

'Five,' said Muddy.

Scuba inserted all the PIPs and tweaked some settings on their skinsuits. 'Whatever planet held theirn fifth assignment, that is where we are going.' She looked over towards the tree line. Thirty or more Dreddax butchers were heading straight for them. 'For piggyback transports we are unable to use skinsuits alone. We must use the hoop. I have configured the hoop for three transports only. It will close and disintegrate when the third transport has taken place. The Dreddax butchers will not be able to follow. Yourn skinsuits will automatically engage transport mode to protect you during travel, then disengage if the destination atmosphere is safe. I will go through first. We do not know what we will find on the other side. Muddy, if we get split up, press these three sections on yourn skinsuit. It is a family suitcipher . . . a code . . . that will allow me to locate you.' Without another word, Scuba stepped into the golden hoop and disappeared.

'I'll piggyback Angel,' said Muddy. 'You take Mrs Magner.' He noticed a little hesitation. 'Bug, you OK?'

Buggy found himself thinking about the scars on Mrs Magner's arms. How her skinsuit had taken so long to attach. He nodded. 'Just nervous.'

'I travelled to another planet before, remember. It's . . . weird,' said Muddy. 'But safe,' he added.

'Even with someone on your back?' asked Buggy.

'That's the alternative.' Muddy pointed at the advancing Dreddax butchers. He knelt down and let Angel clamber onto his back. 'Good girl,' he said. When he stood, he found his vision blocked by white, fluffy material. 'Angel, tuck Little Dog completely inside your skinsuit. He'll be fine there. Good. Now hold tight.' With a final nod towards his friend, Muddy walked into the golden hoop.

Buggy watched as Muddy and the small girl on his back vanished into thin air. He turned towards Mrs Magner. 'Taxi for Magner.'

The old lady took a step towards him, then stopped. 'I've dropped my bible, somewhere on the grass.'

'Mrs Magner! Leave it! There's no time!'

'Always time,' muttered Mrs Magner as she walked away. 'A time to get, and a time to lose; a time to keep, and a time to cast away.' With her back to Buggy, she slipped her hand inside her dress and clasped her bible. She knelt on the grass, next to the body of the Dreddax butcher that Scuba and Muddy had fought. 'I can see it! It's here! On the grass!' She took the bible from her dress, lifted it into the air and waved it.

There was a strange shimmer in the air ahead of the old lady. The next second, a Dreddax butcher appeared, almost on top of her.

'Mrs Magner! Look out!' shouted Buggy.

Mrs Magner gazed up into the yellow visor. She could see the reflection of her silver cross glint on its surface. The Dreddax butcher stared down at her. And did not move.

Still on her knees, Mrs Magner turned her head towards Buggy. 'Take ye heed, watch and pray,' she shouted, 'for ye know not when the time is.' Looking back into the butcher's visor, she smiled and slyly scooped up the small black transporter disc from the grass. The old lady slipped it, unnoticed, into the pages of her bible. She got to her feet and ran at Buggy. 'A whip for the horse, a bridle for the donkey, and a rod for the fool's back!' she shouted as she leapt upon him.

The momentum of the old lady jumping on his back sent Buggy stumbling towards the golden hoop. He kept his footing and clung to her as best he could. With a crackle and an echoing cry of 'Giddy up!' both makeshift horse and manic rider disappeared.

Chapter Eleven

Buggy opened his eyes. He felt warm. He was lying on his back. Flakes of pure white swirled around in the air above him. He watched them swoop and spin on the breeze. He smiled and poked out his tongue, let a few flakes deliver their fresh water parcels direct. This was exactly like the snow that Muddy had told him about. It was ace. Buggy looked around for his friend. But the only other person near him was Mrs Magner. She was standing a few feet away, just staring down at him.

'How long have you been there? Did we land together?' From his prone position, he scooped some snow into his right hand, squashed it into a ball like Muddy had told him, and launched it. It exploded on Mrs Magner's forehead. 'Sorry, I just had to try it out,' laughed Buggy. A snowball exploding on someone's head *was* funny. Just like Muddy had said.

The old lady blinked at him. Her expression didn't change. Buggy frowned. A snowball exploding on someone's head didn't seem to be as funny for the someone. Just like Muddy had said.

The old lady shuffled over to him.

'Mrs Magner. It was a joke. Seriously, I'm sorry,' repeated Buggy.

Without a word, the old lady leaned down and pushed Buggy's arms tight to his sides. She continued to stoop until they were almost nose to nose. Her good eye was red and bloodshot. 'This will hurt,' she whispered.

'Mrs Magner, it was just a ball of snow!'

The old lady placed a finger across his lips. 'Sshhhh. Save your strength.'

Buggy's stomach turned. Mrs Magner looked wild . . . confused . . . the same face he'd seen when she was poking at shadows. Travelling to another planet must have been the last straw. It had sent her over the edge. Buggy knew he had to calm her down . . . think of something to say, something to make her focus. But all he could think was how peaceful and silent snow was. It absorbed sound. Flakes continued to land on and around him. They melted on his face. Tiny drops of water began trickling downwards, towards his neck. He found the sensation calming . . . until that sensation reversed. How could water droplets trickle up his face rather than down? Buggy tried to sit up. Mrs Magner pushed him back down. She straddled his chest, moved so her weight bore down on his shoulders, held his arms firmly in place with her legs. Buggy lifted his head to try and reason with her, but a bright

Catherine wheel of pain fizzed across his eyes. In his ears too - a deep, intense burning, thin and piercing, from his ear lobes all the way to the centre of his brain . . . *needles* . . . Mrs Magner was pushing needles into his eyes and ears! 'Stop! Mrs Magner, stop!' Buggy tried to wriggle free, but the old lady's grip was vice-like. She was strong. Far too strong for an old lady. 'Mrs Magner! *Please* . . . don't do this!' He tried to push her off, but pain stole his strength. His head felt like it was about to explode. He cried out, 'I KNOW WHAT YOU ARE!'

Buggy's body went slack. His new white world went black.

Chapter Twelve

Muddy opened his eyes. He felt warm. He was lying on his back. Flakes of pure white swirled in the breeze above him. A few of the flakes settled on his face. They transformed into dots of water and trickled away. Muddy smiled. Was this the snow of Earth? His eyes traced the zigzagging path of a few more flakes as they made their way to the ground. Snow was great. Buggy was going to love it. He looked around for his friend. But the only other person near him was Angel. She was just a few feet away, playing with Little Dog. Her lips were pursed, and a tiny frown creased her brow. Moving the toy's legs in turn, she pressed each cloth foot into the snow in order to leave a trail of tiny paw prints. She paused for a moment, lifted Little Dog's tail and made him crouch. She blew a quiet raspberry. Then her frown lines deepened. She wagged a reprimanding finger at the toy before standing him back up. To round off her little scenario, she used the toy's back legs to flick snow over the imaginary poop. Muddy smiled again. Angel made life look so simple. Forget the past. Forget the future. Just get on with the now. It made him realise that she was the one most in need of her family. The sooner the better. She was young enough to start over and have a normal future . . . whatever normal turned out to be.

'Angel,' he called. 'You okay?'

The little girl scooped up her toy and held it close.

'You OK?' repeated Muddy.

She didn't respond.

'And Little Dog? Is he okay?'

Angel looked at her toy, glanced at the imaginary poop then patted his sparkling collar.

Muddy got to his feet. 'Good. Shall we go and find our friends, then?'

He held out his hand.

Angel took it.

Chapter Thirteen

Buggy blinked. The pain had gone. He looked to his side. Mrs Magner was right there, sitting cross-legged against the alley wall. She was motionless, staring down at the floor. He noticed that her tatty dress had gone, but he couldn't remember if she'd been wearing it when she'd attacked him. 'You stopped,' he said.

The old lady raised her head. 'What am I?'

'Eh?'

'You said you know what I am.'

Buggy thought for a moment before answering. 'On our planet, when you went back for your bible, a Dreddax butcher appeared right next to you. Why didn't it attack you?'

Mrs Magner poked a finger into the snow. Taking great care, she drew a long, straight line. She stared at it. Then she drew another smaller line through it, making a cross. She studied her artwork for a long moment. 'I knew they were coming.'

Buggy nodded. 'It's OK,' he said. 'It's not your fault. The scratchgas in the air on our planet confused you, made you do bad things.'

Mrs Magner continued to stare at the cross. 'What am I?'

Buggy saw no point tiptoeing around the matter. 'Scuba says you're something called a cyborganic.'

'Is that why she wants me dead?'

'She doesn't want you . . . well . . . she . . . look, Scuba only has suspicions. She doesn't know for sure that you're a cyborganic.'

'And how can we know for sure?'

Now it was Buggy's turn to look down at the floor.

Mrs Magner sighed and stood up. 'A talebearer revealeth secrets: but he that is of a faithful spirit concealeth the matter.'

'I thought we'd already established that I don't speak bible,' muttered Buggy. 'I have no idea what you just said.'

With a chuckle, Mrs Magner began to walk away. 'You are a good, trustworthy young man, Bugger. That is what it means.'

Buggy found himself with a decision to make. Thick snow began to blot Mrs Magner out. If Scuba was right, then it would be wise to let the old lady go.

And yet . . .

'Wait!' shouted Buggy. He got to his feet and scrunched his way towards her. 'When Scuba found us . . . after that machine had moved us, she . . . she wanted to cut you. She said that your blood would be affected by a magnet. Something about nanotechnology in your bloodstream.' Buggy tutted. 'Mrs Magner, I don't believe that you're bad. I've known you for as long as I can remember. You've had years to do bad things. But you haven't. And you could have hurt me or worse just now. But you didn't.' He walked right up to her. 'I *will* help you . . . but you must tell me if you think you're losing control of yourself at any point.'

The old lady grabbed hold of Buggy's shoulders. 'At any point?' she whispered. Her good eye, no longer bloodshot, moistened. Her fingers began pressing and squeezing. 'You want me to tell you if I think I am going to lose control of myself at *any point*?' She nodded to herself. 'Then you need to know . . . that I feel I will lose control of myself at *every* point.' As the passion in her whisper grew, her undulating fingers inched inwards, creeping towards Buggy's neck like thick spider's legs. 'There is a demon inside me, Bugger, gnawing at my brain, filling my mind with thoughts to turn the hair white and the milk sour. You've never known me. You've only known *of* me.' Mrs Magner looked suddenly deflated. 'And yet you offer help. Samaritan.' The old lady sighed. 'So . . . yes. When I learn what I truly am, I will tell you to run. You have my word.' As her fervour subsided, so did her grip. 'What am I?' She turned her hands over and stared at her palms as though seeing them for the first time. 'I am a lost sheep. I need to be found.'

'Then may the good Lord lead us to a magnet,' said Buggy.

He held out his hand.

Mrs Magner took it.

Chapter Fourteen

M uddy took a deep breath. With Angel tight to his side, he stepped out into the main street. There were people. Lots of them. Different features. Different hair colours. Different skin tones. It was astounding. 'Have you ever seen anything like this before?'

Angel looked up at him with big saucer eyes.

Muddy crouched down beside her. 'Listen, Angel, we've been friends for a while now, so you know you can speak to me if you like?' he said. He realised that he had no idea how old Angel was, or if she actually could speak. 'But nodding and shaking your head is OK too, if you don't want to say anything.'

Angel lifted Little Dog. She pointed at her toy, directing Muddy's gaze to the snowflakes that were drifting down onto its fur. The girl's eyes flicked between the snow landing on Little Dog and the snow settling on the black skinsuit that covered her own arm. Flakes that hit fur either settled or were blown away. Flakes that hit her arm melted. Some of the water droplets were absorbed by the black material, some ran off.

'It's amazing, isn't it?' smiled Muddy.

The ever-faithful Little Dog sparkled. And this time Angel nodded.

Muddy wasn't sure if she was agreeing to the snow being amazing, or the skinsuits being amazing, or the people being amazing. It didn't matter. She was communicating. And besides, all these things were amazing. 'There's something else, Angel. You know Scuba, the girl who helped us, she thinks that she can get us back to our families and make us forget everything that has happened over the last few days. Would you like that?'

The small girl stared down at the snow-covered ground.

'Tell you what,' said Muddy, 'check with Little Dog before you answer because the question is for both of you.' He stood back up and continued to marvel at his new surroundings. After a minute or two, he gave Angel's hand a little squeeze. 'So, what do you think? Would you and Little Dog like that?'

Angel made Little Dog's head nod.

'OK, good. Then that's what we'll do. We'll ask Scuba to send us back to our families.' He pushed his forefinger and thumb on the shoulder of his skinsuit, triggering the family suitcipher that Scuba had shown him.

Hand in hand, Muddy and Angel stood at the side of the footpath and waited. Snow drifted down and people drifted by. No one paid them any attention.

It was Angel who noticed Scuba first. She tugged on Muddy's arm and flicked Little Dog's head towards the road. Scuba was halfway across, making her way towards them. As she stepped onto their side of the pavement, she bumped into a passing man. Muddy thought it was an accident . . . until he noticed a brown wallet in her hand.

'So, you're taught how to fight *and* how to steal?'

'No,' replied Scuba. 'We are taught how to defend ournselves and we are also taught sleight of hand.' She flicked through the contents of the wallet. Took out some paper currency. Put it back. Took out a small plastic card. Smiled. 'Credit-based payment system. Encoded magnetic strip composed of iron-based particles. Perfect.' She placed the card on her forearm and allowed her skinsuit to scan it before putting it back in the wallet and running down the street. 'Sir, yourn wallet, you dropped yourn wallet.'

After reuniting the man with his money, Scuba waved for Muddy and Angel to join her at the top of the street. She walked across to a small, square machine that was mounted into a wall.

'What are you doing?' asked Muddy.

Scuba positioned her wrist above a slot in the right-hand centre section of the machine. The sleeve of her skinsuit extended and seeped into it. 'Creating a currency account on this planet. It will make ourn stay here more . . . agreeable.'

Muddy became a little self-conscious. He gave a furtive glance around. 'The people here seem a bit . . . stupid.'

'Stupid humans? Who would have thought it?'

Muddy grinned. 'You know what I mean. More than stupid.'

'I know. I was just making fun,' said Scuba. 'I ran some tests earlier. There is faux scratchgas in the atmosphere. It is mentally numbing the populous.' She took her hand from the machine. 'Done. You realise that this is Earth? The same planet that you transported to before?'

Muddy nodded, pleased that Scuba was relaxed enough to be making fun. 'I guessed,' he said. 'I recognised the feel of it, the smell and stuff, you know. And the snow. But why is there scratchgas in the atmosphere? You said Earth wasn't a scratch planet.'

'I said it was not listed as a scratch planet. And I did not say scratchgas, I said faux scratchgas. It is a replicated version. And that means whatever is going on here is not sanctioned by the Amorphi. But mine scan showed no non-humans in the vicinity. We should be perfectly safe. All in all, it is serendipitous. We can still interact with these people – they will just appear distant, as though in a dream state. At the rate the faux scratchgas is dissipating, the populous should be like this for two or three days. We will be long gone by then. They will not even remember we were here.' Scuba pushed off from the wall. 'Now follow me. I scouted this area before meeting with you. I also used this planet's rather archaic wireless network to research local accommodation. There is an hotel just over there. It appears acceptable. Allow me to do the talking when we enter.'

Scuba led them across the main road. They turned right, down a short side street. An imposing, silver-fronted building sat at the end of it like a glamorous blockade. It was as though the building itself was saying, *what's the point of any more road? Where else would you want to go?* A silver and gold military figure, shield and banner in hand, stood guard above the entrance. Five letters, spread across the silver facade, spelling out the word 'SAVOY'.

Muddy kept his eye on the military figure for a moment, making sure it *was* just a statue. 'This planet seems a bit more . . . I don't know,' said Muddy.

'Opulent?' offered Scuba, as glistening entrance doors slid open before them. 'Yourn planet had a smaller population, prudent, environmentally aware. This population . . . not so much.'

'Opulent,' parroted Muddy. 'You use words that . . . I don't.' The sheer splendour of the building's interior reduced Muddy's voice to a whisper. 'We should find Buggy and Mrs Magner first.'

'It is not that simple,' replied Scuba.

'Well, you found me simply enough. Just use that suitcipher location thing?'

'Only skinsuits with a family link can do that. Finding the others will require a little more effort. I will need water, like I needed water to locate mine team on yourn planet.'

Muddy had a flashback to the moment they'd located Scuba's team. He prayed they wouldn't find Buggy and Mrs Magner in the same state. But he didn't say anything, he just kept quiet and followed.

Ahead of them, across a chequered marble floor, stood the hotel reception. Scuba stepped forward, addressed the lone female behind the counter. 'River View Personality Suite,' she gave a brief glance towards Angel, 'with an adjoining River View Junior Suite. I will put it on mine card.'

The female receptionist nodded and pointed to a tiny box on the counter.

Shielding her actions, Scuba allowed the sleeve of her skinsuit to extend into the slot, just like she'd done at the wall machine. She entered a number, prompting a message to appear on the screen of the box: 'PIN accepted.'

'Thank you,' said the receptionist.

Scuba took her hand from the machine. 'We wish to be discreet. No maid service or butler will be necessary. We will see ournselves to the room.'

'Very well, madam,' said the female, handing a small card to Scuba. 'The lift is just through there. Your suites are on the sixth floor, room 6F5.'

The lift was fast and smooth. On the sixth floor, Scuba found the door labelled 6F5. There was no hole for a key. She hovered the card that the receptionist had given her over the door handle. There was a click. She turned the handle and pushed the door wide open.

Muddy peered in. 'This isn't a room. It's a small country. A small country made of marble.' Beyond the entrance foyer he could see a spacious sitting room with tables and chairs. He could see audio and televisual entertainment equipment, and corridors, lots of them, branching off in all directions. By his side he heard Angel yawn. 'This one needs to go to bed,' said Muddy. 'I'll take her to her room . . . if I can find it. I'll press that suitcipher thing if I get lost. You can come find me.'

The route to Angel's adjoining room led past a balcony. Muddy gave Angel a little nod. 'Let's go have a look before bed.'

They stepped out into the evening air. The skinsuit compensated so quickly that Muddy didn't notice the cold. The first thing to catch his eye was a river. It was dark, murky, not like the clear water of home. It snaked along, curling past a large wheel-shaped structure, viewing pods hanging around its rim. Then the river swept past the base of an old, gothic building. There was a tower built into the right corner, a large circular timepiece at its head. All the buildings in this city looked impressive. The ancient and the new, side by side, each one lit up to show it at its best. Muddy looked down at Angel. She didn't seem as captivated as he was. 'OK, come on sleepyhead.'

Angel's bed was huge and soft as a cloud. Just sitting on it made Muddy want to stop everything, curl up and snooze. He managed to control himself. He tucked Angel in and made sure to tuck Little Dog in right next to her. 'Me and Scuba will be through there if you need us.'

Angel didn't say anything. She pulled Little Dog close and stared at Muddy through the dull light. He decided to stay a while. Compared to the shattered stone building they'd slept in the night before, this was luxury. But Angel was just a child. She was scared. And scared stayed, no matter the surroundings. Muddy shuffled up next to her and stroked her head until she drifted off.

When he got back to the adjoining apartment, he heard the sound of running water. He knocked on the bathroom door.

'Enter.'

Muddy eased the door open a crack.

'I said enter.' Scuba motioned him to come inside.

The sound of running water was coming from a freestanding bath. It was big and white, and the four supports were shaped like animals' feet, complete with claws. The bathroom was as immaculate as everything else. Two fluffy white dressing gowns hung from separate pegs on the wall. Accompanying pairs of fluffy white slippers sat on a shelf below them. Every garment had the word 'Savoy' embroidered upon it in gold thread.

'You may have noticed that yourn suit absorbs a certain amount of water,' said Scuba. 'Water reacts with the living synthetic cells and raphenia. It aids function and gives an energy boost.'

'Is that why I don't sweat?'

'You still sweat, you just do not notice. The suit absorbs all substances from yourn skin and either utilises them, recycles them into yourn bloodstream or expels them. I was able to use moisture from the melted snow earlier to partially track yourn friend and Mrs Magner.'

'They're still together?'

'Yes, but mine results were inconclusive. They must have been on the move. The volume of pure water in this bathtub should give me a better reading.' Scuba turned off the tap and stepped into the centre of the tub. The water was only ankle deep. She pressed parts of her skinsuit . . . more suitciphers, Muddy guessed . . . and then raised her hands above her head.

Muddy couldn't help but smile.

'What?' asked Scuba.

'Nothing.'

'Do not nothing me.' Scuba gave a tiny, angry kick, splashing a bit of water over Muddy. 'What?'

'It's just . . . I saw you do that on my planet. It looked like a halo. That's why I thought you were an angel.' He didn't know if it was just the heat from the water, but Scuba's cheeks reddened slightly.

'That was a nice thought. Now shut yourn face while I scan.' She raised her hands again and a golden hoop appeared.

Muddy was much closer than the last time. In the forest, his view had been obscured by leaves and branches . . . and panic. Now, in this calm bathroom on Earth, he could see everything clearly. The inside of the hoop above Scuba's head was criss-crossed with lines. Thin as strands of hair, some of the lines grouped together, some curved apart. Peppered throughout the circle were blocks and dashes and dots and rectangles.

'Buggy and the cyborganic are still together,' announced Scuba. 'They have definitely moved again since mine last trace though.' She touched thumbs and the hoop disappeared. She lowered her arms. 'They will find a place to stay overnight. I will keep checking theirn location. When they remain stationary, we will have to move fast to find them before they go somewhere else.'

'OK,' said Muddy. It felt good knowing that Buggy and Mrs Magner had made it safely to Earth. 'Have you learned anything else about this planet?'

'Two facts. I told you before that Earth was not listed as a scratch planet. Fact one, it is not listed at all. It is like a forgotten planet. Mayhap that is why the population is so diverse and the planet so . . . discombobulated.'

'The planet is so what?' interrupted Muddy.

'This is yourn language that I am using.'

'Well, I'm sorry, but I've never used that word before and probably never will.'

Scuba tutted. 'Disorganised . . . mixed . . . jumbled up.'

'Oh. Well, why didn't you just say that.'

'I did. Yourn linguistic skills are that of an infant. Mayhap I should use baby talk in future confabulation.'

'Now you're just doing it deliberately.'

'Mayhap I am. Mayhap it will inspire you to learn yourn own language. Now listen, we know for certain that at least three Dreddax butchers have been on this planet because theirn PIPs brought us here. And theirn visit was recent because faux scratchgas is still in the atmosphere, but theirn reason for being here I know not.' Scuba bent over and turned the hot tap back on. 'Fact two, this planet is not mine concern. Mine concern is getting you back to yourn families.' She poured some thick liquid from a bottle at the side of the bath into the water. White bubbles began filling the tub. Muddy began feeling a little uncomfortable.

'I can only speculate,' continued Scuba, 'but mine guess is that the Dreddax butchers happened upon this planet recently and decided to scout it. There is no damage and they have now gone. And thanks to us they will not be coming back.' She pressed a suitcipher at her wrists. Muddy watched as her skinsuit began to retract. First her wrists were slowly unveiled, then her forearms, then her elbows. He thought it would stop there. But the skinsuit continued to retreat. Scuba bent over and pressed a suitcipher at her ankles.

Muddy covered his eyes. 'What are you doing?'

'I am taking the opportunity to bathe.'

Muddy shuffled backwards, one hand over his eyes, one hand feeling for the door handle. 'Err, wh . . . we . . . err . . . we usually bathe alone on my planet,' he mumbled.

'We are no longer on yourn planet,' said Scuba very matter-of-factly.

Muddy kept his eyes covered. 'You're making fun again, aren't you? I can tell, see. I'm getting to know you now. You are making fun. Definitely. Are you making fun?'

'I am merely taking the opportunity to bathe and giving you the opportunity to bathe also.'

'It's alright, I can wait,' replied Muddy, as he continued to back away, 'definitely making fun . . . err . . . but thanks,' he added. As soon as he was out, he closed the door. He was sure he heard a mischievous giggle above the gurgle of running water. But, louder than that, was the sound of his own heart pounding questions in his chest.

Chapter Fifteen

'Did you hear that?'

'No, what was it?'

'My stomach,' said Buggy. 'I'm hungry.'

Mrs Magner nodded. 'Me too.'

Buggy looked along the main road. He felt strangely comfortable in this new world. 'There are plenty of shops and restaurants,' he said. In amongst them, a busy, glass-fronted burger bar caught his eye. He watched people enter, pay for food, go to a table.

'We have no way to pay,' said Mrs Magner.

'I'm not sure that'll be a problem,' replied Buggy. 'People on this planet are weird. They buy stuff but some of them hardly eat any. Come on.' He led Mrs Magner across the road and into the burger restaurant.

'I'll sit down, shall I?' asked Mrs Magner.

Buggy pointed to a table and nodded. 'Just sit there and look normal.' He paused. Mrs Magner wasn't going to look normal in a million years. 'I mean, well, at least try and . . . look a bit hungry. I'll be back in a sec.' He picked up a tray and circled around the tables. The queues at the counter blocked his view of the staff and, more importantly, their view of him. Choosing his moments carefully, Buggy began to commandeer a selection of untouched items.

'Dinner is served,' he said as he placed the tray in the centre of their table. 'OK, we've got some kind of fizzy drink, and this looks like a milkshake. Oh, and I managed to get a straw. These things here are fried potato slices, I tried one. They're good. We can share them. And we have a two-layered burger and a single burger with some cheese on. Which one do you fancy?'

Mrs Magner shrugged, so Buggy took it upon himself to decide. 'OK. Potato slices in the middle. Erm, I'll take the double burger, it's more manly. You get the burger with cheese. I'll have a go at the fizzy drink. And you take the milkshake.' He sat back to admire his distribution skills. 'And since you got the cheese it's only fair that I get the straw,' he joked. He picked it off the tray, slipped it out of its wrapper and pushed it through the slit in the lid of his drink. Buggy took a bite of his burger. It tasted good. He glanced up at Mrs Magner. She hadn't started. He took another bite of his burger. It tasted really good. He slowed down his chewing, surreptitiously watched the old lady out of the corner of his eye. She wasn't doing anything. He gave a little 'mmmm' of encouragement. Nothing. She didn't even pick her burger up.

Buggy could feel her good eye flitting from his mouth to his fizzy drink and back again. There seemed to be an air of . . . anger exuding from the old lady. Suddenly, Mrs Magner's hand whipped out and plucked the straw from Buggy's drink. Bits of the fizzy liquid flicked out over him. A blob got him right in the eye.

Mrs Magner plunged the straw into her milkshake. She let it rest there a moment. She tapped the top of it. Tapped the top of it again. Then she stooped forward and took a giant suck.

Buggy wiped the liquid from his eye. 'Or you could have the cheese *and* the straw,' he muttered.

They ate in silence. Mrs Magner tucked into her burger like she hadn't eaten for weeks. She only stopped every now and again to tap the top of her straw and take another giant suck.

Suffering from a distinct lack of straw, Buggy took the lid off his drink and placed it on the tray. A few moments later, when he moved to pick his drink up and try some, Mrs Magner moved for it as well. Buggy stopped. Mrs Magner stopped. Buggy moved his hand a little closer to his cup. Mrs Magner moved her hand a little closer to his cup. She looked him in the eye, her hand poised. Buggy decided to go for it. But the old lady beat him. She reached the cup first. But she didn't pick it up, she just left her hand resting against the side of it. Buggy sat back in his chair, shrugged and shook his head. What was this old lady doing? Had she lost her mind? Again? He decided to ignore her. He reached for his drink. Still looking him in the eye, Mrs Magner pushed his cup over.

Liquid poured out onto the table. As quickly as he could, Buggy covered it with napkins. He sat back in his chair flabbergasted. 'Well, I guess I'll stay thirsty then.'

The old lady looked around a little sheepishly. She sighed and held her milkshake out, waggling the straw under his nose. Buggy shook his head. 'No, thank you,' he said. 'Keep your precious straw.' He was in no doubt that this old woman, this cyborganic, was utterly bonkers. He couldn't risk any more incidents like that. They were lucky no one had seen it. Mrs Magner picked up her burger. Buggy went back to his and wondered what they should do next. 'We'll have to find somewhere to stay the night. I think these skinsuits will keep us warm, but we should at least find somewhere under cover, out of the snow. Don't murder me in my sleep though, OK?'

'Of course I won't murder you in your sleep,' replied Mrs Magner. 'I'll wait until you wake up.'

Buggy gave a half-hearted laugh. Was that his first encounter with cyborganic humour? It would have been funny if it wasn't so plausible. He scrutinised the old lady, searched for signs that she was just joking. It didn't help. Close up, her white eye looked ancient and evil. Her other eye was the complete opposite – clear blue, youthful somehow . . . twinkling with the knowledge of hidden things. 'Mrs Magner, how old are you?'

The old lady paused mid-chew. 'Cast me not off in the time of old age; forsake me not when my strength faileth. My flesh and my skin hath he made old; he hath broken my bones. He hath set me in dark places, as they that be dead of old.' A tiny bit of chewed bread fell out of her mouth onto her sleeve.

She tipped her head to the side and looked at it through her good eye. 'Oops.' She reached down and flicked it . . . at Buggy.

He wiped the wet blob off his shoulder with a napkin. Mrs Magner's behaviour was beginning to worry him. Maybe he should be a little more subtle with his questioning. 'That silver cross you keep with you,' he said, 'it looks really old.'

Mrs Magner reached for the chain around her neck. Her fingers slid down each link until they settled on the cross. She squeezed it tight and nodded.

'I noticed that there's a hole in it,' said Buggy. 'Is it hollow in the middle?'

She nodded again.

'How long have you had it?'

'Since . . . my childhood,' she said. Her hand squeezed harder on the cross. The silver edges began to dig deep into her skin.

Buggy reached across the table. 'Mrs Magner . . .'

Her grip loosened. 'Yes?'

'Do you remember much from when you were little?' he asked, shuffling his chair a little closer to her.

'Of course.'

Buggy waited for her to elaborate, but instead she went silent. Looked at the floor. Looked at her straw. And back again. Floor, straw, floor, straw. Her eyes moistened. She shook her head. 'No,' she admitted. 'I don't remember. I try. I try to think about it and all I remember is . . . emotion.'

Buggy sensed he was in dangerous territory. He was tormenting the brain of a scratchgas muddled cyborganic. If he continued . . . well, he didn't want to consider what might happen. And yet he wanted to ask so many things . . . *'why didn't that Dreddax butcher kill you?', 'how did you get those scars all over your arms?', 'why do I feel sorry for you despite knowing what you are, what you might do to me?'* He sat back. He couldn't ask those things. He needed to relieve the tension. 'I spent all my childhood with Muddy,' he said. 'Most people think we're brothers. I'm glad he's with us. The things that have happened over the last few days. It's unreal. I wouldn't have picked anyone else to go through it with. I'll be glad when we get back to our families. Get everything back to normal.'

The old lady didn't seem to be listening. 'It's OK, Mrs Magner. We'll be alright here. We'll find the others, and everything will be alright.' His words were lost on her. Mrs Magner was looking past him, just staring through the restaurant window.

'Be sober, be vigilant; because your adversary the devil, as a roaring lion, walketh about, seeking whom he may devour.'

Buggy turned in his chair, followed the old lady's gaze. And he stared too. The remaining piece of burger in his hand dropped to the floor. Walking along the street, passing right by the window, was a Dreddax. Unmistakable. Unbelievable. And the humans around it didn't run, they didn't scream. They behaved as though it was the most normal thing in their world.

It took a moment for Buggy to pull himself together. 'Come on.' He got off his seat, ushered Mrs Magner out of hers. 'Before it disappears.' He led the way out of the restaurant, looked left. The Dreddax had crossed over and was making its way to a fork in the road. Buggy hung back, waited for it to choose its route, then he jogged over to the junction. The Dreddax was nowhere to be seen.

Mrs Magner caught up with him and stopped dead.

'Can you see it?' asked Buggy.

The old lady ignored his question. She had seen something else. Something that was holding her absolutely transfixed. It was a church. Not a simple church, like the ones on their home planet, but a beautiful brick-built structure. The main window was spectacular. It was huge and hexagonal in shape. A large, perfectly circular piece of clear glass sat at its centre. Around that circle, small, uneven glass segments, all different colours, had been patched together. In the darkness, the glass centrepiece shone like the moon. Light spilled from it in four directions, highlighting a patchwork cross.

'Mrs Magner, did you see where it went?'

The old lady just continued to wonder at the church.

Buggy tugged at her arm. 'Over there!' He pointed at the Dreddax. It was coming back their way. 'We need to get out of here.'

Mrs Magner looked at the Dreddax. Then she looked back at the church. 'Discretion shall preserve thee; understanding shall keep thee.'

'Now, Mrs Magner. We need to go now.' Buggy tugged at her arm again.

The old lady turned around. 'I gave you my word . . .' she whispered.

'What?'

Mrs Magner's rheumy eye glowed like the church window in reflected moonlight. Her lips toyed with a smile. 'I . . . know . . . now . . . what . . . I . . . am.' She gave a gentle nod. 'And you need to run from me.' The smile dropped from her face. The old lady sucked in a huge, deep breath . . . 'RUN FROM MEEEEEEE!'

The ferocity of the shout brought sudden clarity. This was the warning she'd promised. Mrs Magner was a cyborganic. Her cyborganic purpose had come back to her. Buggy turned away. He had to run. Anywhere. As he leaned into the night, he heard Mrs Magner's whispered words . . . *'not fast enough'* . . . he felt an impact on the side of his head. It knocked him clean off his feet.

Chapter Sixteen

'Are you dressed?'

Muddy looked in the mirror. The clothes that Scuba had bought him fitted well. 'Yes,' he replied.

'Good. Now, depending on where you want the skinsuit to remain, do the suitciphers I showed you.'

Muddy rolled the top of his socks down and pressed the suitcipher at each ankle. He did the same at his right wrist. The skinsuit began disappearing. He could feel it moving, like someone was running a fine brush over his skin. Within moments the entire skinsuit was just a bracelet around his left wrist. He pulled his socks up, tied his bootlaces. After a final check in the mirror, he walked out of his bedroom and gave a spin. 'What do you think?'

Scuba gave him the once over. 'I think we will blend in much better now.' For herself, she'd chosen blue jeans, big brown boots, a thick dark brown jacket and a woolly hat. 'And what do you think?'

Muddy thought she looked beautiful. 'You look . . . warm,' he said.

'Here.' A black woollen hat came flying through the air. Muddy couldn't tell if Scuba had thrown it to him, or *at* him. 'Without the skinsuits regulating ourn temperature, it may get cold,' she said. 'If it gets too cold you can always re-activate the suit beneath yourn clothes.'

When they got outside, it was still snowing. Muddy frowned at Angel. She was wearing exactly the same outfit as Scuba, only all her clothes were pure white. He pulled her hat off and put his black one on her head instead. 'I don't want to lose you out here. You look like a snowball.' He turned to Scuba. 'OK, which way.'

'The scan last night showed both Buggy and the cyborganic a few minutes from this position,' said Scuba. 'The scan this morning showed one of them in that same location.'

'Stop calling her a cy— wait, one of them? What do you mean "one" of them?'

'Did you not do mathematics on yourn planet?'

'Enough to know one is significantly less than two.'

'There is no need for worry. There are many ways that two can be one. Two halves for example. Put them together and they become one.'

'You're saying Mrs Magner and Buggy have been cut in half?'

'I am saying there is one signal. They may be attached, so close together that the scan cannot distinguish between individuals.'

'What! Now you're saying that Mrs Magner and Buggy are . . . ' Muddy looked down at Angel and covered her ears, 'erm, *attaching?* That's disgusting.'

Scuba sighed and set off. 'I am saying that there is one signal. And the sooner we get to the location, the sooner we discover why.'

Muddy took Angel's hand and followed. 'Well, if we discover . . . *that*, then you can break the news to his parents,' shouted Muddy. 'I'm certainly not.'

It was quiet. The main street was virtually empty. Most of the stores were closed at this early hour. The fallen snow was even and smooth. Muddy liked the gentle scrunching sound it made underfoot. He was warming to the cold planet.

Scuba was a little way ahead. She looked back, waited for them to catch up. 'We are getting close,' she said.

'Hang on,' said Muddy. 'I recognise this place. This is where I landed the first time I was here.'

'And do you recall the way to the police station?' asked Scuba.

'Yes,' replied Muddy. 'Up there, right and then left. I don't think it's that far.'

'Then go and retrieve yourn backpack. I must return to mine planet to get the data regarding the location of yourn family. I may need assistance. Retrieve that master PIP and you will be able to come with me.'

'You mean when you return to your planet to get the information that will get Angel and Mrs Magner home to their families too,' said Muddy. It was obvious to him that Scuba would need reminding of that every now and again.

'I will go to Buggy and the cyborganic,' said Scuba. 'Mine scan says they are very close. I believe I will find them inside that church. Meet us back here when you have yourn backpack.'

'Scuba, please, stop saying Mrs Magner is a cyborganic, especially in front of Angel.'

'Sorry, I would not wish to upset the cyborganic's beacon.'

Muddy blew in frustration. He led Angel to Scuba's side. 'Stay with Scuba, just for a little while.' He held Angel's reluctant little hand up and waited for Scuba's reluctant bigger hand to take it before he left.

As soon as Muddy was out of sight, Scuba let go of Angel. 'You fool the boys, but you do not fool me,' she said. 'I have been watching you every second since we met. You have watched me also. You saw what I did to those Dreddax butchers on the other planet. I will not hesitate to do the same to you should it be required. Walk ahead of me.' She turned Angel around and gave her a push to start her walking.

Nearer the church, Scuba slowed and surveilled the area. She pulled Angel's hood to bring the little girl to a stop. Scuba crouched down, pressed a suitcipher at her wrist, triggering the skinsuit to install beneath her clothes. She needed to be ready for anything. She hadn't wanted to worry Muddy back at the hotel, but with skinsuits, one signal meant one signal. Only one person was inside that church. She didn't know if it would be a friendly human male or a deadly cyborganic huntress. Scuba looked at Angel. 'Come here,' she said. 'Give me yourn toy.'

Angel took Little Dog out of her pocket, squeezed him tight and shook her head.

Scuba took hold of the girl's coat, pulled her close. She snatched Little Dog out of Angel's hands and hurled him towards the gaping black mouth of the church. The toy spun through the air, collar sparkling. It landed a foot or two in front of the entrance. Everything stayed quiet. Scuba poked Angel. 'Well? Go and get yourn toy back . . . *child*.'

With lowered head and shuffling feet, Angel made her way through the snow towards Little Dog. Scuba studied the entrance. Studied the surroundings. Searched for any kind of movement. Any kind of trap. She saw no immediate danger.

Angel bent over, picked up her toy and hugged him.

Scuba rose from her hiding place, had another look around. She made her way to where Angel stood, following the exact path the girl had taken. The inside of the church was now visible. And she could see someone lying on a pew. It was Buggy. Scuba pushed Angel to the large wooden doors and tethered her to one of the ornate doorknobs by her hood. 'Move and you die.'

Scuba entered the church hall. She knelt next to Buggy, gently nudged him. 'Are you OK, Buggy?'

Buggy jumped. His eyes shot open and darted all around the church. He saw no one else. Nothing else. 'I'm fine,' he replied. 'Where's Muddy?'

'What happened here? What happened to yourn face?'

Buggy replayed the events of the previous night in his head. 'I fell,' he said.

'Where is the cyborganic?'

'Where's Muddy? Where's Angel?'

'Angel is waiting outside. Muddy has gone to retrieve his backpack from the police station.'

'Alone?'

'He knows the way. He is more than capable.'

'But what about the Dreddax?'

'What Dreddax?'

'Me and Mrs Magner saw one last night, just walking along the street. No one paid any attention to it. We followed it to this corner, and then . . . we lost it. The church was open, so we . . . I . . . stayed the night under cover.'

'Clarify. Was it a generic Dreddax or a Dreddax butcher that you saw?'

'How can you tell?'

'The ones that came for us on yourn planet were butchers. Five slashes of red colouring on theirn chest plates.'

'I don't know. It was dark. What does it matter?'

'It matters because regular Dreddax conform to Amorphi protocols and may be here solely for the purpose of monitoring the populous. Dreddax butchers, however . . . well, you had better try and remember for the sake of yourn friend.' Scuba had a quick glance around. 'Where is the cyborganic?' she repeated. 'She will know if it was a butcher.'

'I don't know where she is.'

Scuba studied Buggy for a moment. 'You did not fall. The cyborganic did that to you.'

Buggy sat himself up. 'I think something happened to her last night. She . . . left me here. Hasn't come back.'

Scuba nodded. 'The faux scratchgas in the atmosphere of this planet must have been potent enough to finish the job. Hern transformation to cyborganic is complete. We need to leave this place. If there *are* Dreddax butchers here, she will no doubt be working with them. You are bait. They will want to get us all. They may be watching right now, waiting until we are all in the same place. It is fortunate that yourn friend has gone to the police station.'

'She said she'd tell me if she was a cyborganic.'

Scuba prodded the bruise on the side of Buggy's head. 'She told you.'

'She told me to run. She didn't tell me she was a cyborganic.'

Scuba sighed. 'And yourn friend tries to convince me that humans are not stupid.'

'No, no, we can be stupid,' acknowledged Buggy. 'Doesn't mean we're always wrong.' He stood up, a little unsteady on his feet. He saw Angel in the doorway. 'Angel's managed to get her hood hooked on the door handle, poor kid.'

'Yes, poor child,' said Scuba, 'I wonder how that happened.'

'Hey Angel,' said Buggy as he unhooked her. 'Good to see you.'

Angel didn't say a word. She took Buggy's hand and moved close to his legs, hiding her face from Scuba.

'Come on. We need to leave this area,' said Scuba.

'We should look for Mrs Magner.'

'Unless you want another one of those on yourn head, I suggest you follow me.'

Buggy stayed put. Angel stayed with him, both arms now wrapped around his thigh.

'Buggy, I do not mean to be harsh,' said Scuba, 'but this is yourn choice – come with me to save yourn friend or stay here to fall into a cyborganic trap.' Scuba didn't wait for his decision.

Buggy had one last look around. He unclamped Angel from his thigh, took her by the hand and followed Scuba off the church grounds.

Chapter Seventeen

Muddy's heart sank. There were more people around now. Walking in the company of other people should have been comforting. But it wasn't. It was just eerie. These people were . . . hollow. That was the scratchgas. The *faux scratchgas* went Scuba's voice in his head. Maybe without it, things would have been different. Maybe not. He'd never liked being around lots of people anyway. Being with Buggy, Scuba, Mrs Magner and Angel was better. Not the greatest of circumstances. But better, nonetheless. Muddy sat down on a nearby bench. He wanted to take a moment, alone, just to relax. He closed his eyes, shut out the hollow people. Even with his eyes shut, he could tell he was on a different planet. The smells, the sounds, the *feel* of the place. At least it was safer on thi—a particular smell interrupted his train of thought. He'd only come across it once before, very recently.

He turned his head into the breeze. Opened his eyes. Standing at the end of the street, turning slowly from side to side, was a Dreddax. Muddy looked down its armour. Five red slashes on the chest. A butcher. And yet the people of Earth didn't react. They didn't seem worried. It wasn't that they ignored the butcher, but those who looked at it only gave a casual glance, as though they were seeing a statue or monument that had been part of the landscape for years. *Blend in or don't get seen.* Muddy stayed on the bench, hoping the Dreddax butcher would go the other way.

It didn't.

It meandered through the pedestrians, staring at some longer than others, searching . . . getting closer. At the opposite end of Muddy's bench, the butcher paused and peered down. A hollow lady sat munching on a sandwich. The Dreddax butcher dismissed her, took another step. Muddy stiffened. It was right next to him. Its head turned away . . . and then turned back. Muddy felt the reflection from the shining visor creep across his face. Not long ago he'd looked through a visor just like it. Text was about to run across its base, telling the Dreddax butcher that this was not an Earth human. Telling it how much this non-Earth human was worth. Muddy whipped his arm up to engage the shield on his skinsuit and push the butcher away. It took him a second to realise that his skinsuit wasn't deployed – less time to realise that he'd lost the advantage of surprise. Red lasers began to hum. Muddy jumped over the back of the bench and ran. He bumped and banged along, forcing a path through the unresponsive crowd. They had no idea he was running for his life. A quick look back. The butcher was following. It was paying no attention to the other humans. Its visor was fixed on him and him alone. Muddy found an extra burst of speed. He was faster than the butcher. He could outrun it. Up ahead, he saw the police building. The entrance was just around the corner. He jostled through the final group of people and raced up the steps to the front office. As gently as he could, he closed the door behind him. He paused to catch his breath, looked through the glass door at the street below. No sign of the butcher. It couldn't have seen him enter the station. Now he had to work out how to get back to the church and warn the others. First things first, he needed to get his backpack. There was only one member of the public sitting in the waiting area. A different Sergeant stood behind the front desk. He wasn't alone. Muddy recognised the female officer next to him. It was Fourforty. She was just staring into space. *Scratchgas.* It was no respecter of job or rank. Not that it mattered. Muddy imagined there would be very little crime when you combine an atmosphere full of scratchgas and a street full of Dreddax butchers. Even so, he moved around slowly and purposefully, as though he was under the influence of scratchgas too. There was no gap or gate in the front desk, so he walked to the far end of the counter and leaned over. He spotted his backpack, in a clear, sealed plastic bag. Muddy engaged the skinsuit beneath his clothes and waited. When no one was looking in his direction, he slid over the counter and dropped to his knees on the other side. He reached for his backpack. And heard a metallic clink.

He was handcuffed to the shelf.

'You!'

'How . . . ' Muddy gave Fourforty a gentle poke in the arm with his free hand. 'How come you're OK?'

He got a poke back, with interest. 'What do you think you're doing?'

Muddy bobbed his head up and peeked over the counter, then came back down. 'Ssshhhhh!'

'You sssshhh! What the hell's going on?' asked the officer. 'What's happened to everyone? And why aren't you like them?'

'Please . . . Fourforty, be quiet . . . I . . . it's diff . . .' Muddy's attempt at an explanation was cut short by the sound of the station door crashing open. He pulled Fourforty under the desk, signalled for her to take off the restraints.

Fourforty pointed in the direction of the door, mouthed the word *who*?

'It's more of a "what",' whispered Muddy. 'Do you have weapons?'

Fourforty nodded. 'Asp,' she replied, pointing to her belt.

Muddy felt his stomach turn. A stick against a Dreddax butcher.

The butcher's distinctive dull buzz grew slightly louder. It was moving towards them. Pointing to the asp, Muddy shook his head, he pointed at himself, then at Fourforty, then used his thumb to motion slitting his throat.

Fourforty didn't seem fazed. She looked around, quietly unlocked the cuffs. She signalled for Muddy to wait, then crept to the Sergeant's side. She tugged a small lever underneath a screen next to him. A CCTV camera in the corner of the room moved. Fourforty adjusted its angle. The Dreddax butcher appeared on screen. Its weapons were ready, each strand of spaghetti searching independently for a target. Now Fourforty looked a little more concerned. Her hand moved away from her asp. She edged nearer to the Sergeant, reached up, unclipped something that looked like a gun from his belt. All the time her eyes were locked on the CCTV screen. She waited, signalling with her outstretched left hand for Muddy to be still.

Suddenly she pointed. Muddy didn't need telling twice. He grabbed his backpack and ran towards the rear door. He grabbed the handle, turned and pulled. It wouldn't budge. He looked back at the Dreddax butcher. Red dots were spinning, aiming straight at him.

Fourforty rose smoothly to her feet. She fired the weapon. Two metal pins zipped through the air towards the butcher. They punctured its visor, embedding themselves in its head like tiny anchors. Black liquid began spurting through the cracks. Fourforty jammed the weapon into the Sergeant's hand and squeezed his finger down on the trigger. She too turned and ran to the rear of the front office.

'It won't open!' shouted Muddy.

Fourforty just looked at him. 'Of course it won't open.' She pulled a card from her pocket. 'The likes of you can't just go wandering around a Metropolitan Police facility.' She swiped her card through a black box near the lock. There was a click. She pulled the handle. The door opened. The officer and Muddy ran into the adjoining corridor, leaving the juddering Dreddax butcher behind.

'You used me as a distraction.'

Fourforty ignored him. She led the way through the station and across the back yard. 'Start talking,' she ordered. 'Everyone changed after you'd escaped from the police cell. Where did you go? Why is everyone different?'

'Don't blame me! The creature you just shot is a Dreddax butcher. It's from . . . somewhere else. I don't know why it's here. I'm human, like you. I'm from . . . somewhere else.'

'That's one of the most ridiculous confessions I've ever heard,' muttered Fourforty. She ushered Muddy through the yard's main exit. 'And I've heard a few.' She turned back to ease the solid metal gate shut behind her. 'First things first, where did—' Fourforty didn't finish her question.

Muddy turned around to see the officer on the floor. Scuba was on top of her. 'No, Scuba! She's OK! This is the law enforcement officer I told you about.'

The scuffle stopped, but neither female released her hold. They looked like they'd tied themselves into a knot. Muddy couldn't tell who had the advantage. There were arms and legs everywhere. Fourforty was older, bigger. She looked like she could handle herself. Muddy reckoned her law enforcement training would have seen to that. But he wondered if she was capable of doing what he'd seen Scuba do.

Scuba's legs were scissored around Fourforty's neck. She had one of the officer's wrists in a lock. She squeezed it. 'Then explain to me why she is unaffected by the faux scratchgas in this atmosphere.'

Fourforty winced and took a breath. 'What's scratchgas? Maybe I'm immune. I've only ever had chickenpox.'

'How much contact did you have with Muddy when you first encountered him?'

'I was the only one to have *any* contact with him.'

'Physical contact alone would not be sufficient to negate the effects of scratchgas.'

'Scuba,' interrupted Muddy. 'Please let her up. She just saved me from a Dreddax butcher. You can trust her.'

His plea fell on deaf ears.

Fourforty nodded to him, appreciating the effort. 'I've never had a prisoner escape before,' she said. 'I wanted to find him. I took his backpack, cut into it and searched it.'

'Still does not explain,' said Scuba squeezing her legs a little tighter.

Rather than retaliate, Fourforty released her hold and raised her open hands. 'What about if I ate one of the biscuit things I found inside the bag . . .' she said, looking a little embarrassed.

Scuba frowned, relaxed her own grip.

Fourforty shrugged her shoulders as best she could. 'What?'

'Is it commonplace on yourn planet for law enforcement officers to eat evidence?' asked Scuba.

'It was the end of a long shift. I was hungry. Now get off me.'

'Or what? You will eat me too?' Scuba unhooked her legs, stood up. 'You and Buggy should get along splendidly. He also eats things he should not.'

Chapter Eighteen

'There are five of us here,' explained Muddy. 'This is Scuba. She's getting *all* of us home – this tiny thing is Angel . . . and her friend Little Dog . . . then there's me, Mrs Magner and . . .' Muddy turned towards some movement to his right, 'and speak of the devil, my best mate, Buggy.'

'Hi,' said Buggy, nodding to the new addition. 'There are four of us, not five. Mrs Magner's done a runner. Scuba might have been right about her.'

'Are you sure?'

Buggy shrugged. 'I'm not sure about anything anymore.'

'Then we should go find her.'

'That's what I said.'

'We *will* locate the cyborganic,' said Scuba, brushing herself down. 'So that we can avoid it and avoid the Dreddax butchers that it is no doubt working with. Or, more accurately, working *for*.' She turned to Fourforty. 'The substance in the atmosphere that has made yourn population behave like automatons will dissipate in a few days. Everything will go back to normal then. Meanwhile, you can be of help to us should you wish.'

'Go ahead,' said Fourforty.

'Does yourn law enforcement use canine units?'

'Yes.'

'Are the canines kept in quarantined conditions?'

'No. Why?'

'I could have used a canine that was not affected by scratchgas. They have a gift when it comes to sniffing out Dreddax.'

'What if a canine had eaten some of that biscuit too?'

'That would be . . . fortuitous,' said Scuba.

'Oh, so now it's OK to eat evidence all of a sudden,' muttered Fourforty. 'Luckily for you, I am part of the specialist canine unit. And even luckier for you, I share food with my dog. I'll go and fetch him.'

'No,' said Scuba. 'I need to speak with you. Muddy, you or Buggy fetch the canine. You had them on yourn planet, did you not?'

'Yeah, of course,' said Buggy. 'I'll go and get it. I've got a way with dogs.'

Fourforty reached out to him. 'It's a different entrance. Take this pass. There's a small black box at the entrance door. Swipe the card to get in. The kennels are just around the corner. Keep the building to your left. Kennel nine. All the dogs are sleeping except mine.'

'What's its name?'

'*His* name is Chisel.'

'Chisel. Hmmm,' said Buggy as he walked away. 'That's a good name.'

Scuba clicked her fingers to get Fourforty's attention. 'Listen, Fourforty,' she said, 'you will not know if this has happened before because you would have succumbed to the scratchgas with everyone else, but that creature you saw in the police station: have you seen anything like it while you have been *compos mentis* the last few days?'

Fourforty clicked her fingers in Scuba's face. 'No.'

'Do you remember anything unusual prior to scratchgas release?'

Fourforty clicked her fingers in Scuba's face again. 'No.'

'Anything at all?' Scuba caught hold of the officer's hand before she could raise it to click her fingers again. 'I apologise for clicking mine fingers earlier. It was disrespectful.'

Fourforty lowered her hand. 'I don't remember anything unusual at all.'

Scuba sighed and turned away.

'We should help this planet,' whispered Muddy.

'I have got enough on mine plate helping you.'

'Even so, we can't leave Fourforty alone with a bunch of Dreddax butchers. The one in the station nearly got us both.'

'It is not up for discussion.'

'Oh, here we go. Black and white.'

'Erm,' interrupted Fourforty. 'If you're going to have an argument you could at least involve me. I love a good argu—' The officer's attention suddenly switched to Buggy. He came running around the corner towards them . . . then through the middle of them . . . then past them.

'What is *that*!' exclaimed Muddy.

Fourforty gave a sharp whistle. The monster ended its pursuit of Buggy and padded up to her side. 'Everyone, meet Chisel.'

Buggy had his head down, hands on his hips, gasping for breath. He looked up to see everyone staring at him. 'What?' he shrugged. 'I got him here, didn't I?'

Muddy laughed and turned to Fourforty. 'Got a way with dogs, you see. Canines aren't . . . weren't that big on our planet. What do you call this breed?'

'He's a cross breed, Belgian Malinois and Rottweiler.'

'He's magnificent,' said Muddy.

'Thank you.'

'Has he been trained to follow scents?' asked Scuba.

'Of course. It's part of his job.'

Scuba nodded. 'Good. And you are law enforcement?'

'The villains in the metropolis will rejoice the day I retire,' confirmed Fourforty.

'Then please take yourn canine on a patrol. If you find Dreddax butchers, note theirn positions, but under no circumstances engage them. As you are a native of this planet, they will assume you are under the influence of scratchgas and ignore you. Do not give them cause to think otherwise. Now, yourn animal will need a target scent.' Scuba jogged away from the group. She disappeared around the corner of the station building, heading in the direction of the front office. A few moments later she reappeared carrying a severed Dreddax head.

Muddy was horrified. 'What are you doing! Surely you didn't have to bring its entire head! One of its tentac—'

'The head is easiest to remove,' interrupted Scuba. 'You do not understand the difficulties involved in removing Dreddax . . .' Scuba frowned, 'testi—'

'TENTA . . . cles,' shouted Muddy with an involuntary wince.

Scuba pushed past him. 'May I?' With a nod from Fourforty, Scuba held the Dreddax head under Chisel's nose.

Chisel whined a little. Pattered to and fro. Gave a little snarl. He knew danger when he sniffed it. Scuba dropped the severed head and kicked it over towards the boys. 'Dispose of this while I speak with Fourforty.'

Scuba guided the officer and her canine to the end of the street. 'Begin yourn reconnaissance outside that church.' Scuba glanced back at the boys. They were far enough away. 'As you were made aware, Fourforty, there was a fifth member of ourn group. An older lady. Long white hair. Distinctive left eye, damaged, white in colour. She is dressed entirely in black, with material like this . . .' Scuba lifted her sleeve to show Fourforty the skinsuit. 'And she wears a striking, yet simple silver crucifix. If she gets a chance, she will kill both you and yourn canine. Do what you must. I have to go off planet. You can give me a situation report on mine return.'

'No way,' said Buggy.

'Go on! That thing nearly killed me! You're supposed to be a mate. The least you can do is put its head in the bin!'

'Listen, I dealt with one severed head back home.'

Muddy thought about that. 'Fair enough,' he conceded. 'But this planet has so many different bins.' He looked at the labels on each one. 'You think a Dreddax head will be recycled?'

Buggy shrugged.

'General waste, then.' Muddy picked the head up by the visor and stuffed it into a big grey bin.

'Scuba seems . . . motivated,' said Buggy. 'But I guess you would be if Dreddax butchers had just killed your team.'

Muddy pushed the lid of the bin shut. 'I think it's more than that,' he said. 'I had a sneaky look in her backpack on our planet. There was a piece of cloth inside with writing on, child's writing. I think Scuba had a sister who was murdered by Dreddax butchers too.'

'You remember what any of the writing said?' asked Buggy.

'That's the thing. Scuba said that my skinsuit had initiated some new facility for audio and visual translation of other languages,' Muddy paused. 'It really hurt when the suit did that by the way!'

Buggy thought back to his landing on Earth. Mrs Magner's bloodshot eye. Her own skinsuit must have hurt her first. Maybe she hadn't been trying to kill him after all. Maybe she just knew his skinsuit was about to do the same to him and was trying to help? He decided to keep that to himself. 'What's your point?' he asked.

'Well,' continued Muddy, 'she also said she didn't think any languages had been uploaded into it yet. But when I looked at her cloth, my eyes behaved like a camera. It was as if they took a picture of the cloth, then overlaid the symbols with a translation. So, if no other languages have been uploaded, I guess the writing must have been in Scuba's native language and the skinsuit, being linked to my brain, translated it. Since it was the first thing I've ever read in an alien language . . . ' Muddy smiled. 'I memorized it.'

'Nice one. Off you go then,' prompted Buggy.

'OK, it went like this . . . *May-Yania, Tinta. Little sister. They have taken your life. And they think me dead. They will think again. I am weak. I am worn. I will be reborn. This promise begins with your blood and ends with mine and theirs. May-Yania, Tinta. Little sister. I will be your sorrow. I will be your tomorrow. My name is May-Yania* . . . and that's where it stopped, the rest was destroyed.'

'Seems pretty conclusive,' agreed Buggy. 'Sounds like Dreddax butchers killed Scuba's sister and thought that Scuba was dead too. Maybe that's why they weren't lying in wait for her after killing her team. Wow.' He shook his head. 'No wonder she hates them.'

'Shhhh. She's coming back. Don't say anything about the cloth. She didn't see me looking at it.'

'OK. Nothing about the cloth. But I can definitely mention her saying testicles instead of tentacles, right?'

Muddy smiled. 'Best not say anything about that either. She's still learning our language. It's not easy. She might be a bit sensitive about it.'

'You two look guilty of something,' said Scuba.

'Just wondering if we're helping this planet now?' lied Muddy.

'Not unless we have to.' Scuba looked at Buggy. 'Can you analyse data?'

'Probably,' he said.

'He can,' piped up Muddy. 'Since the age of eleven. Started when he wanted a new guitar. He analysed how many chickens he'd have to buy, how many eggs they would have to lay, the price he would charge per egg, target sales per day, estimated time it would take to raise enough to cover the guitar . . . left no stone unturned. It was impressive.'

Scuba looked quizzically at Buggy.

'Oh yeah,' he nodded. 'I'm that good.'

'And did you get yourn guitar?' asked Scuba.

'He didn't get the chickens,' said Muddy.

Scuba sighed. 'You both look guilty of something again. Nevertheless, I am going to link you wirelessly to the police computer network. Yourn skinsuit will project a virtual screen before yourn eyes. Experiment with it. Learn how it works. Then I want you to scrutinise the police databases. Look for patterns or anomalies. Just see if anything stands out. There is no rush, we may be gone for a while.'

'Gone?' queried Buggy.

'I have a different database to retrieve. It is on mine planet. It contains information regarding the new location of yourn parents and the relevant PIP code I will need to reunite you with them.'

'Can't we all go and get it?'

'Mine home planet does not allow piggyback entry. Only authentic security-coded PIPs will get you there. And since you ate yourn, you stay here. Keep the law enforcement officer with you if she returns before we do. Avoid Mrs Magner should you see her.'

'And babysit Angel too?' asked Buggy.

Scuba gave a single nod.

Angel had been sitting on a nearby bench swinging her feet. On hearing this, her feet stilled, and her head lowered. She began to snuffle. Slipping off the bench, she walked up to Muddy, tugged his hand.

'What's up, Angel?'

The girl took Little Dog by the scruff of his neck and held him out.

'You want Little Dog to look after us while we're away?'

Angel nodded, thrusting her toy towards him with an insistent frown.

Muddy looked at Scuba and grinned. Scuba walked away in disgust, went over to talk privately to Buggy. Muddy looked back down at Angel. 'Thank you. That's really nice of you, but only for this journey.' He stuffed Little Dog into his backpack. 'And while we're gone, you'll have Fourforty's big dog looking after you. How good is that!' Muddy squeezed Angel's hand. 'When I get back we'll swap. OK?'

Angel turned around and went back to foot-swinging on her bench.

'Come on,' shouted Scuba. 'We will leave from the police yard.'

Muddy nodded a goodbye to Buggy. Scuba used her cashpoint trick to swipe through the entry gate. 'I took a copy of Fourforty's card.' She tapped her sleeve against Muddy's. 'Now you have a copy too. Try it.'

Muddy let the door close and held his sleeve up to the black box. The skinsuit material automatically extended into the slot. The door clicked open and he strode through. It felt good having access to secure locations.

Inside the yard, both Scuba and Muddy stacked their Earth clothes in a neat pile. Scuba placed the master PIPs into their skinsuits. A little smile crept across her face as she did so.

'Don't do that,' said Muddy. 'It's unnerving. Last time you smiled a bunch of Dreddax butchers attacked us and we nearly died.'

Scuba's smile only broadened. She pressed the transport cipher on their suits. 'I cannot help but smile. I am going home.'

Chapter Nineteen

Muddy heard a loud "thloop". A memory came back, of when he and Buggy used to go to the river. They'd choose thin, saucer-shaped stones, hurl them into the air and try to make them thud into the water on their spinning edge. A split second later he entered water with that same splashless thud. Reborn in mud on one planet. Baptised in water on another. He held his breath, tried to orientate himself, and realised the skinsuit was over his face . . . and his mouth. Before he had time to panic, a hand grabbed his shoulder and pulled him upwards. When he broke through the surface of the water, the material automatically cleared from his face. 'You could have warned me we'd be landing in water,' he gasped.

'It was a lesson,' said Scuba.

'I already know how to swim.'

'Not a lesson in swimming. A lesson in relying on yourn skinsuit.' Scuba swiped her hands down her body, as though presenting a new set of clothes. She rose out of the water. 'Did you see me do this on yourn planet?'

'Yeah. It messed with my head. That and the halo thing.'

Scuba raised her eyes to the sky. 'Do what I just did. Wipe yourn hands down the sides of yourn skinsuit, not a straight line, a curved one.' Scuba moved behind him and held on to his waist as he began to rise from the waves. As soon as she let go, he crashed back into the water.

Muddy kicked for the surface. When his head broke through, he was greeted by Scuba laughing like he'd never seen her laugh before. 'Finally . . . ' He spat some salt water from his mouth, 'I've learned what makes you laugh. People drowning. That's weird.'

'*You* are weird,' retorted Scuba. 'Like a baby taking yourn first steps.' She helped him up again. 'We learn this straight from the womb. Yourn suit will repel water with just enough force to compensate for yourn weight. But in order to aid the function, you must visualise what you want to happen. The skinsuit is connected to every fibre of yourn being. As you bond with it, it will begin to respond faster with less physical instruction. It is a living organism remember, an extension of you. Try again. The surface of ourn undulating ocean is a good place to learn this skill, so take advantage.'

Muddy concentrated and slowly let go of Scuba's hands. 'I've seen insects do this on ponds,' he said as his arms began to flail. 'And if they can do it . . . there! How do I look now?' His legs began to do involuntary splits.

'Absurd,' said Scuba.

Muddy shuffled in a big, awkward circle, saw deep, purple water in every direction. 'So, this was your planet?'

'Is.'

'It's very . . . watery.'

'Well, there is no doubting yourn formidable observational skills,' said Scuba, hiding a smirk. 'The pull of ourn moons sculpts the oceans. It means the entire surface of ourn planet is submerged for much of the time. During those months, violent storms ravage the atmosphere, but ourn homes are . . . were . . . always protected beneath the waves. You will see where we lived . . . what was destroyed . . . on the way to the unit.'

'The unit?'

'Yes. You will see. Come on. Should you wish to speak when we are submerged, we will be able to hear each other clearly if we are touching.' Scuba's skinsuit spread over her face and head and she slipped elegantly beneath the ocean.

Muddy looked at the waves. Thought about going below. His skinsuit spread across his face, small ovals covered his eyes. He could see through them as if they weren't there but he knew they were as black as the rest of the material. He looked around the surface a little longer. Looked at the two suns, the pale pink sky, the purple water. He felt a hand on his ankle . . . 'Come on,': Scuba's voice in his ears. With a lot less elegance than her, he fell beneath the waves. And panicked. He couldn't do it. He couldn't make himself breathe under water. It felt so . . . *unnatural.* Muddy went straight back up, gasped for air. Above the surface, even with the material over his face, it was as though there was nothing covering his mouth, but in the water . . . A hand on his ankle again: 'Come on. You can do it.'

Muddy composed himself and tried again. Just below the surface he forced himself to breathe out. But the breaths that followed were fast and shallow . . . panic inducing.

Scuba moved towards him. She took hold of his hands. 'Close yourn eyes,' she instructed. 'Now imagine you are above the water, on land, but it is dusty and windy, so you have placed an handkerchief over yourn mouth to keep the dust out. Breathe slowly, breathe deeply. Good . . . Again . . . Now open yourn eyes. Continue to breathe. Slow and deep. Good. Yourn skinsuit maintains optimum possible air quality for lung function. In effect, you inhale the same breath of air with new oxygen added each time, either filtered from the surrounding elements, in this case from the water, or created chemically by yourn skinsuit. You will not suffocate. It is exactly like breathing above the surface, only a little more effort is required.'

Muddy nodded. Breathing underwater was so alien it was frightening . . . and yet it was one of the most amazing things he'd ever experienced. 'I . . . think . . . I'm OK now,' he managed. 'Thank you.'

Scuba stayed facing him for a while longer. 'Breathe with the ocean. Slow and deep.'

Muddy responded to her words, timing his breathing as the ocean gently heaved them to and fro. In. Out. In. Out.

'OK,' said Scuba, 'Now follow me. And do not forget to breathe.'

Seeing Scuba swim away had a focusing effect on Muddy. He swam to her side, reached out and took hold of her hand.

Scuba turned her head. 'Yes?'

Her voice in his ears took him by surprise. 'Erm,' he said, realising what he'd done. 'Yeah, I just wanted to ask . . . ' Laboured breathing meant laboured speaking. It gave him a few more moments to think of something to say. The first thing that entered his head was the cloth he'd seen in her backpack . . . her sister . . . but that was too personal. And now he was feeling awkward. He'd been holding her hand without saying anything for way too long, 'Why aren't,' he took another breath, 'there any fish?' He couldn't see Scuba's face beneath her skinsuit. He was glad. He pictured a look of disdain – brought on by a stupid question from a stupid human.

'Mine planet was a scratch planet, like yourn, remember. All living things were taken.'

'Of course. Sorry,' said Muddy. 'I forgot.'

Scuba drove deeper into the darkening water. But she didn't let go of Muddy's hand. 'Keep looking down,' she said.

The ocean was vast. Muddy felt tiny. Insignificant. Lost. And the deeper they went, the darker the water became. Occasionally a shape would form in the depths – the suggestion of a tower or turret, but Muddy wasn't sure if they were real, or just his eyes trying to comfort him, forcing the familiar on the foreign. 'Were there cities down here?' he asked.

'Yes,' said Scuba. 'All crushed by the Amorphi machines. You do not realise how spectacular some things are until they are gone. They were truly beautiful. The rock moss and quartz here produce oxygen naturally. It formed immense caves and caverns filled with breathable air. We just built up from there, using the same materials. Let nature do the rest. And nature knows what it is doing . . . mostly,' she added.

'Why hasn't your planet been restocked yet?'

'Because . . .'

Muddy had started to become wary of the pauses in Scuba's speech. At first he thought it was a language thing, that she was trying to think of the appropriate words, but he was beginning to think that she was filtering how much she wanted to say to him. 'Because?' he pushed.

'A deal with the Amorphi.'

'You made a deal with the Amorphi?'

'No. We shared this planet with another species. They made the deal . . . without ourn knowledge.'

'What other species?'

Scuba stopped swimming. She pressed a cipher on her skinsuit, making the material on her face transparent. She did the same for Muddy. They hovered like that for a long moment, swaying gently with the current. Then Scuba looked him straight in the eye. 'The Dreddax,' she said.

'Dreddax!' Muddy wondered how the skinsuit would cope with an unexpected bowel movement. 'Here?!'

'This is a massive planet. A divided planet. And this was theirn home planet also. Dreddax and Quarasians lived side by side. I am Quarasian. Quarasians are humanoid with skinsuits. Like I told you, we lived above the oceans when we could, and also in the natural air-filled structures below the oceans. The Dreddax are humanoid reptilian, naturally amphibious. They are capable of operating above ground but lived in the water, beneath the oceans. They were the majority. There had always been tension between the two species, but we co-existed well enough. Until the Amorphi arrived. They came to make mine planet a scratch planet. Pure chance meant they made contact with the Dreddax first. When the Amorphi saw theirn amphibious capabilities, theirn self-contained weaponry, they decided to recruit them to help service all scratch planets. A one-hundred-year contract was signed. Ourn planet was emptied. The Dreddax agreed to serve the Amorphi for the entire period and the Amorphi agreed to let the Dreddax, and the Dreddax alone, reclaim this planet and fill it with whatever stock they desired at the end of the contract.'

'All Dreddax agreed to this?'

'It was complicated. Most ordinary Dreddax were against it but remained silent. Some Dreddax were completely on ourn side. It was the separate Dreddax butchers who saw it as the opportunity of a lifetime. When things turned bad and the butchers took over negotiations, the silent majority did nothing to stop it. The few Dreddax on ourn side died with us when the machines came.'

'Why did the Amorphi allow this? I thought they were in the business of buying and selling lifeforms?'

'The Amorphi abided by theirn agreement and took no interest in mine planet. They had no idea that the Dreddax butchers were wiping Quarasians out instead of moving us on.'

'But didn't the Amorphi have to control the machines?'

'No, no longer. Dreddax scientists introduced some brutal ingenuity. They captured some of mine people alive, used Amorphi technology to defragment theirn memories, but not the full clean defragmentation. Theirn defragmentation procedure uses a burrowing worm that destroys minds. It leaves geographical knowledge and minimal motor control only. In essence the captured subjects were turned into navigational zombies – empty, soulless, totally beyond repair. These zombies were wired into the Amorphi machines. They knew the terrain, knew the significant targets, so were able to guide those machines with pinpoint accuracy. It accelerated mine planet's destruction.'

A wave of nausea washed over Muddy. 'That's . . . horrific.'

Scuba ciphered the skinsuits back to black. 'The Dreddax butchers have since split from the main Dreddax nation in order to pursue theirn own interests. They stole an Amorphi ship, known as a serpent, and are the only ones who still use that awful mind destroying technology. They capture native inhabitants of each planet they raid, use the worm on them, fill the serpent, destroy the planet. But enough history. Dwelling on these things serves no purpose.' She tugged on Muddy's hand. 'We kept some places hidden from the Dreddax. From ourn own people even. We are going to a survival vault, deep in the quartz bedrock. It is the place mine team use as a base. It remains untouched. The database we require is in there.' Talking done, Scuba let go of Muddy's hand and headed off.

They worked their way down through the ruins, wriggling past large sections of rubble, occasionally having to heave fallen rocks aside in order to continue. Muddy felt his skinsuit become tighter, more solid, the deeper they submerged. But it remained pliable. Scuba guided him to the base of a purple quartz mountain, so deep in colour it was almost black. She stopped swimming and allowed her momentum to carry her towards a curved indent in the rock. She eased herself sideways into a thin crack, motioned for Muddy to follow.

For a while he couldn't see a thing. He had to rely on touch alone. The first section was so narrow he was sure he was going to get stuck, but a little slime on the quartz and a little panic in his heart helped him squeeze through. Round and round they went, in an ever-ascending spiral. Some rocks along the route glowed, sending streaks of faint purple light through the silent water. Eventually, the gaps widened, allowing them to swim freely. The wider sections contained a sprinkling of plant life and anemones. They released flashes of colour, then shied away as Muddy passed by. He wondered what Scuba's ocean would have been like in its prime, before it had been drained of all life. It must have been a purple paradise. Ahead of him, Scuba veered sharply upwards and disappeared. Muddy kicked hard and followed her route, up into a cylindrical tunnel. She was waiting for him at the top. It was a dead end. She reached out, guided him to her side, kept contact with his skinsuit so that he could hear her speak. 'Keep yourn back pressed against this dark section of quartz. Engage this suitcipher when I say.' Scuba showed him the cipher, waited for him to nod. She pressed her back against the quartz too. 'OK, now.'

Chapter Twenty

Muddy's skinsuit automatically retracted from his head. They were clear of the water, but he could still feel rock at his back. 'Did we just travel through the quartz?'

'We did,' said Scuba.

'I feel cold.'

'That is a normal, brief side effect. Ourn scientists had to work hard to make what we just did possible. On other planets, quartz is one of the only substances that ourn skinsuits cannot transport through in such fashion. It can only happen here because natural elements present in the skinsuit are also present in the quartz of ourn planet. We will be absolutely safe. No scan can penetrate this place. And only authentic skinsuits containing the master PIP of a fully authorised team member can get in. There is no physical entrance door, you see.'

'So how did you even build it?'

'A special keyhole surgery was used initially, to make a space big enough for people to transport in and begin proper construction. From outside it appears to be a solid quartz mountain. It is the perfect place for a survival vault.'

Muddy looked around. It was an amazing achievement. The size . . . the design . . . the equipment. The room was full of lights and machines and screens. 'It's . . . big,' he said.

'Hmm,' nodded Scuba, 'congratulations on yourn impressive choice of adjective.' She twisted along a bank of desks, pressing buttons and flicking switches as she went. 'Do not touch anything without first asking.'

Muddy made an extravagant show of pretending to press a few buttons. Scuba didn't react. 'Is it OK to go and have a look around this . . . *big* place?'

Scuba waved him away.

Dark purple quartz made for a spellbinding structure. It wasn't a uniform purple. Numerous shades curled and swirled within the walls. Muddy found his eyes following the swirls as he walked along. It was calming. Everything about the place was calming. The colour. The lighting. The temperature. The safety. He noticed what looked like a natural indent in the wall. He traced his fingers across it. A bright dot of pink flashed beneath his fingertips. At the same time a section of the quartz wall appeared to turn to liquid and just fall away. It was a door. Muddy closed it. And opened it. And closed it again. Each time the quartz wall fell away, or returned, he could hear a sound like a droplet of water plopping into a bucket. He never thought he'd find a door so mesmerizing. He opened it again. The room was filled with boxes. Nothing interesting. He walked a little further along, looked for other possible doors. He found one – opened it – and his jaw dropped. The quartz that made the walls in this room was dark. And the room itself was only dimly lit. Around the perimeter of the room, set on individual plinths, were giant glass containers. They were triangular in shape, open fronted. Inside each one was a tiny rotating planet. As spectacular as the display looked, the room had a simple, poignant aura about it. Some of the planets looked in a bad way.

'These planets were not as lucky as mine and yourn.'

Muddy jumped. He hadn't realized Scuba was behind him.

'Sorry,' she said.

'That's OK.'

Scuba motioned towards the containers. 'At least ourn planets are in one piece. These are miniatures of planets destroyed by the Dreddax butchers. Ourn skinsuits take visual data during PIP transportation, so mine team created holographic, scale versions of the planets. We constructed this room as a memorial.'

'They look beautiful, but . . . sad somehow. You know them all?'

Scuba nodded. 'Part of ourn training is to learn the history of these planets.'

Muddy looked around the room, picked out the greenest sphere. 'Tell me about that one.'

'That planet never had human stock, only reptiles and insects. The market for reptiles dwindled and the Amorphi abandoned the planet. The Dreddax butchers invaded it for sport. They hunted the reptiles to extinction and the planet died. It has not been used since.' Scuba went to a control panel near the doorway, swiped her forearm across a scanner. 'I completed a little research in the other room, regarding the planet we were just on.' A small replica of Earth burst into life in the centre of the room and began gently rotating. 'Earth was once stocked with enormous reptiles too, then the Amorphi made it a scratch planet, sold some reptiles, enhanced others, relocated them all. This was a long, long time before the Dreddax became involved. When Earth recovered, the Amorphi re-stocked it with smaller reptiles and first-generation humans. The history log shows that Earth has been a scratch planet on at least five occasions. That is quite incredible. The human stock currently on the planet are aware of these anomalies in theirn history and refer to them as "mass extinctions". Theirn scientists search for something they call "the missing link", a specific human form to show natural progression in theirn "evolution".' Scuba smiled. 'It is beyond theirn comprehension. They have no idea that they were taken off the planet, relocated, modified by higher life forms, put back.' Scuba closed the panel and the planet disappeared. 'But Earth has not been touched for tens of millions of years. It is almost as if that planet has been forgotten.'

'Not by the Dreddax butchers we saw,' said Muddy.

'No. Apparently not by those Dreddax butchers.'

'What about that planet?' Muddy pointed to the planet that made him feel most melancholic. The darkest globe on display.

'Destroyed just a decade ago. You would not think it now, but that planet was once white, the majority of it covered in ice and snow. The warmer parts were covered in white sand. It was inhabited by a small population. A secretive race of fighters called the Lupelli. From what we know, it was an harsh culture, but one full of . . . wonder. The young went through an extraordinary rite of passage. Ourn accumulated data gives a good general overview, but is obscure regarding specifics. The story is a little . . . fantastical. Researchers described it as a supernatural "happening". Artefacts they uncovered described the process as "the merging of beast and baby" or the "combining of savagery with soul". The rite of passage took place when a child reached the age of six. The child was sent, alone, across the frozen wasteland to the white forest.'

'How could a six-year-old survive alone?'

'It is understood that most did not. But the cold was not the worst danger. The forest was filled with packs of giant white wolves – again, not all details are known about them. They were certainly an intelligent species, mystical, unlike any other in all the worlds. The alpha wolf would have been twenty times the size of the canine called Chisel. It had fur so white it could blind you, and theirn eyes . . . theirn eyes were haunting - one ice blue, the other shimmering green. An alpha wolf would grant protection to any wandering child that survived the harsh conditions, study it, assess it, judge it. From what we understand, if the child was deemed worthy, the alpha wolf would sacrifice itself, allowing its spirit to be absorbed by the child. And if the child was not deemed worthy . . . the pack would rip the child to shreds and consume it. Children that survived and returned home, did so with a wild, burning fever. It would rage for weeks as the child's body fought to contain and control the white wolf spirit. Some children survived, some did not. The few that survived were revered. A female child would earn the title "Lupella", a male child, "Lupello". It is said that the spirit of the white wolf would fill theirn bodies when they fought, making them the most savage warriors in existence. Theirn enemies named them "Bicandemonica" – it translates to "Two-Legged Dog Demons"'.

Muddy stared at the rotating globe. He was totally absorbed by Scuba's story. He tried to picture the places, the people, the creatures. 'How did their planet end up like that?' he asked.

'When theirn planet was selected for scratching, the Amorphi sent in the Dreddax to complete the task. But the Lupelli surprised the Dreddax with theirn strength and theirn ability to overcome the effects of scratchgas. Even the white wolves came from the wasteland to fight. And they did some serious damage to the Dreddax numbers. For the first time in theirn history, the Dreddax made the decision to retreat. They spoke with the Amorphi, explained the special qualities of the inhabitants and convinced the Amorphi to let the planet be. Unfortunately, the Dreddax butchers, who were now acting alone, saw profit. They returned. And they returned with theirn Amorphi serpent. It was chaos. The butchers captured a dozen inhabitants, carried out the corrupted defragmentation procedure. As with mine planet, the zombified inhabitants were installed into the Amorphi serpent. They knew instinctively where to guide it, what and who to target . . . ' She looked towards the model of the burnt planet, then her gaze dropped to the floor.

Muddy didn't want her story to end. 'But if the butchers won, why did they destroy the whole planet?'

'The butchers did not win. They did not destroy the planet. The Lupelli did.'

'What?'

'There came a point when the Lupelli understood that theirn entire planet was about to be enslaved, theirn culture destroyed, theirn lands and creatures mutilated. But surrender was never an option for them. So, they made a brave decision. They enticed as many Dreddax butchers as they could to the surface of theirn planet . . . then the Lupelli ignited the atmosphere. The entire planet was scorched. No survivors. A rich and wonderful history, gone in the blink of an eye.' Scuba shook her head. 'I would have given anything to meet the Lupelli. They did the right thing in mine opinion. I wish they had killed every last Dreddax butcher. I wish they had been able to destroy theirn stolen Amorphi ship. But nothing can compete with an Amorphi serpent.'

Muddy felt the change in Scuba's mood. Talking about the Amorphi serpent affected her. He didn't like it. 'These things I'm seeing, the things that you're telling me . . . they're incredible . . . and some parts are just sickening. I couldn't have even dreamt it up, any of it, never in a million years,' he said. 'I think my dreams are generally a bit more pleasant, a bit more . . . basic.' Muddy shrugged. 'At least they used to be.'

'What were they . . . yourn dreams when you were little?' asked Scuba.

'Oh, you know, be an astronaut, fight a dragon, get the girl . . .' Muddy blushed a little. 'That kind of thing.'

His confession seemed to lighten the mood in the room. It brought a moment of silence and he was pleased to have changed the subject . . . until Scuba erupted with laughter.

'What now?' he asked. 'I don't seem to be drowning, so why are you laughing at me again?'

'I am not laughing at you,' replied Scuba, trying to control herself, 'I am laughing with you.' She shook her head. 'No, I am laughing at you. Sorry. It is just . . . you humans. I dreamt of becoming the leading microbiologist in all of the worlds, you dreamt of, how do you say . . . tales about fairies.'

'Fairy tales,' corrected Muddy. 'Yeah, well. I was little. And that's what being a kid is all about . . . dreaming fantastical dreams, not dreaming about becoming the leading geek in all the worlds.'

Scuba laughed away his defence. 'Ooooh,' she said, 'I shall fight dragons dressed as an astronaut and find the beautiful love of mine heart! Come dragon, bring yourn dragon friends, I will beat you all . . . ' Scuba doubled over.

'Oooooh, I'm going to be the biggest geek in the multiverse,' countered Muddy, ' . . . and say "yourn",' he added as an afterthought.

Scuba stood bolt upright. The smile dropped from her face. 'You did not have to learn an entirely new language in just a few days. I am going to find the database and download it.' Without another word she stormed out of the room.

Muddy didn't follow. He just stood there fighting the urge to shout "tentacles".

Chapter Twenty-One

'Bug.'
     'Bug.'
     'Bug.'
  'Bug E.'

Buggy turned from the virtual keyboard, saw Angel standing next to him. 'Look, Angel, I'm trying to go through all of this information, like Scuba asked. I've almost finished. Just go and sit on the bench for a little longer. I know you must be really bored.'

'Oh, on the contrary, I've found my time with you to be most fascinating. And I truly believe that the only future worth having is a fascinating one.'

Buggy stopped what he was doing. He blinked. He turned back to Angel, stared at her for a moment. 'Wha . . . what did you say?'

'Bug. Bug. Bug. Bug E,' came the childlike words. They were followed by a huge grin.

Buggy shook his head. He had imagined it. Surely. 'No .. . I meant after that.'

Angel gave a delighted little laugh. 'I'm just joking. Of course I know what you meant, silly. I said I'd found the time I've spent with you to be most fascinating. And then I said that I truly believe the only future worth having is a fascinating one. You know what I mean? This is me talking. Isn't it strange? I've been quiet for so long. Blaaa bluurrrr bluuuubb blub bloooo. I just made those sounds up,' she said, nodding with admiration. 'Oh yes.'

Buggy pushed aside the virtual keyboard and it disappeared.

'Now don't be afraid,' smiled Angel. Another little laugh. 'Actually, I'm joking again. You should be afraid. But it won't do you any good. Now listen . . . are you listening . . . you are listening, aren't you?'

'I . . . I'm all ears.'

'Actually, you're mostly oxygen, carbon and hydrogen. Then you have a myriad of other chemicals in miniscule quantities. Nitrogen, calcium, phosphorous, potassium, selenium, vanadium and so on and so forth . . . .'

Buggy gaped at the small child. She hadn't spoken in all the time he'd been with her, and now the vocabulary and knowledge spewing from her tiny mouth was extraordinary. Fear shot through him at the sheer *wrongness* of it all. Her words drifted in and out. He couldn't concentrate on them.

' . . . separate states. It's been very frustrating not being able to talk. So, excuse me if I go on a bit. Now, individually, these chemicals are not that interesting. However, assembled all together in the form of a human, with the always intriguingly debatable inclusion of a soul or intellect or spirituality if you will, you suddenly become much more . . . shall we say . . . desirable. A collectable, even. Speaking of spirituality, I wonder where Mrs Magner has got to.' Angel shook her head, as though momentarily distracted. 'Anyway, that's by the by. I am a cyborganic, as you've no doubt been told by your friend from Quarasia – did you know that's where she's from? Which makes her a Quarasian! Watch how I say it . . . KWA . . . RAY . . . ZEE . . . AN . . . did you get that? KWA . . . RAY . . . ZEE . . . AN . . . "Crazy 'un" for short. How funny is that? The Dreddax love her, by the way. And when I say "love" her, I do, of course, mean hate her. They may even sign me up to obtain her one day. She used to be enemy number nothing, but, since her fellow Quarasians are no more, and since she got involved in this kerfuffle, she's been promoted! Yes, enemy number one, the crazy 'un. See? Hard work does pay off. And if you think that's funny, and it is, well, wait until I show you this—'

'Is Mrs Magner with you?' mumbled Buggy.

Angel looked around in an exaggerated fashion. 'Can you see her? No? So, she isn't with me then, is she?' The small blonde child curled her bottom lip and made a sad face. 'And she's not *with* me with me. Mind you, she's not with you either.' Angel curled her bottom lip again. 'She's not right in a million years that one. You can tell she's not one of you humans, though, eh? A right religious nutter. My guess? She's a cyborganic who's been contracted to obtain your friend, just like I was contracted to obtain you. I'm sure she'll collect him when he returns. At least *you* don't need to worry about her, though. No. *You* need to worry about me. Where was I, yes, obtaining you . . . right, are you watching? Are you? You are watching, aren't you?' Angel's right eyeball blackened and twisted. She turned to face the wall. Light sprayed out onto the bricks. 'Now listen. This is *GREAT*. I was hired by a collector who uses the Dreddax as his middlemen. They've been an excellent source of information since their allegiance with the Amorphi. As soon as the collector discovered that your planet was to become a scratch planet, he tried to hire his usual little trio of greedy Dreddax, but they weren't available, so he hired me instead. More expensive, yes, but far more efficient too. You get what you pay for, don't you think? And guess what, this was my assignment. There were five items to be appropriated from your planet for my client's private collection. The first four items were insects, you were the fifth . . . and, for me, the most exciting. I've captured a human before. But this was a long time ago. Yes, Homo Heidelbergensis, I believe the species was called. Your brain size has increased since then. And you are not as muscular. Or hairy. But that's by the by. I've watched you, you know. You and your friend Muddy. Fascinating. Humans themselves and human interactions are absolutely fascinating. And when I say fascinating, I do actually mean fascinating on this occasion. Usually, I'd say fascinating but actually mean dull. But I'd tell you so. See. Fascinating. Truly. You two are very similar. And yet very different. I see you tapping, listening to sounds. Perhaps a musician? I'm right, aren't I?'

Buggy gave a bewildered nod.

'Muddy however, he takes in the same things as you, but he seems to process them in a different way. And when we were walking on your home planet, you preferred to walk in the sun, Muddy in the shade. More... goodness, I really don't know. I do wish I could spend more time with you . . . but anyway, that's by the by. I digress... now yes, yes, challenging . . . you were the most challenging item, and you weren't an insect ... but, and here's the funny bit. This is how I labelled my five assignments.'

With one eye still on Buggy, Angel pointed to the wall. The light split into five segments. There were pictures of insects in each of the first four segments, two types of fly, a beetle and a cornhopper. Buggy recognized them but didn't know all their names. Below each picture was a label.

'See?' smiled Angel. 'See the labels?' There was excitement in her voice, 'Bug A, Bug B, Bug C, Bug D and then . . .'

In the last segment there was a picture of him.

'Bug E,' he said.

'Bug E!' squealed Angel. 'Yes! Bug E! Bug E! Buggy! Buggy! Buggy! You see what I mean? How funny is *that!* Seriously. I would have peed in my pants a little had I not been cyborganic. I don't have a need to urinate you see. You humans have to urinate, but I don't. All moisture is reused internally. I'm quite amazing really."

'Amazing.'

'Yes. I knew you'd agree. But do you know what? I *can* wee if I need to! Just to fool you. It wouldn't be normal for a human not to wee, would it? So, since I'm . . . *disguised*, shall we say, as a human, I do actually nip to the toilet now and again. So, there *wee* have it. Enough fun. I have already delivered bugs A to D. Now to complete my assignment by delivering . . . ' Angel looked at Buggy and gave him and encouraging nod. 'Hmmm? Hmmm?'

'Bug E.'

'Yes,' nodded Angel. 'Bug E, Bug E, Buggy, Buggy, Buggy! It's the gift that keeps on giving. Now, well, time for us to leave. Just follow me. I know where to go. And don't think of trying to escape. I am harmless. But I'm harmless in a very, very harmful way. I will hurt you, but I won't kill you. I have to deliver you alive. Goodness, I've missed talking.' Angel paused and thought for a moment. 'Do you need a wee before we go?'

Chapter Twenty-Two

S cuba held up a small datapod.

'You got the information?' asked Muddy.

'Yes,' replied Scuba. 'Everything I require has been downloaded onto this.'

The look on Scuba's face wasn't one of triumph. Muddy had the distinct feeling that she was hiding something. 'And our parents are on it?' he asked. 'Plus the location of the planet they were sent to?'

'Yes,' snapped Scuba, ' . . . and yes,' she added, a little more calmly. 'Everyone is named on the database.'

'Good.' Muddy put her frostiness down to his comment about her language skills. 'Sorry about earlier,' he said. 'I wasn't being serious, you know, just stupid teasing.'

'Accepted,' replied Scuba. 'Let us not dwell on it.'

Scuba had placed the datapod on the edge of the table. 'What else is on this thing?' asked Muddy. He reached for it.

Just as his fingers were within touching distance, a tiny shield popped out of Scuba's hand, blocking his path.

'Do not touch,' she said.

'How did you do that?' asked Muddy. Her tiny hand shield was different to the large one that he and Buggy had been shown on his home planet.

'Shields are a basic skinsuit function. We learn the different types when we are children. Usually by playing games. Here, let me show you. Sit opposite me.' Scuba demonstrated the required movement and explained the thought process behind it. She guided Muddy through it a couple of times. When he was competent, she explained the game to him. 'A sweet was placed on a table between two seated children. The first child would produce a hand shield to cover the sweet. It was the second child's task to produce a stronger hand shield to displace the first one. Then the first child would try to displace the new shield and so on. Strongest shield wins the sweet. The more you practice, the better you become and the stronger the shield you produce.'

They sat and played for a while, using the datapod as the sweet. Needless to say, Muddy didn't win.

'You're good at this,' he said.

'Yes, I became a very fat child.'

They both laughed.

'You're certainly not fat now. How did you slim down?'

'By learning to fight,' replied Scuba.

'You fought the other children? For sweets?'

Scuba smiled, shook her head. 'Fight pit,' she said. 'A round pit, like a well, with a corridor at the bottom. You enter the pit alone and stand at one end. Synthetic copies of enemy creatures are generated at the other end of the corridor. You choose one and fight it. Different enemies require different techniques, different strategies. It was a tough way to learn. The best way to learn. You remain in the pit until the fight is over. Win or lose.'

'Lose?'

'Yes, yourn aim is to kill the enemy. And of course they have the same aim. But there are safety protocols in place. The fight pit . . . it makes constant observations, calculations and predictions. An enemy can deliver a killing move, a kill shot, or apply a killing hold, but the fight pit will still the enemy at that exact moment to prevent . . . mishaps.'

'So, there were times when you were "killed"?'

'There were.'

'How many?'

'More times than I remember. There is no shame in it. How else do you learn to adapt and overcome? I can die many times inside the fight pit, but outside the fight pit I can die only once.'

Muddy nodded. She had a point.

'Go and have a look at one first-hand if you like. There is a new one opposite the memorial room. I have a few more things to do here. I will retrieve you when I have finished.'

Muddy took the hint. Scuba wanted some alone time. 'Yeah, I'd like to see one. Maybe I'll be able to win some sweets from you afterwards.'

'I doubt that,' said Scuba.

When he reached the pit, Muddy was a little disappointed. There wasn't much to see. It was a deep circular hole in the ground with a sand covered floor. He walked over to a double rail, bolted to the top of the pit wall. There was no ladder attached to it. No way to get to the base of the pit. Muddy held onto the bars and leaned over for a better look. As soon as he touched the metal, a series of glowing purple rungs materialized, cascading downwards. Muddy slipped off his backpack. He smiled to himself, took Little Dog out and balanced him on top of the pit wall. 'There you go, Little Dog, a ringside seat. You can tell Angel all about it when we get back.' Swinging his leg over the rail, he tested the first rung. It seemed solid enough. He began to descend. As he went lower, his heartrate went higher. He hadn't expected to be so nervous. What was the worst that could happen? No harm could come to him. Scuba had said so. And he hadn't been much use to her so far. Maybe he could gain some experience now, in safety.

Fixed into the purple quartz at the base of the pit was a panel. It was at the end of the short corridor that Scuba had described. The panel looked simple enough. On. Off. Left and right arrows. A select button. He took a deep breath and pressed ON. The pit came alive. The brickwork glowed purple and the rungs of the ladder disappeared. No way out. Opposite him, the other end of the corridor also lit up. A beam of red light shone down onto a circular base. Muddy pressed the arrow on the wall next to him and stared down the corridor. The red light flickered, went black, came back on. Standing in the beam was a creature that looked like a giant spider. It was four times his size, skittering and jumping at the beam. Writing appeared around the base of the podium – "Passive Enemy". Well, passive enemy or not, Muddy pressed the button again, hoping for something smaller and with fewer legs. The spider was replaced by a thing that looked like a floating stick with a green spiky light at either end. He didn't fancy that either. He flicked through a few more. The writing across the base changed to "Active Enemy". A robot figure materialised, similar to the one he'd seen Scuba go after, followed by more creatures that were at least human-shaped. Muddy figured the passive enemies were creatures that only attacked if they had to, perhaps if you accidentally came across them. The active enemies were more likely to be creatures that you'd had a bit of previous with. As if to confirm his theory, a Dreddax butcher appeared. Muddy paused on it. He'd had enough of those for the moment, but it would be a good idea to come back to it. Practice against Dreddax butchers would help him to help Scuba. Muddy turned his back to the opposite podium and faced his panel. He couldn't just keep flicking through the options until he found a nice one. That's not how real life worked. The next opponent would be his, whatever it was. He pressed the arrow. Pressed select. Then turned around. A tall, slender creature stood in the red beam. Its skin looked smooth and shiny - colourful, like oil floating on water. It looked naked except for a series of ornate rings that looped around its elongated neck. Its head was small, its nose and mouth long, every bit as smooth as the rest of its body. Muddy couldn't tell if it was male or female. It stepped off the podium. Headed towards him. With purpose. That was the moment Muddy realized what a stupid idea this had been. He didn't know what he was doing. He had no idea what this creature was, what it could do, or how to even begin fighting it. The creature coming at him appeared to have no such worries. It began to run. Its hands reached towards its neck. It pulled two curved knives from the bands. As it did so, there was a quiet popping sound. Spikes burst from its skin. Muddy just stood there. Two knives came spinning through the air. They were aimed at his feet. The creature wanted to root him to the spot. Muddy instinctively lowered both of his hands and formed two separate shields from his knees to the floor. The fight pit beeped. The creature froze. The quartz wall turned red. A message – "Prediction Fatal" – began flashing across the brickwork. A polite female voice verbalized the same message. Muddy looked up to see the creature's horned tongue just millimetres from his face. The tip of the horn glistened. It had tiny, hooked sections on it. They looked loose, like they'd detach on contact. And they were moist with a thick green liquid. Poison, Muddy guessed. The knives the creature threw at his feet had just been a distraction. Lesson learned. Dead . . . but still alive. He flopped back on the sand. He'd done nothing, yet he felt exhausted. As the walls returned to their normal colour, the creature disintegrated, bursting into a billion tiny dots before completely vanishing.

Muddy looked up to see Little Dog's collar flashing. He laughed. 'Don't worry, Little Dog!' he shouted. 'I'm fine.' He got to his feet and leaned against the wall. Having confidence in the pit's safety protocols gave him confidence in himself. Perhaps he really could learn to fight in here. He dusted himself down. Ready to go again. At the end of the corridor there was a flicker. Had he accidentally nudged the panel? He looked to see what kind of creature was up next. What he saw confused him. At the end of the corridor, standing on the podium, was Scuba. Her skinsuit had deployed to cover her head and face. Muddy laughed. 'Scuba!' he shouted. 'What are you doing?'

'Busy,' came the distant reply.

Muddy glanced again at the body that was slowly making its way towards him. The reply hadn't come from that direction. The skinsuit sparkled, as though it wasn't solid, as though the fight pit hadn't quite finished making it. Maybe fighting other members of your community was an option? Muddy shouted to Scuba again: 'Why would you practice fighting each other?'

Silence.

A moment later, Scuba's face appeared over the side of the pit. 'Get out, NOW!'

'I can't, it's locked in, the ladder retracted, what's wro—'

'THEN FIGHT!' screamed Scuba.

Muddy looked at the oncoming skinsuit. Whoever was inside it was big . . . strong. Two words went through his mind – *prediction fatal*.

A blade-shaped shield came slicing through the air towards his head. Muddy ducked, felt the wind from the blade flick at his hair. He initiated his own shield, raised it over his head just in time to stop a second blow from cutting him in half. The fight pit wasn't stopping this one.

Blow after blow pinned him to the ground. Muddy curled into a tight ball, domed a shield around his whole body. Through it, he could see the skinsuit standing over him. Even now, it didn't seem completely solid. But the blows felt solid enough. Another blade crashed down. The next made a hairline crack in his dome. Muddy was in no doubt that he was about to lose this game of shields. Another blow; this time the edge of the blade pierced Muddy's shield completely. Bright sparks fizzed through the air as the blade was heaved loose and raised again. At the top of its swing, Muddy closed his eyes and concentrated on making his shield as strong as he possibly could. If there was ever a time for his mind to bond completely with his skinsuit's capabilities, it was now.

He waited for the blow. And waited. He opened his eyes. And saw Scuba.

'We can get out now. I have overridden the system. The ladder is back.'

'Where did he go?'

'It,' said Scuba. 'Where did "it" go.'

'What do you mean?'

'That skinsuit belonged to the last member of mine team. The body we had to leave behind on yourn planet. His name was Mezko.'

'What? Well, what's Dead Mezko doing here? And how can he be attacking me if he's dead!'

'I have no answers for you. What we just saw is not possible. Skinsuit technology does not work on deceased Quarasians. That was not Mezko. I will download ourn archives relating to reanimation, see if any such thing has happened before.'

'Will he come back?'

'It!' snarled Scuba. 'Mezko was an he. That *thing* was an "it". And *it* only fooled the security protocols temporarily. Without living tissue interacting with the skinsuit, it could not stay materialized within these quartz walls. It was recognized as an imposter and ejected. It will not be back.'

'How did it find us in the first place?'

Scuba had something in her hand. She held it up. Her words froze Muddy's heart.

'Little Dog brought him here. Little Dog is the beacon.'

Chapter Twenty-Three

Buggy reached out and touched the barrier. It was thick and slightly frosted. It felt like glass, but it wasn't smooth. He couldn't hear anything through it, but he could see blurry figures on the other side. He recognized the size and shape of Angel. A blob of blonde on top of the little figure provided additional confirmation. It was her for sure. And she must have seen him pressing his face up against the barrier because she had the cheek to turn, give him a little wave and a thumbs up. There were Dreddax sized silhouettes around her. She was obviously holding court. Buggy pitied them for a fleeting second. Now that Angel had started speaking, he couldn't imagine her ever shutting up.

He pushed off from the barrier and took a closer look at his surroundings. His cell – at least he presumed it was a cell – had stone sides and a solid rock wall at the back. Sections of it were covered with brown ceramic tiles. Each tile was decorated with a simple, white image – some had a candle, some had a cross, some had an outline of hands in prayer. There was definitely a church theme going on. The artwork looked old. So did the haphazard wooden shelving on the rear wall. Both the shelves and the floor were littered with objects . . . dusty pots . . . urns . . . wooden plates. A stringed instrument caught Buggy's eye. He picked it up, gave it a strum. It was horribly out of tune. That was sacrilege anywhere, not just in a holy place. He shrugged. If he was going to be an exhibit in an ancient, holy display cabinet, he'd at least make sure the instruments were in tune. An old coin in one of the pots served as a makeshift plectrum. Buggy began plucking the strings one by one, adjusting the tension as required. When he finished, he propped the instrument back up against the shelf. Grit and dirt crunched beneath his feet. The crunch led him to a tiny avalanche of shale in the far corner. Buggy turned away from it. It wouldn't be wise to show any interest in that right now. Instead, he returned to the front of his cell and rested his forehead on the barrier. He stared at Angel's silhouette. She looked animated, excited. She was obviously taking great pleasure in recounting her story. He sighed. Scuba had warned him, *Keep yourn wits about you when we go off planet, something may happen*. Well, his wits had gotten him captured by a little girl. No ordinary little girl, though. Scuba had been right about that. Angel was a cyborganic. A cyborganic working for who knows who. Buggy tried to take some consolation from that fact. What chance did he have against a cyborganic?

Eventually the figures beyond the barrier drifted away. Buggy shuffled over to the front corner of his cell, where glass met stone. He squashed his face against the join, tried to get an angle to see what was next to him. It was another cell. And there was a dark shape in the centre . . . maybe a person. The thought that he might not be alone heartened him. He turned his attention back to the little avalanche in the rear corner, wondered just how loose the rocks were. Was there even any point trying to escape from one cell into another? But if there *was* someone else in there . . . Buggy moved along the side wall, testing the strength of each section as he went. It was the last part, above the avalanche, that felt weakest. The loosest rocks sat just above head height. But even they felt pretty secure, and they looked pretty heavy too. Again, Buggy wondered if it was worth the effort. Maybe he should just kick back and play the lute thing for the rest of his caged life. No. If Muddy could dig his way out of the ground after a cave in, he could dig his way out of a cell by moving a few rocks.

Buggy set to work. He used his fingers and the makeshift plectrum to scrape away the grout and tiny pebbles that surrounded the larger rocks. One by one he wiggled and twisted them until he could get a decent enough grip to heave them out. After each success, Buggy pressed his face to the gap and called out, 'Hey, you in there, help me make this wider!' Nothing. After half an hour of hard graft he called out again. Still no response. He worried that he wouldn't be able to break through the wall before Angel and the Dreddax butchers returned. As a precaution he carried each rock over to the centre of his cell and arranged them to look like a body, sitting in his chair. The more cut and grazed his fingers became, the more his enthusiasm began to wane. Buggy paused and looked up at the hole. It didn't seem to have increased in size. But his doubts had. Then, totally out of the blue, a thought entered his head. He smiled. His mum's cupcakes. They had a reputation. A reputation for turning out heavier and harder than the rocks he was moving. And he'd managed to eat and digest a few of those, not just move them from one place to another. What he wouldn't give for a few of those cakes now. He could use them as cannonballs. He'd be through the wall in a heartbeat. He gave another fruitless call through the gap.

Trying to keep the negative thoughts at bay, Buggy got back to it. And the gap grew. When it was big enough, he pulled himself up and peered through. It *was* another cell – smaller . . . plainer than his, with a deep pit at the back of it, but a cell, nonetheless. More importantly, there *was* someone in it – someone sitting so still that a chill went rippling down Buggy's spine.

He hoisted himself up and slid through the hole. It felt like entering an ancient tomb, complete with corpse. Even the noise of stones skittering along the floor didn't disturb the body. Buggy stayed in a crouch next to the wall. Nothing bad happened, so he tiptoed towards the centre of this new cell. On the chair, as motionless as a mannequin, sat a human. It was a male. Most likely an Earth one. He looked about thirty years old. And he was alive. There was a pulse beating in his neck . . . his chest rose and fell with slow, shallow breaths. Buggy waved a hand in front of the man's face. A blink response - nothing more. There was a tiny silver disc fixed to his temple. Buggy gave it a gentle poke . . . and snatched his finger back when he received a mild electric shock. It wasn't the strength of the shock that affected him, just the surprise. He steeled himself and went for it again. This time he picked it clean off. The man in the chair didn't budge. Buggy examined the tiny disc. It barely covered the top of his finger. There were rings carved into it, making it look like a little slice of metal tree trunk. Illuminated threads connected the different sections, some followed the rings, some looped over them. Only the side that had been against the man's skin was illuminated. The side that faced outwards was plain and flat and silver. There was a second disc, a duplicate of the first, on the man's other temple. As Buggy picked the second one off, he heard the sound of sliding doors. He'd forgotten all about the Dreddax. The front panel of the cell started to rise. There was no time to escape back through his hole. Buggy eased the chair onto two legs and slid it to the rear of the cell. He tipped it until the man's body fell into the pit, then he ran to the centre of the cell with the empty chair. He stamped on the two tiny discs until the lights went out. After giving them a quick polish, he licked the inside of each one and stuck them to his own temples. The cell door rose further. The Dreddax butchers weren't facing him. They'd chosen to deal with the occupant of the opposite cell first. The extra seconds were crucial. Buggy sat down and tried to slow his breathing and beating heart.

A human female stepped down from the opposite cell – she too had a shiny metal disc on each temple. She walked to the centre of the room. She stopped. She waited. The Dreddax turned to Buggy. He did his best to copy the female. He rose slowly from his seat, eyes wide open, stepped out of the cell and fell into line behind her. As he did so, he noted that the front of his original cell hadn't lifted. Whatever was planned for the two Earth humans hadn't been planned for him. Buggy patted himself on the back. If he hadn't put in the effort to get through the wall, he'd have missed this opportunity to escape. He vowed to always put in that extra effort in future. The female began to move. Buggy followed her out. One Dreddax butcher lead the way and one brought up the rear.

They walked through cold, semi-dark corridors – each one as quiet and empty as the next. Brown tiles lined the route. They all had simple cross and candle designs on them, like the ones from his cell, suggesting to Buggy that they were still within the confines of the church building. He wasn't big on religion, but he prayed for an opportunity to escape, nonetheless.

No such opportunity arose. Their Dreddax escort didn't leave them alone for a second. Eventually they were shepherded into a small room off one of the corridors. Buggy was glad the Earth female was in front of him. He could just mirror her movements. And if anything terrible was going to happen, it was going to happen to her first. He felt a little bad about that, but not bad enough to move in front of her. To compensate, and despite his previous silent prayer falling on deaf ears, he sent out another one, thanking the Earth female and hoping she would be fine.

In the corner of the room stood another Dreddax. Buggy hadn't seen one like it before. This one was smaller, its body armour plain and silver – noticeably shinier than the Dreddax butchers' armour. It carried no insignia. And it wasn't just this new Dreddax that looked pristine. The entire room hummed with the universal smell of the clinically clean. Buggy's gut was telling him to run . . . now. In his peripheral vision he could see that both Dreddax butchers had moved to the door. It was the only exit. He was going nowhere. In the centre of the room, a circular chair rose from the ground and spun to a halt. The silver Dreddax stepped forward, took the Earth female by the arm and guided her towards it. When she was seated, he adjusted her head so that her face was towards him and slightly raised. He turned to a table by his side. The middle tendril on his left arm wriggled free from its clasp. Its barb dipped into three separate metal jars, one after the other. The middle tendril from the right arm did the same, only its barb dipped into a single, larger jar at the end of the table. The two tendrils sought each other out. Their barbs interlocked and began to spin, slowly at first, then faster and faster until they were just a blur. For a moment the conjoined barbs shone like a tiny sun. They stopped dead and separated. A cylindrical pill dropped into the waiting Dreddax hand. The pill glowed, deep red and black. After waiting for the glow to fade, the silver Dreddax leaned towards the female. It placed the pill, gently, precisely, onto the female's face, a fraction below her bottom lip. It stuck firm but didn't seem to burn her skin. A ripple of tiny bumps rose and fell along its surface. As it cooled further, a crack developed. This was no pill. It was a chrysalis.

And something was trying to get out of it. The crack spread. There was a dull ting as the bottom half of the chrysalis broke off and dropped to the floor. Buggy's eyes flicked back up to the Earth female's face. A grey, gaseous worm crawled from the remaining section of shell. It stretched. It squirmed. It gently probed her skin, getting its bearings. Slowly but surely the tiny worm slinked over the female's lips and settled into the groove beneath her nose. It paused briefly, then, with apparent eagerness, it hurried towards her left nasal cavity . . . and disappeared. A line of blood trickled down the female's nostril. It flowed along the ridge of her lip and settled in the corner of her mouth. Her eyes rolled back in her head. Buggy's blood ran cold. He was zero for two with his prayers. And he was next in line for the worm. He silently cursed himself. If he hadn't put in the effort to get through that wall, he'd still be safe in his own cell. He vowed never to make that extra effort in future.

Not that he saw any future.

Chapter Twenty-Four

It was dusk. Muddy landed in a crouch – a feat that brought a smile to his face. He was beginning to get to grips with skinsuit transportation. Being able to recognize the *fizzy* feeling as his body reassembled enabled him to move into a particular position, rather than end up flat on his back. A flash of movement in the distance made him stay in a crouch. Caution overrode his desire to get back to the police station and make sure Buggy was OK. He stared through the darkness. This was exactly where he'd landed on his first visit to Earth. Rain had washed the snow away. It made the place look different . . . more sinister somehow. Another flash of light – Muddy focused in on it. He could make out the top half of a visor. The Dreddax butcher it belonged to was standing outside a building, next to the church. Etched into the building's brickwork was the word 'Crypt'. Why was the butcher there? Was it waiting for him? But Scuba had told him that skinsuits only allowed you to materialize in secure locations, where scans showed no sentient being or machinery present to witness your arrival. So, if the Dreddax wasn't there for him, perhaps it was guarding that building? The whys about that didn't matter right now. Muddy just wanted to leave. The Dreddax head moved and dipped as though it was in conversation. Muddy took advantage. He began to edge backwards, towards a tube station entrance. As he eased down the first step, he caught sight of something reflected in the Dreddax visor. It took a moment for him to register what it was. When he did, fear and disappointment surged through him in equal measure. No time for caution now. He began to run. He ran through the underground passageway. He ran through the furthest exit. He ran into the streets beyond.

The back gate of the police station was deserted. It was deathly quiet. Muddy scoured the area for any sign of Buggy. He could see nothing except the small datapod that his friend had been using. It was lying on the floor. He walked over to it, reached down and—

'Where have you been?'

'Scuba!' Her camouflage had made her invisible in the half light. 'You almost made me jump out of my . . . your sister's . . . skin.'

Scuba placed a finger over Muddy's mouth, pressed the cipher on his skinsuit to fully engage it, then another to make it go into camouflage mode like hers. She kept hold of his shoulder. 'We can talk freely like this, like we did in the water. No one else can hear us.'

'What's the point!' asked Muddy. 'Buggy is missing. Mrs Magner is missing. Angel is missing. Fourforty is missing. Everyone is missing.'

'Buggy was here,' said Scuba. She held up the datapod. 'Working on the analysis like I had asked.'

'So where is he now?'

'Captured.'

'What do you mean captured?'

'You left yourn friend isolated on an alien planet with cyborganics,' said Scuba. 'What did you expect?'

'What did I expect? I expected him to still be here! What did you expect!'

'I expected him to be captured.'

'So why did you leave him?'

Scuba gave Muddy a little shove. 'From the moment you insisted on bringing those cyborganics off yourn planet I warned you that any consequences would be on you.'

Muddy didn't know how to respond to that. It was harsh. But it was a fair comment. He remained silent.

Scuba inserted the datapod into the sleeve of her skinsuit. 'The last thing he typed was "Angel",' she said. 'The cyborganics have yourn friend for sure.' Scuba's tone softened. 'But I do not believe that any harm will come to him. They will not complete any transaction without having you both,' she added.

'And what if we aren't both being sold to the same buyer?' asked Muddy.

'Then they will complete the transaction without having you both,' snarled Scuba, abandoning her efforts to make things sound better than they were.

'There was a Dreddax butcher guarding a building by the church when I landed,' said Muddy. 'It was communicating with someone.'

'Clarify "someone"?'

'I didn't see a face. I did see . . . something, though.'

'Clarify "something".'

Muddy was hesitant. And he didn't know why. He just didn't want to say it. It would be like admitting he'd been wrong all along. 'A reflection in the butcher's visor from whoever it was talking to. A glint . . . lines . . . silver . . . ' he sighed, '. . . it looked like a silver cross. Mrs Magner wears a silver cross around her neck.'

'Be still!' commanded Scuba, 'someone is coming.'

They both pressed themselves against the back gate, camouflaged, silent.

A familiar, fur covered face appeared from around the corner of the wall. Chisel looked dirty. There were fresh cuts along his face and nose – sharp diagonal lines. He sniffed the air, padded forwards.

'He knows we're here,' said Muddy. 'And why you want to hide from a dog I'll never know.' He pressed the cipher on his suit to go back in black and retracted his facial covering. Chisel wagged his tail. 'He looks like he needs a drink.' A pool of rain and melted snow had settled in a ledge on the building. Muddy scooped some water from it. He knelt down and offered his cupped hands to the dog.

Chisel lapped up every last drop, tail wagging. He lifted his head expectantly.

Muddy gave him a little fuss and stroked his neck. 'Those cuts look sore.' He pointed them out to Scuba. She looked disinterested. Muddy slipped off his backpack and had a rummage. 'These are medical wipes, right?'

He got a reluctant nod from Scuba and set to work cleaning up Chisel's wounds.

Scuba caved in and took a closer look. 'Raised and inflamed. Poison from Dreddax barbs can cause that reaction. The crisscross pattern of the cuts also suggests Dreddax barbs,' she said.

Muddy had another rummage through the medical pack. 'Will this help?' he asked, pulling out a small tube of cream.

'Do not waste that antivenom on a canine!' fumed Scuba.

'Ah! So, it will help,' said Muddy. 'Good.' He unscrewed the top and smeared the ointment along the cuts on Chisel's nose. Chisel squinted as the concoction was massaged in. He seemed to be enjoying the fuss. When Muddy had finished, he gave the dog's neck a final ruffle and turned away to tidy up the backpack. Immediately, a tentative nose nudged him in the ribs. Chisel wasn't quite ready to give up on the attention. Muddy eased him aside. 'Let me tidy this medicine away first.'

Not understanding the words, but getting the message, Chisel padded off.

A moment later, he gave a low rumbling growl.

'TAC,' whispered Scuba.

Muddy had become proficient at entering two different suitciphers into the arm of his skinsuit. TAC – take active camouflage, and BIB – back in black. He went TAC.

The fur around Chisel's neck raised. He growled again. Both Muddy and Scuba scanned the street, saw nothing. Muddy moved forward, patted and stroked the dog. The growling stopped.

'Just a trick to get more fuss?' offered Muddy. Chisel's tail started wagging again.

'And it worked.' Scuba tutted.

Muddy went back in black. That's when he noticed a Metropolitan Police uniform across the street. 'BIB,' he said to Scuba. 'It's just Fourforty.'

When Scuba came out of camouflage mode and he saw her face, Muddy toyed with the idea of asking her to cover it again. She looked angry. He guessed it was his fault for using her precious antivenom cream on Chisel. But his concerns went deeper than that. 'You still want to get me and Buggy home, right?' he asked. 'I mean . . . that's still your priority?'

'Of course, why?' asked Scuba.

Muddy shrugged. 'Just wondered.'

'Wondered what?'

'You seem angry. Sometimes I wonder if revenge is higher on your list than getting us home.'

'Mayhap if yourn eyes had seen what mine eyes had . . . ' Scuba went quiet.

'Scuba, I'm sorry, I didn't mean to question you. I know I've been lucky up to now.'

'Forget what I said. It makes no difference.'

'Fine,' said Muddy. 'Look, just promise me that you won't do anything rash if you see Mrs Magner or Angel. Since you rescued us, you've had to go at a hundred miles an hour, acting on instinct . . . but right now maybe we should take a step back, just for a moment, and think about what to do next, make sure whatever we do is the best thing. You know?' Muddy paused. He couldn't tell if his plea had sunk in. Scuba was too difficult to read. 'Anyway, Fourforty might know more,' he continued. 'She must have been on patrol with Chisel. Maybe she saw something that will help. Are you going to tell her about Angel and Mrs Magner being cyborganics?'

'It is time Fourforty understood exactly what we know,' replied Scuba.

The officer nodded a hello. 'Muddy, Scuba. Is Chisel OK?'

'Yes, yourn canine is fine,' said Scuba. She walked forwards to meet the officer. 'And we need to—' Scuba generated a spherical hand shield and smashed Fourforty in the head, knocking her clean out.

'Scuba!' shouted Muddy. 'What have you done!' He ran to the officer's side, knelt down, checked her pulse. She was still breathing. He rolled her into the recovery position.

Scuba stood over him, watching impassively.

Muddy glared up at her. 'I *just* said don't do anything rash!'

'You said not to do anything rash if I see Mrs Magner or Angel. I did not see Mrs Magner or Angel. I saw Fourforty. And this is not a rash act. She is a cyborganic.'

Muddy was dumbfounded. 'You need help. Seriously. You've got some kind of cyborganic paranoia.' An image of the cloth from Scuba's backpack sprang to his mind - her words only moments ago - *mayhap if yourn eyes had seen what mine eyes had.* It took the edge off his anger. 'Whatever happened to you in the past has made you think that everyone you meet is a cyborganic! First Mrs Magner, then Angel, now Fourforty! Who's next? Me? Buggy? . . . Chisel?'

'The mild antidote in yourn food bars would have negated the effects of scratchgas in a canine such as Chisel, but not in an adult human. I understood this from the beginning but did not see Fourforty as a danger when we first encountered her. However, now . . . ' Scuba pointed to one of the shiny silver number fours on the officer's shoulder. 'This is the silver that you saw glinting in the Dreddax visor. This is why hern own canine growled at her.' Scuba leaned towards Muddy. 'Yourn world has changed. Yourn thinking needs to change also. You knew nothing of cyborganics previously. Circumstances dictate that we will encounter a disproportionate number of them now.' Scuba flicked her wrist. A small shield blade extended from her sleeve.

Muddy instinctively created a shield of his own underneath it. 'Can you just calm down for one second!'

Scuba generated a stronger shield, bumping Muddy's effort out of the way. She challenged him with her eyes – the game she'd taught him on her planet, only this time the prize was not a sweet, it was a life. Muddy responded, displacing Scuba's shield with a more powerful one of his own.

Scuba just huffed. She fired a shield into his chest, throwing him onto his back. Before he could recover, her blade sliced into Fourforty's arm.

Blood seeped onto the concrete slabs.

'Come here, NOW!' ordered Scuba.

Muddy got to his feet, took a wary step to her side.

'One skinsuit is not enough to generate the kind of power we need,' said Scuba. 'Link yourn arm through mine.'

Muddy obeyed. As their arms linked, Scuba's sleeve merged with his. She pressed a suitcipher.

'What are you doing?' asked Muddy.

'Generating a magnetic force.'

He didn't ask any more questions. He just watched on in horror as Fourforty's blood began to wriggle and slither towards the magnet like a scarlet slug. 'How . . . I mean, they had no idea we'd end up on this planet. How could she have known to lie in wait?'

'She was not waiting for us. We were a surprise. Perhaps a bonus. The data that Buggy found shows a cycle. Crime patterns are standard for five-year periods, then there are a glut of missing persons. Fourforty is a hibernating cyborganic, triggered by scratchgas every five years to facilitate the activities of Dreddax butchers. She will think she is a normal human law enforcement officer the rest of the time. When scratchgas is released, it sends these Earth humans into theirn distant, disaffected state, but it activates her. When the scratchgas dissipates, the humans return to normal, and Fourforty returns to the belief that she is one of them.'

'But she saved me from a Dreddax butcher. Don't kill her.'

'I could have killed her when we first met. I knew she was not human then,' Scuba reminded him. 'But not everything is black and white,' she added, with only a hint of sarcasm.

Despite the circumstances, it drew a smile from Muddy. 'We should help this planet,' he said.

'How many times must I tell you? This planet is not mine concern. I have a limited window of opportunity to integrate you and Buggy into yourn new lives. That window has narrowed due to ourn unexpected difficulties. It closes at midnight. Now that Fourforty has been in contact with the Dreddax, I believe her to be a threat to us. We need to put her somewhere secure before we leave.' Scuba slipped off her backpack, took out some tiny pieces of metal and electronic equipment. She began to assemble a small spiderlike structure. 'You have been inside one of the custody cells in this police facility. Would it hold her?'

'Yeah. I suppose so,' answered Muddy. 'What's that?'

'It is a tracknid. We need to locate Buggy fast. Mine own scanning capabilities will not pinpoint him accurately enough. This is a bit... radical, but it will do the job.'

'And just what is a tracknid?'

'A stealth machine, designed to hunt and destroy Quarasian PIPs that have fallen into the wrong hands. Mine team have used them against Dreddax in the past. The tracknid knows no obstacle. It will burrow through metal, brick, bone . . . do whatever is necessary to locate the PIP. It will then physically retrieve the PIP, slot it into this central compartment and self-destruct.'

'But Buggy's PIP isn't in the wrong hands. It's in the wrong stomach.'

Scuba released the tracknid. It scurried to the wall. Its body went through a variety of colour changes until it settled on a white and green mix. Scuba walked over and pressed the centre of it. The tracknid froze. 'That is correct. But we need to find Buggy quickly and this is the most efficient way. The tracknid *will* find him . . . then it will eat through his stomach and retrieve the PIP. So, let us ensure we are present in order to stop that last part from taking place.'

Chapter Twenty-Five

Her skin paled right in front of him. Her cheeks hollowed. Her eyes, once shining brown, faded until they were the same metallic grey as the gas worm that had entered her head. A single tear rolled over the edge of the Earth female's long lashes. All that she was. It rolled down her cheek to the curve of her chin, held on for the briefest of moments, then let go, falling to the floor and splashing into oblivion. Buggy's heart ached. The change in the female had been tangible. He had *felt* it somehow. She had been something. Now she was nothing. And he was next.

The empty woman stood. A Dreddax butcher moved forward, five red slashes on its breastplate. Buggy noted an additional insignia beneath the slashes – a serpent – and writing beneath that – *Pilot segment 1*. Its visor slid aside. Two tendrils extended from its head. One went to the right of the woman's forehead, one to the left. The barb on the end of each tendril began to drill, ever so delicately, into the discs on her temples. They stopped spinning, held there for a moment, then retracted. When the Dreddax butcher closed its visor, a mirror image of the female's eyes appeared on the shiny surface . . . brown eyes . . . the eyes that had been. It looked so wrong that Buggy's stomach turned. The butcher headed to the door. The empty woman followed. What had they done to her? Why would the Dreddax butcher need to see through the woman's eyes? Buggy could make no sense of it. His brain had so many things bouncing around inside it, he couldn't think straight. And any second now, something else would be bouncing around inside it - a gas worm. He had no idea what to do. He couldn't run from the room. But he couldn't let the worm enter his nose, either. And if they found out the silver discs on his temples were just stuck on with spit . . . well . . .

He needed time. He had to act like the female had acted, just for a while longer. The silver Dreddax led him over to the seat. Buggy sat. He watched the barbs that had produced the chrysalis dip into the same pots. Maybe he should just run now? The barbs connected and began to spin. Buggy could feel the heat from the tiny ball of light that they generated. As he stared at it, his thoughts drifted . . . home . . . the sun . . . him and Muddy chatting and laughing on the grass, eating flavoured tubes of iced water until they felt sick . . . how could things have gone so bad so quickly?

And then things got worse.

Before he realised it, the silver Dreddax had placed the chrysalis on his face. The grip it had was astonishing. It gave off a distinctive odour: hot metal; volcanic rock; smoke. Then the squirming started. There was a crack. Buggy heard the 'ping' of shell hitting floor. He felt a rippling movement on his lower lip; the worm was stretching upwards, moving towards his nose. Now there was no choice. He had to run . . . pick the worm off his face and just run. Buggy went to raise his hand. He couldn't. Something about the chair. He was immobile. The worm moved again, stretching across his lips. Buggy closed his eyes.

Chapter Twenty-Six

With Fourforty secured, Scuba and Muddy returned to the back gate. Muddy was relieved to see the tracknid still attached to the wall. He put the visions of tiny metal legs cutting through Buggy's stomach to the back of his mind . . . for a while at least. Scuba pressed the tracknid's body. It began skittering around in circles.

'What's it doing?' asked Muddy.

'Determining which PIP frequency to lock on to, depending upon the coding and half-life signature of each trace.'

'Erm . . . baby talk,' requested Muddy.

'Every PIP leaves a trace that diminishes over time, like a scent. The tracknid is establishing the correct scent to follow.'

'Spider's on the hunt,' said Muddy.

'Spider's on the hunt,' nodded Scuba.

The tracknid went through some more colour changes, this time settling on black and grey. It sprang from the wall and headed off along the street.

Muddy watched the creature . . . *the machine?* . . . like a hawk. The first time it disappeared into a clump of snow, his heart skipped a beat. He looked at Scuba. Scuba looked down at her forearm. There was a display on her skinsuit – a tracking device for the tracking device. Muddy didn't need any device to tell him they were heading for the church. He glanced towards the Crypt, just for a fraction of a second. When his eyes found the tracknid again, it had crawled to the edge of a small drainage hole. Muddy's heart missed more than a beat this time. The tracknid dropped down the hole.

'It's gone! How can we follow it down there! It's going to eat through Buggy's stomach!'

'Calm yournself.' Scuba checked the monitor on her forearm. 'The tracknid is directly below us. Moving slowly.'

Muddy pointed to the Crypt. 'That's where I saw the Dreddax butcher. Parts of the church must stretch beneath ground.'

Scuba nodded. 'The tracknid is no longer moving horizontally. It is burrowing downwards. There must be lower levels. We should be able to reach them via The Crypt entrance.' Scuba started to move but stopped suddenly. 'TAC,' she whispered. She kept her arm in contact with Muddy's skinsuit. 'That Dreddax butcher you saw. It is still there. Guarding the entrance.'

Beneath his skinsuit, Muddy paled. Visions of metal spider legs and torn flesh came back with a vengeance.

Chapter Twenty-Seven

'Fascinating.'

Buggy recognised the voice. He opened one eye. Angel was standing in front of him, staring at the worm on his face.

'And when I say fascinating, I do of course mean, in this instance, horrifying.' She reached out and pinned the worm down, just before it entered Buggy's nasal cavity. The worm reacted, protecting itself by forming a new shell. 'You do know there's no coming back from this type of gas worm?' muttered Angel, as she picked the thing off his face. 'It literally eats away ninety-nine point six-seven-five percent of your brain. Just leaves the tiny bit they need. And trust me, there is no fascinating future in store for a brain-dead Bug E zomb E locked in an Amorph E serpent.'

The danger from the worm was gone. But Buggy wasn't sure if it was safe to reveal he was OK. Surely that would just take him out of the frying pan into the fire. Not that there was much difference between frying pans and fires these days. He decided to keep up his act. 'I do not know you,' he said in a flat monotone voice, 'I belong to the Dreddax. Look at the discs on my temples,' he added. Right on cue, one of the tiny metal discs lost its spit stickiness and fell to the ground. Buggy's despairing eyes followed it as it rolled to a stop by Angel's feet.

Angel watched it too. And burst out laughing. 'Fascinating,' she repeated when she'd managed to gather herself. Buggy sighed. Angel handed the solidified gas worm to the silver Dreddax. 'Try using it on the correct subject next time. This one is not destined for a segment in your Amorphi serpent, abhorrently beguiling machine though it is.' Angel nodded to herself. 'I am *definitely* going to take a trip inside that serpent at some point,' she declared, 'just to see it go about its business. In fact, I'm putting that top of my to-do list.' To the Dreddax butcher by the door she said, 'Of course this little incident is all the more horrifying because I am currently on my way to collect payment for this specimen, and if you *had* sucked out his cutely malfunctioning brain . . . he was trying to escape, you know . . . imagine that! What a genius escape plan.' She turned back to Buggy momentarily, held his face in her hands and gave his cheeks a few friendly slaps. 'I know – I'll swap places with someone who is about to have their brain removed.' She shook her head. 'Now, where was I? Ah yes, removing what little brains he has would have rendered him worthless. My buyer hired me to capture him for his human abilities. If I hadn't come along when I did, I might have found myself having to blame the Dreddax in this little facility, and goodness, that wouldn't have been pretty. I know all about you and your strange physiology you know. Hmmm. No. Not pretty at all.' Angel paused, gave her threat time to weave its magic. 'But that's by the by. Now, if one of you would kindly take him back to his cell, I will go and collect my payment and we can forget all about this little incident.' She continued to mutter as she exited the room. 'I should be paid double. I feel as though I've had to capture this slippery fish at least twice.'

Buggy was still mightily disturbed by the change in Angel. She was just a sweet little girl at first, vulnerable, abandoned, sad. She didn't look any different now, she hadn't grown or anything, but she exuded . . . exuded what? Buggy couldn't think of any way to describe it other than a cheery aura of imminent threat. And that made her even more disturbing. From the reaction of the Dreddax butchers, he wasn't the only one who felt uncomfortable in her presence. They remained motionless as the cyborganic passed by... and they didn't move until Angel's mutterings had faded well into the distance. Only then did a Dreddax butcher step forward. A tendril coiled out from its arm and curled around Buggy's wrist.

Chapter Twenty-Eight

S cuba touched skinsuits again. 'Follow me closely. Stop
when I stop, move when I move.'

The Dreddax butcher was patrolling methodically –
walking from crypt entrance to church entrance and back
again. It moved fast, constantly looking behind, then ahead.
There was no opportunity to sneak by. Muddy tapped Scuba
on the shoulder, signalled for her to wait. He found a
surviving patch of snow and scooped some up. As the butcher
began to turn away from the church, Muddy threw his
snowball. It arced through the air unseen and skidded into the
black church entrance. The butcher paused. It turned back
towards the noise. After what seemed like an age, it went
inside the church to investigate. Muddy and Scuba slipped
quietly through the crypt entrance and scurried down the
spiral staircase that greeted them.

The main hallway was deserted.

'BIB,' commanded Scuba.

Muddy pressed the relevant suitcipher. The skinsuit material lost its camouflage and retracted from their faces. Scuba looked at the scanner on her forearm. 'The tracknid is still below us, but not too far ahead. We will go down level by level until we find it.'

Muddy looked around. The staircase stopped on this floor. The room and hallway were both huge, but all on one floor. 'There *are* no lower levels.'

Scuba began checking the walls. 'The tracknid disappeared below ground. And it is below us now. There must be lower levels.' When she got to the wall behind the staircase, she knocked, listened, knocked again. 'This is it. Come here. Put yourn back to the wall, like we did on Quarasia.'

Scuba was right. They found levels on the other side. Lots of them. She took the lead as they descended a new spiral staircase. Four levels down she looked at her tracker, nodded and stepped off. Through dimly lit passageways, empty rooms and silent hallways, the tracking signal pulled them ever deeper into the crypt's underground web.

Muddy kept pace with her . . . until they entered one particular corridor. He stopped. He stared. There was a second corridor, running parallel to the first. It had been purpose built – purpose built for an Amorphi serpent. And the serpent was there, hovering with ominous intent. Muddy almost cowered. It was massive. Close up, it looked as deadly as Scuba had made it sound. The entire body swayed gently. Its outer shell, formed from a dark, shimmering metal, had been fashioned and decorated to look like scaled skin. The enormous head was split, designed to function like an actual jaw. Both the top and bottom sections of the mouth were filled with pointed, razor-sharp fangs. Deep in the serpent's throat, Muddy could make out the end of a tube, charred and blackened – the source of the flames that had devoured his home. This serpent was part dragon. He was drawn to the eyes in the top section of the head. Huge black ovals. He wondered at the horrors they must have seen over the years. The entire serpent structure was held together by the spine. It breached the outside surface and ran from tip to tail, serving to lock the segments in place. There were at least twenty of those, double segments, starting behind the head and running down beyond the belly of the beast. If what Scuba had told him was true, and he had no reason to doubt her, then inside each of those segments would be a mere shell of a human, its brain stripped, capable only of soulless search and destroy.

He turned to Scuba. The serpent had her full attention too. 'Is this planet your concern now?' asked Muddy.

Scuba didn't answer straight away. 'This is they,' she whispered, almost to herself. 'The group responsible for the destruction of so many planets, mine planet included. This serpent was also on yourn planet. Dreddax butchers from this thing killed mine team. They must have come straight here. Earth is where they hide it.' She looked to the floor, shook her head ever so slightly. 'But you and Buggy are still mine priority.'

Muddy heard effort in her words. Like she'd had to force them out. It made him wonder just how true they were. The way she'd spoken about the Amorphi serpent before . . . there was so much more than hatred between her and this machine. 'How did it get so far underground in such a confined space?' he asked.

Scuba pointed towards the far end of the room. There was a circular structure, similar to the transporter that Scuba's team had used, only this one covered the entire wall.

Muddy was stunned. 'What? This is a giant underground parking bay? But if the Amorphi serpent is here, then Earth must be next on their "to do" list.'

'No. Not according to Buggy's findings. Earth is just a base. It is an entire planet off the grid. The strength of Dreddax butchers on this planet – there must be ten, maybe fifteen – it is hardly big enough for an assault force, never mind an entire scratch planet unit. They are here purely to man it . . . deal with business in the local area. The faux scratchgas covers theirn movements. They must take a handful of humans every five years to make a little extra profit and top up theirn trade. No doubt there will be a ship in the outer atmosphere with theirn main force aboard. Theirn transport capabilities are not as good as ourn. They can only transport over short distances. To transport the serpent and stolen goods to and from raided planets, they would need to carry them in the larger ship.'

'You should stop them, stop the Amorphi serpent. You may never get another opportunity.'

'I cannot. I have no team.' Scuba masked her disappointment well. The words came out easier this time. 'Like I said, mine priority is you and yourn friend. We find

Buggy, I encode yourn PIPs and you leave.' She took a resolute step away, but then paused, looked down at the tracknid monitor, made a decision. 'Stay here for just a moment.' She began retracing her steps. 'I can at least go inside the serpent . . . see if it is manned, assess its stage of readiness.'

The corridor went deathly quiet. It made Muddy's ears hurt. And it stayed like that for a little too long. He started feeling anxious. Not just about the presence of the Amorphi serpent, but about the tracknid too. He and Scuba had stopped moving, but that vicious little machine hadn't. And without Scuba's tracker, he had no idea how close it was to Buggy. Muddy took a cautious step into the serpent's bay. 'Scuba,' he whispered. 'Scuuuba?' He moved in deeper, right up to the base of the ramp that Scuba had ascended. At the top was an entrance to the central segment of the serpent's body. The darkness that filled the entrance hung in the air, dense and deep. Muddy eased his way up but didn't call Scuba's name. His mouth was as dry as a bone. The hairs on his neck rippled a warning. He moved to the edge of the darkness. And a hand pushed him gently backwards.

The skinsuit material retracted from Scuba's face. Muddy wondered how she'd gotten so close . . . how she'd gotten so pale. 'What's wrong?' he whispered. She didn't reply. 'Scuba . . . what?'

'It . . . the serpent, inside . . . there is . . .' A light started flashing on Scuba's sleeve: red – danger. It snapped her back into the moment. 'The tracknid has sighted its target! Go!'

They both turned to run.

And the attack came out of nowhere.

The force of the hit floored Scuba. She crashed, headfirst into the wall. Muddy was stunned by the speed of the attack. The identity of the attacker stunned him even more. She must have been hiding inside the Amorphi serpent, waiting. She had pounced from that all-consuming darkness, kicking Scuba to the ground with her first strike. Now the old lady moved like an athlete, shoving Muddy out of the way and rushing at the fallen girl.

'Mrs Magner! Stop!' shouted Muddy. 'Buggy's in trouble, we have to get to him now!'

The old lady glanced back . . . but continued her assault. A blade extended from the sleeve of her skinsuit. She stood over Scuba and raised it. Without thinking, Muddy ran and threw himself at her as the blade came down. Instead of cutting into Scuba, the blade sliced through the straps on her backpack. Scuba stirred, shook the cobwebs from her head. She grabbed Mrs Magner's legs, dragged her away from Muddy. A powerful shield pulse sent the old lady spinning down the corridor on her back.

Mrs Magner swivelled her body and rose to her feet before she'd even come to a stop. She turned around. One good eye and one white rheumy eye glared at Muddy and Scuba. But instead of returning to the fight, Mrs Magner picked up Scuba's backpack and ran.

'You hurt?' asked Muddy.

'No time,' winced Scuba. She pointed at her sleeve. 'The tracknid . . . Buggy. We must move.'

They charged along the corridor, following where Scuba's flashing tracker led.

'She tried to kill you,' panted Muddy.

'I think mineself and mine team were the targets all along. You and Buggy were just bonuses. Cyborganics must have been placed on yourn planet knowing it was the next scratch planet . . . knowing mine team would be there. Since Little Dog was the beacon, I am not even certain Angel and Mrs Magner are working together. It appears to be a free-for-all.' The flashing on Scuba's arm changed to a high-pitched screech. 'The tracknid! It is close!'

Chapter Twenty-Nine

Buggy sighed. Despite his feelings about Angel, he couldn't deny that she'd been right. His escape plan had been ridiculous. If that worm had entered his brain, he would have escaped alright . . . permanently. And what was he supposed to do now? Allow himself to be led like a dog back to his cell? Knock out a few tunes on the lute? He stared up at the side of the Dreddax visor. It was disconcerting not seeing a face, no matter how alien or unfriendly. But it would have been more disconcerting seeing his own eyes staring out of that butcher's visor. Buggy tugged on the tendril that was wrapped around his wrist. 'Who am I being sold to?'

The Dreddax butcher turned to look at him but didn't stop walking. There was a momentary whizz – a sound like the revving of a tiny dentist's drill. A red pulse shot down its tendril. Buggy flinched as the barb jabbed into his wrist.

Burning fluid rushed through his veins. Poison! Scuba had said that barbs could inject poison! Its effect was immediate. He felt drowsy, disorientated. Fire ants crawled over his skin. Whispers filled his head. He felt light. Were his eyes open or closed? A rumbling – the cave-in that started all this, and his parents, way, way in the distance . . . out of reach . . . their faces becoming blurred . . . another noise, clattering, a shout . . . Buggy tried to look, but lifting his eyelids was like lifting an iron drawbridge . . . 'Wha . . . what was that?'

The butcher raised a hand, ready to strike. But the clattering that roused Buggy had caught its attention too. Voices. Shouting. A scuffle? Buggy couldn't quite make it out. The sounds were echoey and distorted, but they weren't just in his head. The Dreddax butcher began charging the weapons on its raised arm. More noise. Running. The tendril gripping Buggy's wrist loosened. The butcher pushed him to the wall, held him by the throat with enough pressure to prevent him from calling out. Buggy wriggled his head to the side as best he could, succeeded in raising the iron drawbridge just a fraction. Was that movement? Along the corridor? It was difficult to see . . . as though parts of the wall were bending. Then it struck him . . . it wasn't the wall . . . it was camouflage . . . someone had camouflaged their skinsuit. It was Scuba! It had to be. He'd seen her do the same trick crawling through foliage towards her team. He tried to follow the path of the distortions, but they were too fast, too difficult for his drowsy eyes to keep up. A blur of movement right beside him. The pressure on his throat was suddenly gone. He began a gentle slide to the floor. At the same time, he saw the Dreddax butcher that had been holding him fly through the air and smash into the opposite wall. It gave him a warm, strangely satisfying feeling. As he slid further down, he stared up at the ceiling. Something small and metallic scurried around the edge of his vision, but Buggy didn't have time to focus on it. He was yanked to his feet. Was somebody messing with his PIP? This didn't feel like a friendly rescue anymore. It didn't feel like a friendly anything. Three fingers punched a suitcipher on his chest. His skinsuit hardened. Everything went black.

Chapter Thirty

S cuba hurtled along the corridor, only glancing at the tracker once. She skidded around a corner and almost fell over a Dreddax butcher. It was laid out on the floor, its visor smashed in. Its tendrils were hanging loose but still squirming with life. Scuba stood over it, pummelled its chest until the tendrils became still. 'The cyborganic has taken Buggy,' she hissed.

Muddy dropped to his knees behind her. 'We'll never find him in time.'

'The tracknid did not get to him.' Scuba pointed to the spidery contraption. It had scurried into the shade of a Dreddax boot. It froze and began going through colour changes. Scuba reached towards it, allowed her sleeve to extend into its body.

'What are you doing?' asked Muddy.

'The tracknid is analysing the transport signal. It is still hunting the PIP in Buggy's stomach. Like I told you, it will never stop. I need to extract the location code before it . . . '

The tracknid turned black and disappeared in a flash of gold.

Chapter Thirty-One

Buggy still felt groggy from the poison in the Dreddax barb. He had travelled. That much he knew. But he wasn't travelling any more. His suit had gone completely malleable again. Someone had grabbed him. They must have also encoded his PIP with a planet location and initiated transport. He had no idea where he was. This wasn't home. And this wasn't Earth. It was warmer for a start, and breathing the air wasn't pleasant. It didn't seem . . . fresh. Things smelt burnt, but there was no fire, no smoke. A few fingers of sunlight reached into his new cell and poked around. Buggy's eyes poked around with them. It wasn't a cell. There was no concrete. No rock. The structure was made from wood. He was sitting in the corner of a charred, blackened cabin. Minuscule pieces of ash floated in the air, like the snow of Earth. Black flakes circled on the currents, landing on and around him. Across the other side of the cabin sat Mrs Magner. Buggy stared at her. She had a disturbingly familiar look – distracted, obsessed, stark raving mad. The old lady had obviously learnt a thing or two about skinsuits if she'd managed to encode a PIP and transport him. Buggy sat back in wonder. Maybe she'd known about skinsuits all along? Who knew anything about Mrs Magner anymore? He thought back to the escape from his home, just before they'd transported to Earth. He'd seen a Dreddax butcher appear right next to her – it hadn't even touched her. And the skinsuit itself . . . when she'd first squeezed that black cube... the material had struggled to spread, as though it was unsure whether or not to merge with her. He should have said something to Scuba there and then. At the time though, everything was so sudden, so . . . unbelievable. Besides, he'd actually warmed to the old lady during the time they'd spent together. But now, that no longer mattered. It was obvious. Mrs Magner was a cyborganic. And she was working for the Dreddax, or for someone higher than them. The Dreddax *knew* her. That's why they hadn't attacked her. And now she'd whipped him away from under Angel's nose so that she could be the one to claim payment.

The old lady began searching through a backpack. Buggy felt behind him. He still had his on. So, whose backpack did she have, Scuba's or Muddy's? Mrs Magner tipped the bag upside down and shook the contents out. After a quick rummage, she paused, placed one of the items aside. She refilled the backpack, rose to her feet and left the cabin with it.

Buggy wasn't sure what to do. He stood, looked over to where Mrs Magner had been crouching. In the poor light it looked like she'd been sitting by a rectangle of charred and burnt sticks. He needed a closer look. Before he had chance to move, the old lady returned - without the backpack. As she closed the rickety door behind her, the whispering began. It grew louder as she made her way towards the rectangle of sticks. She sank back into her crouch, bible in hand. Still whispering, she began rocking forwards and backwards, occasionally stopping to pat her black leather bible. Then the whispering stopped. The rocking stopped. Mrs Magner's finger traced the silver embossed cross in the centre of the bible's cover. She nodded. Buggy tried to subdue the feeling of panic that was rising inside him. There was something inherently unstable about this old woman. Mrs Magner's good eye flashed him a look. It was as though she had sensed him observing her. 'Not long now,' she said. The rocking began again. 'They will be here soon.'

Buggy felt sick. Kidnapped by a tiny cyborganic girl, re-kidnapped by an old cyborganic woman. And now the Dreddax were on their way.

Chapter Thirty-Two

'Did you get it?' Muddy could hardly contain his panic. Scuba looked confused.

'Scuba! Did you get the PIP location code? Where's the tracknid gone?'

'I know this code!' There was genuine surprise in Scuba's voice. 'I know where the cyborganic has taken Buggy. It must be a base also, or at least hern hide-out. It is a perfect choice. It is considered a dead planet, uninhabitable.'

Muddy watched closely as Scuba entered a code into her PIP. It suddenly struck him how hard she was working. Always doing her very best to help him and Buggy. That's what she'd been doing from the first moment she'd appeared. 'I'm sorry.'

Scuba frowned. 'Pardon?'

'I said I'm sorry,' repeated Muddy. 'I should have believed you about cyborganics. I should have trusted you from the very start.'

Scuba placed the PIP back into her skinsuit. 'Then trust me now,' she said. 'The cyborganic has taken Buggy. I will transport to the planet and get him . . . alone. Today is deadline day. If you do not integrate into yourn family unit before midnight, there will be no other opportunity.' Scuba tapped a cipher on Muddy's forearm. A series of numbers and glyphs lit up. 'Enter these symbols into yourn PIP. This is the cipher for the planet on which yourn parents now reside. Press the transport suitcipher and you will automatically pass through the Amorphi memory defragmenter and re-join them. The defragmenter field currently surrounds that planet. When you arrive on the surface, you will be . . . OK. The skinsuit will recognise yourn mental change and disintegrate. You will forget you ever wore one.'

'But . . . '

'Please. No time to argue. I will find Buggy before the deadline and send him to his family too. He will be right behind you. Yourn skinsuit is a little low on energy, but it will self-charge and be ready for travel in a few minutes.' Scuba pressed a separate cipher on Muddy's suit. A familiar snake appeared in the corner of his eye and began chasing its tail. 'When the timer runs out, yourn suit will be ready. Enter the cipher and then transport. Do not linger more than you have to.' She moved towards Muddy, paused for a moment, as though lost in thought. She hugged him. 'Goodbye. I am sorry things did not go smoother,' she said.

Before he could put up any further protests . . . before he could say all the things he wanted to say to this strange girl, she stepped away, entered a cipher into her own skinsuit and disappeared.

Muddy found a shortcut back to the surface. He saw no Dreddax butchers. It was as though they had abandoned the area. No guard at the Crypt entrance. No random patrols. He decided to head for the police station. It wasn't far. And he was thankful to be able to walk feely above ground and get some fresh air. He felt like he needed it. Seeing Scuba leave had hurt. Far more than he'd expected. After being sucked into her weird and wonderful whirlwind, he'd become . . . attached, and now it felt like he'd been set adrift. He would never see her again. And once he'd travelled through the memory defragmenter, he wouldn't even remember her. It seemed . . . *wrong*. His home planet, too. He'd never see that again. Even the planet he was on right now, Earth – it was addictive, a melting pot of people and cultures, all living in such close proximity. Imagine experiencing such a planet when the population was no longer under the influence of scratchgas. Maybe he could just stay here? He didn't *have* to enter those symbols into his PIP.

When he reached the police station, Muddy leaned against the back gate and sighed. He couldn't stay. He had a new life to start. A new old family to join. And Scuba was sending Buggy, so he'd have a new old friend to meet too. He closed his eyes, watched the snake chase its tail for a while. Not long now.

The snake soon lost its appeal. Muddy re-opened his eyes so he could enjoy his final bit of Earth. And his heart leapt. Scuba had come back. She was standing across the street. He took an excited step forward. Just one. As quickly as his heart had leapt, it sank back down like a stone. He'd made this mistake once before. In the fight pit on Quarasia. The skinsuit moving towards him was larger than Scuba, more masculine. Muddy retreated until his back hit the cold metal of the police station's main gate. The black material covering the head of the approaching figure retracted . . . revealing pale, rotting flesh, cold grey eyes. Dead Mezko was back.

Chapter Thirty-Three

Muddy blinked. The snake had almost caught its tail. He only needed to hold out for a minute or so. But running from his alcove wasn't an option. Dead Mezko was too close. And fighting? He wouldn't last a minute against this opponent. His experience in the fight pit had taught him that. Wait! He didn't need to do either! Muddy reached for the gate lock. His sleeve extended, formed the security pass that Scuba had programmed into it. He pushed open the heavy metal door, slipped inside just as Dead Mezko reached out for him. The door crashed shut. There was an audible click as it locked. Muddy dropped to a crouch and took some deep breaths. That should do it. Now he could just wait it out. He checked on the snake. Almost there. As soon as his . . . Muddy stared at the door – a section of it seemed to distort. He squinted, looked closer. There it was again – the centre –

curving ever so sli . . . Muddy reeled back as the outline of a face began to stretch through the wrought iron. Dead eyes stared. A mouth opened into a gruesome yawn as it struggled to form words.

'Tak . . . Tak . . . ' it groaned. Dead Mezko's neck and shoulders pressed forwards. A hand pushed into the metal . . . and another. The squirming body sagged, just for a moment. Forcing its way through the door was exhausting it.

Muddy wasn't about to wait for it to recover. He got back to his feet, ran through the police yard and kicked open the caged custody area. He darted inside. Behind him, he heard a metallic snap. Dead Mezko was through the main gate. Muddy watched from the cage as the corpse steadied itself. Its dead eyes took in the surroundings. When it caught sight of Muddy, it pushed off from the brickwork and began pacing across the yard. Muddy slammed the cage door, engaged the lock. But a solid iron door hadn't stopped this killer cadaver - a wire one stood no chance. Dead Mezko grabbed the outside of the cage. Rage flared in his dead eyes. 'Tak . . . Taka'an dehz . . . ' he hissed as he forced a hand through the wire and reached out for Muddy.

Muddy checked on the snake. It evaporated. His skinsuit was ready. He just needed time to enter the cipher into his PIP. But Dead Mezko wasn't about to give him that time. The rest of his body was almost through the wire. Muddy had no choice but to keep running. He sprinted into the corridor that linked the police station to the custody cage. Behind him, Dead Mezko screamed, 'Taka'an dehz venk'eya tuk . . . VENK'EYA TUK!'

Muddy had no idea what the words meant, but there was no mistaking the venom in their delivery. He repeated them like a mantra as he ran, sure that they'd be the last words he'd ever hear.

Or maybe not.

This section of the corridor was familiar. He'd run through it once before. It led to the front office. He could lose Dead Mezko among the people and the streets outside. A quick look back. No sign of the corpse. The office door came into view. Muddy reached for the handle . . . just as the entire door was ripped off its hinges. Three barded tendrils cut through the air towards him. Muddy whipped his head back. A Dreddax butcher! Still on Earth! Back down the corridor, Dead Mezko was closing in – a hideous grin across his rotting face. 'Kas'ood Quarasian on famik'yun bi depaar,' he shouted.

Muddy froze. A Dreddax butcher in front of him. A living corpse behind him. No time to put a cipher into his PIP. There was a corridor to his right. But that was a short wing, lined only with cells - a dead end . . . literally. He'd be trapping himself. And yet all he needed were a few precious seconds to encode the PIP. The cells . . . he could lock himself inside one. The doors were heavy, much thicker than the gate and the cage. Surely he'd have enough time to enter the cipher before the Dreddax butcher could break in, or Dead Mezko could break through? Muddy made his decision. He turned towards the dead end. The nearest cell door swung open. Another figure blocked his path.

'Duck.'

Muddy ducked. Electrified wires rocketed past his head and pierced the Dreddax visor. 'You did mean me when you said duck?' he asked.

'I did,' confirmed Fourforty.

'There's another problem about to—'

Before Muddy could finish his warning, Fourforty gave a short, shrill whistle. There was a snarl and a growl. Skinsuit and fur came flying round the corner, both sliding to a halt near the officer. 'Release!' commanded Fourforty. Chisel let go of his hold on Dead Mezko. Fourforty drew a second taser from her belt. She fired. Both the corpse and the Dreddax butcher shuddered like puppets on electrified string.

'Why are you helping me?' asked Muddy.

'Your friend was right. I'm a cyborganic. And it *was* me that you saw at the Crypt. I was trying to negotiate with the Dreddax butchers to get Chisel back. They'd taken him and barb whipped him to punish me.'

'Punish you for what?'

'They knew I killed the butcher in the front office. They believed I had also killed my three Dreddax overseers. They never returned to their Crypt base from the last scratch planet.'

Muddy felt a pang of guilt. 'I think we may have killed those three on my planet. That's how we ended up here. We took their PIPs. I'm sorry if it got Chisel hurt.'

Fourforty squeezed down harder on the triggers. 'It doesn't matter. Now they're gone and I don't answer to anyone. I saw what you did for Chisel. How you gave him water and treated him with the girl's medicine. And I thank you. My dog means more to me than this Dreddax scum ever did. Consider us even.' Fourforty smiled at the confused frown on Muddy's face. 'Surprised that cyborganics have emotions, heh?' she said. 'Well, now you know. And now you should go. I will take care of things here.'

Muddy didn't need telling twice. 'Fourforty . . . thank you,' he said. He slipped into the open cell.

'No need to thank me. I love a good fight,' shouted Fourforty. She squeezed down on the triggers again.

With the sound of shuddering bodies and electrified wires crackling in his ears, Muddy entered glyphs and numbers into his PIP. He had one final look around. The last place on Earth. He put the PIP inside his skinsuit and pressed the transport cipher.

Chapter Thirty-Four

Scuba made no sudden moves. Dreddax butchers almost always left a tri-team on empty scratch planets in order to monitor the conditions and any intrusions. She had no reason to believe it would be any different on this planet. And she had no wish to attract their attention. All she needed to do was take Buggy from the cyborganic, program his PIP and send him to the same planet as Muddy. Of course, she had to find him first . . . and find him alive. She checked the timer that she'd set in her own eye. It was gone. Muddy would have transported by now. She felt bad for not telling him the whole truth, but at least he was safe. And the defragmenting process would strip his memories. Now he would never learn that she had lied. That fact didn't make her feel any better. Scuba gave a heavy sigh and concentrated on the job at hand. She scanned the horizon. Neither Dreddax butchers nor cyborganics came into view. The hard way then. She knelt down and scoured the immediate area for tracks. A gentle breeze caressed the ground, lifting and redistributing the thin layer of black ash. Any anomalies were soon covered in such conditions, but only superficially. Dents from fresh footsteps could still be followed . . . if you could find them in the first place. Touching the warm ash brought memories flooding back. She'd been here before, with others . . . they were all dead now. Scuba pushed her hand deeper, scooped up some of the pure white sand, scooped up more memories with it. She let the sand run through her fingers, the memories run through her mind. She wondered now what she'd wondered then . . . how long had this planet burned? Who would make the Dreddax butchers and their Amorphi serpent pay for what they had done? She arrived at the same conclusion. One day, *she* would. Whatever it took.

Scuba sensed movement. She gave herself a silent reprimand. Her anger at the Amorphi serpent had distracted her. Engaging her skinsuit, she charged up a shield and spun round.

'Hey.'

'You . . . YOU IDIOT,' snarled Scuba. 'What the . . . pop are you doing here? You should be away, safe! Have you lost yourn mind! I cannot believe this. You simpleton!'

'It's good to see you again, too,' muttered Muddy.

'How?' Scuba demanded.

'I watched you enter this planet's cipher into your own PIP. I memorised it.'

'That is the how. And now the why?'

'Look, I appreciate that you wanted me safe. But Buggy is like my brother. I'll go when he goes. If he doesn't make it, nor do I.'

Scuba took a feisty step forwards, intending to knock this halfwit out, enter the cipher into his PIP herself and send him on his way. But the spark inside her fizzled out as quickly as it had ignited. Only moments earlier she'd been thinking about her own friends . . . her own family. Scuba stood still and stared.

Muddy swallowed, hard. 'What are you doing?' he asked.

'I am counting to ten in mine head,' replied Scuba. The anger in her eyes slowly gave way to understanding. She turned away and went back to tracking the cyborganic.

Relieved at the drastic shift in attitude, Muddy trudged after her. 'Dead Mezko came back,' he said.

A slight pause in Scuba's step. 'How did you get away?'

'I had help from a friend.'

Silence followed. Scuba didn't seem interested in pursuing the details. But Muddy was. 'Dead Mezko said something,' he continued.

'What?'

'I can't remember exactly, it sounded something like "taken days venky took".'

'Taka'an dehz venk'eya tuk,' said Scuba.

'That's it! That's what he said.'

'It is Quarasian,' said Scuba.

'So why didn't it translate in my head? I thought all that pain in my ears meant I'd understand other languages,' said Muddy.

'As I said. It is Quarasian. I am Quarasian. These suits are Quarasian, made by and for people who speak Quarasian. Why would translation of Quarasian be included in the translation software?'

'Oh.' Muddy frowned. Something about that didn't quite sit right with him. He couldn't work out why. 'OK. Fair enough. So, what does it mean?'

'"Taka'an dehz venk'eya tuk".' Scuba took a moment. 'In yourn language it means the equivalent of, "Inside this I come for you all".' She shook her head. 'Its existence is mine fault. I should have made the time to extract and destroy the raphenia cube and send that last body back.'

'You couldn't. I was there, remember? There *was* no time. You did what you could by camouflaging the coffin. If you'd have stayed any longer there would have been another Quarasian corpse. Some human ones too.' Muddy moved to her side. 'So . . . you didn't know the Dreddax butchers could make corpses do what they want?'

'It is not the Dreddax,' said Scuba. 'It is much worse. As I explained to you, Dreddax scientists were able to abuse Amorphi technology to create the zombies that are placed in theirn serpent. But to actually inhabit a corpse . . . a Quarasian corpse . . . ' Scuba sighed. 'There were once rumours of a nefarious individual – an Amorphi – outcast by the Amorphi council for experimenting with such things. If he is the one overseeing the dealings of these Dreddax butchers . . . ' She shook her head, trying to nip some appalling thoughts in the bud before they could fully form. 'Did the corpse say anything else?'

Muddy nodded. 'I only remember the first bit. It used the word "Quarasian" and something like "kosood famiklaa bee depaar"'

Scuba turned away. She felt another pang of guilt. *It* knew. But translating that for Muddy would bring . . . complications. 'No. I am sorry. I do not understand the words you are trying to say.'

'Scuba! There!' Muddy pointed to a discarded backpack. It was open. Items were strewn across the sand. 'Why did Mrs Magner steal your backpack? Everything is here . . . no, wait, your cloth is missing . . . '

'What do you mean mine cl—' Scuba rushed at him.

Muddy took a step back, held her backpack out. If she wanted it that badly she could have it. 'Here!' he said. 'You only had to ask!'

Scuba jumped over him, used her weight to pull him into a stoop as she landed. A line of molten red projectiles zipped through the air above them. 'Butchers!' she said. 'The tri-team have spotted us.' She risked bobbing her head up for a look. 'I can see only two of the three. We need to find cover. Follow me.' They ran to the crest of the burnt dune. 'Over there . . . the cabin. Go!' commanded Scuba.

Muddy kept his head low and ran, Scuba just behind. They were both acutely aware of the clear trail of footprints being left in their wake.

'We must enter the cabin,' said Scuba. 'They will not just follow us straight inside and kill us. They will take time to decide the best course of action.'

'And what's the best course of action?' asked Muddy.

'To follow us inside and kill us,' replied Scuba.

'Great.'

As they drew nearer to the cabin door, they could see a body lying near the entrance. Scuba pulled Muddy back and took the lead. She didn't want him to see that body if it turned out to be Buggy.

But the body wasn't human. 'The third member of the Dreddax tri-team,' said Scuba. 'It has been here for a long time. There are no combat wounds or burns.' She frowned. 'It would not have starved or gone thirsty. The tri-team would be well supplied with food and this planet has underground running water. And yet, if it had died of natural causes its team members would have retrieved it, buried it or sent it home.' Scuba went for a closer look. The creature's skin was shrunken and dried. It was covered with small, discoloured patches. 'Do not touch it,' she warned. 'It has been poisoned.'

'Believe it or not, my first thought wasn't to touch the dead wrinkly old Dreddax butcher,' Muddy replied.

'Shush.' Scuba pulled Muddy towards the cabin door. She stood and listened for a moment. No sound. She created a shield and eased the cabin door open. The two of them walked in side by side. And stopped dead. Sitting over in the corner was Buggy. He raised a finger to his lips, then pointed. The light that streamed in from the open door illuminated Mrs Magner. Buggy could now see that she wasn't sitting cross-legged at the head of a pile of burnt sticks, she was sitting cross-legged at the head of a pile of charred bones. The bones were bordered by a series of ornate, metallic tubes.

Mrs Magner didn't react to the new arrivals. She continued tending to the bones, muttering, rocking gently. Muddy eased the door closed. He and Scuba moved sideways and huddled next to Buggy.

'What is the cyborganic doing?' asked Scuba.

'Beats me,' shrugged Buggy.

Mrs Magner unfolded a cloth. Muddy's eyes widened. He leaned towards Scuba. 'That's your cloth,' he whispered, 'from your backpack.'

Scuba frowned at him. 'Remember I told you that mine training included visiting a planet that had been destroyed by Dreddax butchers?'

Muddy nodded.

'This is the planet I chose to visit. That is why I recognised the PIP code I extracted from the tracknid. You saw this planet in ourn memorial room. The burnt planet. I retrieved that cloth from here. From this cabin. From beneath that child's remains. I took it because it . . . affected me. It gave me strength to do what I do.'

Muddy was at a loss. 'So, what's a cyborganic doing with it? Has she been hired to retrieve it? Is it just a collector's item, like me and Buggy?'

Scuba had no answer.

Mrs Magner continued to go about her business, oblivious to everything and everyone around her. She re-folded the cloth, placed it gently under the skull of the small skeleton. She sat back, closed her eyes and spoke. Her words echoed around the cabin. 'May-Yania, Tinta. Little sister. They took your life. And they thought me dead. They will think again . . . '

Muddy's heart pounded. Mrs Magner was reciting the text from the cloth off by heart. It was *her* cloth; those were *her* words. He'd automatically assumed that his skinsuit had translated Quarasian. But Scuba had only just explained that Quarasian wasn't even in the language database. His skinsuit must have translated Mrs Magner's native tongue!

' . . . I was weak. I was worn. I have been reborn. I have finally found them.' Mrs Magner held up the PIP that brought her here. 'I made you a promise that began with your blood. It will end with mine and theirs.' She created a tiny skinsuit blade and rested it on the side of her head. Muddy winced as the old lady pushed the blade into her skin. She cut deeply, drawing the blade from her left ear, across her hair line, to her right ear. Blood began pouring from the wound. It gushed down her face, forming a glistening red mask.

Muddy reached for the medical equipment in his backpack and tried to get up. Scuba wrenched him back down to the floor. She shook her head. Muddy didn't struggle. Trusting Scuba had been a problem before. Not anymore. He settled back to a crouch and watched.

Beneath the crimson curtain, the old lady's features softened, her wrinkles began melting away. Blood soaked into her white, straw-like hair . . . it became shiny and sleek . . . from root to tip, its colour slowly changed to a vibrant blonde. Snaps and cracks echoed through the cabin, quiet and muffled at first, but they soon grew sickeningly loud. Mrs Magner's shoulders began to realign . . . her back straightened . . . her posture became solid, more assured. Silent tears rolled down the red mask. The pain must have been excruciating. Muddy glanced at Buggy. There were no words. It was unbelievable. Mrs Magner was getting younger in front of their eyes.

The cut across her forehead began to seal. The blood that remained on her face contracted and expanded, as though breathing. Slowly but surely, it pooled around the old lady's – the young woman's – damaged eye. The red liquid hardened into a sparkling crystal eye patch and transformed into a deep, unfathomable blue. For the first time since she'd cut herself, Mrs Magner opened her good eye. It had become an exquisite, vivid green.

Muddy felt Scuba squeeze down on his arm . . . hard. Next came an incredulous whisper, 'She is a Lupella . . . *Mrs Magner is a Lupella.*'

From where an old lady had squatted, a teenage girl rose from the ashes. She strode through the cabin, assembling the thin metal tubes from around the skeleton as she went. 'May-Yania, Tinta. Little sister. I was your sorrow. I was your tomorrow. My name is May-Yania, Magna, and I am your twin. I am your soul. I . . . am . . . your . . . *vengeance!*' She had spoken softly at first, but that last word was delivered with such venom it rocked Muddy and Buggy back on their heels. The girl, Magna, thrust her spear through the side of the cabin with malicious intent. She twisted it . . . and wrenched it back. Planks shattered as a skewered Dreddax butcher burst through. Black blood spattered the inside of its visor. It was dead. It just didn't know it yet. Magna ripped the spear from its chest and pointed it at the creature's neck. She stared deep into the visor. 'May-Yania, Tinta was her name,' she hissed. The final thrust of the spear was accompanied by a guttural, almost inaudible snarl. Magna spat on the Dreddax corpse as it fell at her feet. She stepped over it and stomped through the hole that she'd made in the cabin wall.

Scuba, Muddy and Buggy rose in unison and gathered by the same hole. They got there just in time to see Magna take the remaining Dreddax butcher to the ground. 'Call every Dreddax in your command to this location,' she demanded.

Scuba rushed out and placed an arm on Magna's shoulder. 'May-Yania, Magna, think about what are you doing. You cannot call them all. There are too many of them. And they have an Amorphi serpent.'

Magna gave Scuba a one-eyed stare, more piercing than any spear. 'I've been thinking about what I am doing for over a decade! And the LORD God said unto the serpent, Because thou hast done this, thou art cursed above all cattle, and above every beast of the field; upon thy belly shalt thou go, and dust shalt thou eat all the days of thy life.' She turned back to the Dreddax butcher. 'Call them. CALL THEM ALL!'

The Dreddax butcher obeyed. Two tendrils extended, clicking into separate sockets on the side of its visor. Magna waited – just long enough for the signal to transmit. She helped the butcher to its feet. It looked around, unsure of what to do, where to go . . . whether to go. Was it being given its freedom?

Magna leaned towards it. 'Her name was May-Yania, Tinta.' The spear twirled. The Dreddax butcher fell. Magna stared into the visor for a long while, waiting for the life to drain from the creature's eyes.

Scuba stepped away. The damage was done. No point dwelling on it. She turned to Muddy and Buggy. 'You have time before they get here. The Dreddax cannot transport like us. Individuals can only transport short distances. To transport to the surface, they will need theirn main ship in this planet's atmosphere. That means theirn ship will have to fast travel from Earth to here. But once here, theirn entire force, Amorphi serpent included, will transport to the surface. Anyone found on this planet . . . will not fare well. The window of opportunity to get you to yourn families closes in fifteen minutes. You need to leave.'

Muddy and Buggy looked at each other. It was such a simple decision . . . and yet . . .

'Tell us when we have five minutes left,' said Muddy. 'We need to talk, privately.' He placed his arm on his friend's shoulder and they walked back into the cabin.

'Have faith.'

Buggy glanced back. Magna's green eye was staring at him. *Have faith*, she mouthed again, *Samaritan*.

Inside the cabin, out of earshot of Scuba and Magna, the two friends sat facing each other. There were no smiles. They sat in silence for a minute or two, partly processing their own personal thoughts, partly wondering what the other would say.

Muddy began. 'We should leave.'

'We should,' agreed Buggy.

'Well!' Muddy slapped his knee, 'that was simpler than I thought it would be.'

They both gave a half-hearted laugh and shook their heads. If it had been so simple, they wouldn't have been sitting there discussing it.

'If things hadn't gone wrong when Scuba first found us, we'd already be gone, no question,' said Buggy.

Muddy nodded. 'We were under the influence of scratchgas though. I don't think we really knew what was going on. So, we weren't capable of making any kind of decision back then.'

'Wish we had some scratchgas now,' said Buggy.

Muddy allowed himself a cautious chuckle at the memory. 'She didn't like that, did she? We used up her whole canister. But you know what, things going wrong forced us to spend time with Scuba, forced us to learn . . . that's why I'm finding this decision so hard. If we hadn't made it this far . . . or if our "window of opportunity" had already run out . . . ' Muddy huffed. 'I don't know, maybe it would have been easier if this decision was out of our hands, but it isn't, and since it isn't . . . it's the biggest decision of our lives. Whatever we decide we can *never* look back and regret it. We've got to be sure. One hundred percent.'

They went quiet for another minute.

This time it was Buggy who broke the silence. 'Scuba said we'd be happy in our new lives. And we'd still be in a family, with the same people. I'd like that.'

Muddy nodded. 'Me too. But something about it just doesn't sit right. When I wouldn't believe Scuba about cyborganics, she told me my world had changed and I needed to change with it. I knew she was right, in more ways than she meant. It's harsh, but the fact is . . . me and you . . . we can *never* go back to our old world, and we can never be with the family we knew. We've already lost them. That realization hit me hard in the police cell on Earth. If we go back to our families, they would *look* the same . . . but they would *be* different. And the thing is . . . *we* would be different too. The only way to stay *who we are right now*, is to stay here. Leaving would almost be like killing our current selves.'

'With an army of Dreddax butchers and an Amorphi serpent on the way, staying would be *exactly* like killing our current selves.' Buggy blew in frustration and put his head in his hands. It was an impossible decision. And a terrifying one. The sensible choice was to leave. The Dreddax, the Amorphi, the entire business would be erased from their brains. More importantly, they'd be alive. A different life, maybe, but a life nonetheless. Buggy nodded to himself. Decision made. But . . . *have faith* . . . Why had Magna said that? Have faith in what? She'd called him Samaritan, like she had that night by the fire when she'd still been an old lady. And just now, he thought she'd kidnapped him from Earth. Turns out she'd rescued him *from* being kidnapped. Buggy was only sure about one thing. He was sure that he was unsure. And being unsure about everything didn't help when it came to making the most important decision of his life. Was Magna asking for help? Help to exact revenge on the Dreddax? But did he want to sacrifice his life for her revenge, because surely that's what would happen? They owed Scuba a lot, perhaps both Scuba and Magna . . . but did they owe them their lives? The choice seemed stark – go and be different, stay and be dead. 'I think we'd be stupid to stay,' he said.

'We've always been stupid,' replied Muddy.

Buggy spread his arms, guilty as charged. 'We have, haven't we,' he agreed. *Have faith*. 'Well,' he said, 'why change now?'

'No doubts?'

'Plenty of doubts,' said Buggy, 'but stupidity appears to have taken precedence.'

'FIVE MINUTES!' came the shout from Scuba.

Two dark brown eyes and one bright green eye stared at the boys as they came out of their dilapidated conference room.

'We're staying,' announced Muddy.

The three eyes widened.

Chapter Thirty-Five

'It is the worst place for combat that I have ever seen. To be so heavily outgunned and outnumbered in such an open space . . . it . . . ' Scuba didn't say any more. She didn't need to.

Magna closed the door. She knew the Quarasian wasn't complaining, merely stating facts. It was obvious that no matter where combat took place, they would be at an extreme disadvantage. To stand even a glimmer of a chance, their plan needed to be exceptional.

Scuba addressed Magna directly, 'Ourn skinsuits will need to be operating at peak efficiency when we engage the Dreddax. Water would be useful, we need to allow the raphenia to absorb as much as it needs to aid function and enable peak shield power. We should also drink water ournselves. Ourn bodies – and what brains we have, require it too.'

Muddy and Buggy smiled at that. They weren't the only ones feeling a bit dumb.

Scuba continued, 'The skinsuits will extract moisture from ourn bodies should the battle be prolonged, so we cannot afford to go into it dehydrated. Not that this battle will be prolonged,' she added.

This time Muddy just raised an eyebrow at Buggy. That wasn't so funny. Scuba spoke her mind, regardless of the cost to morale. She'd already made it clear that their skinsuits would not have enough power to transport them after extensive use of both camouflage and shields. So, there would be no disappearing in the middle of the battle. This was all or nothing.

Magna walked over to the far corner of the cabin and knelt down. She moved aside some broken wood, swept away some ash and sand to reveal a large metal plate. She heaved the plate up onto its hinges and pointed. Beneath the ground, a stream bubbled by. Scuba crouched over the hole, leaned in to scoop some water into her hands.

'No,' said Magna, firmly. 'The water contains poisons, harmful bacteria, placed in to kill Dreddax in case they returned. Use these.' Magna handed each of them a large straw from a concealed storage pouch attached to the underside of the metal plate. 'It filters out the poisons.'

Buggy thought back to Earth. Magna's bizarre behaviour in the burger bar with the straw and the drink suddenly made sense. He shared an understanding glance with her. No need for apologies or explanations. He was warming to her again.

They all shuffled around the opening and bobbed their heads down, sucking as much water as they could take through their straws. When they were done, one by one they lowered themselves in, so that their skinsuits could also top up. Scuba went first, but only after she'd convinced Magna that the skinsuit would automatically neutralize and expel any poisons it absorbed. Magna was the last to slip into the stream. She addressed everyone as she lowered herself down. 'The wolf and the lamb shall feed together, and the lion shall eat straw like the bullock: and dust shall be the serpent's meat.'

No one understood, but everyone gave a polite nod. It was a strange way to prepare for a battle.

When Magna came out of the stream, she took everyone to the centre of the cabin and cleared away more debris. There was a panel on the ground. It consisted of a raised button surrounded by five circles, four of which were red. 'When the main Dreddax force has landed, I can ignite the atmosphere at ground level. Each circle corresponds to a section of the land. These red circles are no good because that land was ignited during the last attack all those years ago. This green circle is the only section of land left to ignite; it wasn't used before as it has great religious significance. That's why the majority voted not to destroy it. Well, now I'm the majority and I'm voting to use it. It leaves us with a big problem, though. Since this is the only section of land that I can ignite, we're going to have to make all of the Dreddax butchers congregate in this region. Igniting the atmosphere worked before and it will work again. It will absolutely decimate them. It will kill them all.' Magna addressed Scuba directly. 'If the four of us are together when the atmosphere ignites, would a combined skinsuit shield protect us against the shockwave, the intense heat and the initial loss of oxygen?'

'Oxygen is not a problem with a fully engaged skinsuit. The raphenia will initiate the necessary chemical reaction if there is no oxygen available directly from the surrounding atmosphere. Regarding the shockwave and heat? If the four of us are together, under a combined shield, I think it would protect us,' replied Scuba. 'But the initial Dreddax ground force will just include basic troops. Even if yourn fire destroys most of them and we are able to deal with the remainder, we will still be left with two major problems, the troops on theirn ship and . . . ' Scuba paused. The thought of the second major problem filled her with a rage she was finding more and more difficult to contain.

'Their Amorphi serpent,' Magna finished. 'I know. I'm hoping it will arrive with the main force and be destroyed in the fire . . . ' The way Magna's voice trailed off suggested that this was unlikely.

'In ourn situation, hope is not a good plan,' stated Scuba.

Magna looked to the ground for a moment then turned to Muddy and Buggy. 'Please excuse us,' she said.

Magna gathered her bible and led Scuba to the corner of the cabin. At Magna's request, both women initiated full skinsuits. Magna reached out, making contact with Scuba's shoulder so that they could speak privately. Even without being able to see their mouths or hear their voices, it was apparent to Muddy that Magna was doing most of the speaking and Scuba most of the nodding. The discussion stopped briefly. Magna opened her bible. She circled a few lines of text, then folded and tore out an entire page.

Muddy had assumed Magna wouldn't be religious – that she had used religion as a tool for her disguise as an old lady. But the bible, and the words it contained, obviously meant more to her than that. You could take the Lupella out of the religion, but you couldn't take the religion out of the Lupella, it seemed. Their private conference looked like it would go on for a while. Muddy left them to it and wandered over to the cabin door. He peered through a slit in the planks. The sky was darkening. A breeze rushed across the desolate landscape, agitating the surface. Every few metres the wind would dig deep into the ground, sending a wild, spinning spiral of sand and ash shooting upwards. Muddy knew them as dust devils. It struck him as strange that these ones didn't flow with the breeze, they congregated and formed a slow-moving forest that meandered back and forth, trapped in the same section of the landscape.

'Check this out!'

The shout snapped Muddy out of his dust devil hypnosis. Buggy was sitting cross-legged on the floor by the centre console. As soon as he had Muddy's attention, he whipped up some of the ash by his side. He waited for a second, then domed a shield around himself. Muddy grinned and shook his head. Buggy in a bubble. He'd obviously been practicing. Outside Buggy's dome, the ash settled, but inside it continued to swirl around. He looked like a snow globe from the shops on Earth. Muddy gave him the thumbs-up and turned back to the dust devils. The grin dropped from his face.

Dreddax butchers had started to land. He tried to gauge how many, but the dust devils obscured his view. 'Scuba! They're he—'

A massive explosion ripped through the cabin. Muddy was blasted aside with splintered planks and posts.

Chapter Thirty-Six

'I am May Yania, Magna, last of the Lupelli.'

Buggy looked to his side. Magna was sitting right next to him. He had no idea when she'd arrived. Her shield had merged with his. She had cut a nick in the side of her nose. A tear of blood trickled down her face. 'I fight for this blood.' She reached across, cut a nick in the side of Buggy's nose, 'and I fight for this blood.'

Buggy registered pain in his nose but didn't react. He was still confused by the dull ringing in his ears . . . the deep hum in the centre of his brain. He felt frozen . . . unable to object to anything that Magna was doing. A bomb. Some kind of bomb had just landed next to him. If he hadn't been messing around with the skinsuit shield at that exact moment . . .

'Buggy.' Magna took his chin in her hand and turned his face to hers. 'You're in shock. But I need you to help me. Like you did before, Samaritan.' She handed him her bible. 'That night by the fire . . . I was adrift . . . you started reading a passage to me. Please, finish it.'

Buggy took the bible, blinked and looked back up at Magna. 'Am I . . . are we . . . ' He lost the words but found Magna's green eye. That eye was young and bright now, not an old lady's eye, yet it still expressed a lifetime of – of what? Of too much? A word that made no sense came to Buggy's mind: desensitized.

'Where's Muddy? And Scuba?' he asked.

'It was a concentrated explosion. The Dreddax targeted the console with the heavy gun from their ship. They must have learnt from their last encounter with the Lupelli on this planet. The console is destroyed. We can't ignite the atmosphere. You were right next to the explosion. Your skinsuit shield saved you. Muddy was on the outskirts. Scuba will find him. Then they're going first.'

'Going where first?'

'To the battlefield.'

In his head, Buggy heard *to their graves.*

Chapter Thirty-Seven

Muddy stirred. Ash swirled in bizarre patterns over his head. Through the gaps he could see nothing but destruction. He felt a hand on his arm. 'This way.' Scuba's voice. He realized that his skinsuit had automatically deployed to cover his face. He sat up, looked over towards Buggy. He could just about make him out, sitting under a dome shield with Magna. Another heavy shell crashed into the cabin.

Scuba dragged Muddy to his feet. 'We move now, under cover of the smoke.'

'What about Buggy?'

'He is with Magna. You are with me. For us, the safest place is amongst the Dreddax butchers. Theirn ship will not shoot into its own.'

Smoke from the last explosion whirled violently around them, grabbing at them, trying to pull them this way and that. It obscured their view, only allowing them to see the scorched ground every few moments. Scuba trudged towards a huge open plain. It had an enormous bowl-shaped crater in its centre. Dreddax butchers and dust devils were dotted about everywhere. More Dreddax were appearing on the surface every second, stirring up the already lively ground.

'The cabin is destroyed,' said Muddy. 'Can we still ignite the atmosphere?'

Scuba shook her head. 'No.'

'Then we don't stand a chance. We need to get out of here. All of us.'

Scuba shook her head again. 'No. We make ourn stand here. Now. We rely on May-Yania, Magna.'

'And what is Magna relying on exactly?'

'Magna has hern faith . . . and she is relying on us. Let us not disappoint her.' Scuba pointed to the crater. 'That is the land that Magna identified to me. You and I have business on the other side of it.'

'And just how are we supposed to get—' A Dreddax butcher materialized right in front of Muddy, knocking him to the ground with a shoulder barge. A barb whipped out towards his face. Muddy threw up his hand, creating a shield to block the barb. Realisation dawned. This was not the fight pit. Hiding behind a shield there led to an imaginary death. Hiding behind a shield here would lead to a real one. Muddy drew back his free arm and swung. A blade extended from his wrist, out over his hand. It cut into the Dreddax butcher's knee. The butcher began to collapse. Muddy dug his elbow into the sand, held firm and pointed his blade directly upwards. The Dreddax butcher fell onto its point. Weight and momentum drove its body down the full length of the blade. The butcher slumped and rolled by Muddy's side, lifeless. Muddy stared at it. Time stood still. He'd killed his first Dreddax butcher. And he felt sick.

He didn't see the second butcher approaching. But Scuba did. And she made short work of it. She generated a serrated shield mid run and smashed it into the side of the butcher's head. The butcher rocked back. Scuba set the shield spinning and sliced the creature down in a flurry of dust and ash.

Scuba stood over Muddy. 'To answer yourn question,' she said calmly, 'we get across the crater by doing exactly that.' She pointed to the corpse by his side. Muddy's blade was still firmly stuck in its chest. 'Only next time, do not sit back to admire yourn work.' For the second time in the space of a few minutes, Scuba took Muddy's hand and pulled him to his feet. 'Getting to the other side is just ourn first goal.'

Muddy didn't care to ask what their second goal was. The first was impossible enough. They both switched to active camouflage and jogged to the lip of the crater. The other side seemed miles away. Scuba didn't hesitate. She started down the slope. Muddy took a deep breath and followed.

The dust devils helped and hindered in equal measure, sometimes providing cover for them, sometimes providing cover for the enemy. Scuba didn't waste time fighting unless she absolutely had to. In fact, she was constantly improvising and changing her route, deliberately avoiding the Dreddax butchers. Occasionally she would generate a shield and bash one to the ground if it appeared in her path, then she would be gone before it could track her footprints. She was all about goal one. Progress was good. Heart pumping, Muddy followed her lead. But the deeper into the crater they got, the tighter a sense of impending doom gripped him. He just couldn't shake the feeling. Active camouflage would only work for so long. Avoiding Dreddax butchers would only work for so long. Some of them had already assembled into small groups, systematically tracking and following footprints. Thankfully, the dust devils were helping out on that score, constantly stirring up the ground, destroying trails. A quick look back to check how far he'd come only made Muddy feel worse. All he could see were puffs of ash as more and more Dreddax butchers transported to the surface. He looked towards the flattened cabin. Neither Buggy nor Magna were visible in the sinister smoke cloud that enveloped the entire area.

'Concentrate on us, not them!' came the shout from Scuba.

Muddy refocused on goal one. Scuba's tactics had got them across the entire flats of the crater virtually unscathed. But the ground wasn't even anymore. They were both breathing heavily. Moving through sand was exhausting. And worse was to come. Now they had to tackle the slope.

'Take Little Dog from yourn backpack,' instructed Scuba. 'And do not let go of it.' She turned away and began the punishing ascent.

Muddy slipped his backpack off, pulled Little Dog from the pocket as quickly as he could. After the near disaster on Scuba's home planet, he had no idea why she'd told him to keep the toy. He guessed he'd be finding out very soon. He set off again, thighs burning and chest heaving. Even though Scuba only had a few seconds head start on him, catching up with her was a struggle.

About three quarters of the way up the slope, Scuba was waiting for him. She had found some temporary cover. As he passed by, she pulled him to a crouch. 'Rest for a moment. Yourn skinsuit will extract the lactic acid from yourn muscles and enhance yourn circulation. You will recover quickly.'

From his hidden position, Muddy could afford to look out over the crater. The dust devils were evenly spread around the outer perimeter. They hovered, moving only slightly to and fro. There was something soothing about them. Something greater than wind and dust. But their beauty was nullified by the presence of Dreddax butchers. There must have been a hundred or more now. Muddy looked beyond the flats, to the top of the opposite ridge. Swirling smoke still clung to the shattered cabin like a curse. On the edge of the curse, he caught a momentary glimpse of Magna.

Chapter Thirty-Eight

They hadn't moved from the rubble of the cabin. On Magna's instruction, Buggy had stayed hidden while she nipped in and out, monitoring the progress of Scuba and Muddy. Buggy felt safe hiding amongst the wreckage. If only he could stay there until it was all over. He toyed with the idea of saying a prayer, since all his others had been so successful. Before he had chance, Magna came up to him and slapped him on the shoulder. 'They've made it to the other side. Too many Dreddax butchers are landing and heading their way. We need to draw some away. We need to get involved.'

'Get involved?' Buggy gripped the plank that he'd been hiding behind a little tighter.

'It's OK,' said Magna, 'I've been where you are. Don't think, just do. Take it moment by moment. You'll be fine.'

Buggy took no comfort from her words. He reckoned that's what everyone told everyone else just before they were about to be killed. It wasn't as if you were going to come back from the dead and say, "Hang on a minute, you said I was going to be fine!"

'Listen,' continued Magna, 'The strength of the Dreddax is in their reputation, not their actual abilities, at least not these ground troops,' Magna tapped her tricep, 'and they protect the brachial region of their upper left arm for a reason.'

As Magna stood advising him on tactics and offensive moves, Buggy took in the scene. Dreddax butchers were crawling all over the crater. Dreddax butchers were heading towards the ruined cabin. More Dreddax butchers were transporting to the surface. 'Look at them all. How can you not be scared?'

Seeing that her seeds of advice were falling on stony ground, Magna changed tack. 'The first time, I was scared. And every time since . . . until I get started. There is no room for fear. Fighting is a confession for me. Every Dreddax I kill is forgiveness. I let my feelings out when I fight. It's good for you. Watch.'

Magna went to active camouflage. She ran at a group of Dreddax butchers that had climbed over the lip of the crater. There were four of them. Magna's spear crashed through visors and into heads. Then there were two of them. For no good reason she went back in black and placed her spear on the ground. She looked back, making sure that Buggy was watching. She was visible. She had no weapon. The two Dreddax butchers began raining down blows on her. Each blow was met with a blocking skinsuit shield and a step back. It was a lesson. Magna was showing him that he could survive using just the shields. He didn't need a spear like hers. The Dreddax began charging their weapons. That was Magna's cue to move in. She generated a blade from her right arm and manoeuvred left, so that the first Dreddax butcher would conceal her from the second. She cut the first one down. The second could do nothing about it. Now it was one on one. Magna changed her sword for a shield and bumped the remaining Dreddax butcher back towards her spear. She went TAC, picked up her spear and finished the lesson by skewering the butcher in the chest and head. Buggy couldn't help but be impressed. Treating battle like a confession was good for Magna, but it certainly wasn't good for the Dreddax. And for that, he was glad. Magna had given him an inspiring exhibition. She'd proven he could have confidence in her – as well as confidence in his own skinsuit. Even so, he knew he could never fight like that. But he had to try. Or why had he even made the decision to stay? And yet . . . that was just a group of four butchers. The crater was full of them.

Magna returned, black blood staining her hands and face. 'See,' she said. 'At their core, they are creatures of water. They don't like my planet. I'm going to make them like it even less.'

Buggy nodded, tried to press the suitcipher to fully engage his skinsuit, but his hands were shaking too much. 'Don't go too far away,' he said.

Magna moved towards him. 'I won't. You know about BIB and TAC, right?'

Buggy nodded.

'Good. I'm going to put your skinsuit on intermittent camouflage. You'll find it easy to stay out of trouble when you can't be seen. Use a blade when you are camouflaged and do as much damage as you can to any Dreddax butcher near you. When you go BIB, use a dome shield to protect yourself and evade all Dreddax as best you can. TAC fight, BIB avoid. In the woods you told me that you're a musician, right? So, get into a rhythm.' Magna gave Buggy an encouraging slap on the back. 'Forte, Bugger, forte. We are about to create our magnum opus.'

Buggy appreciated the musical reference, but, if anything, it would be a Magna opus, because he couldn't see himself having any influence on the piece. And the only rhythm in his head was his heartbeat. It was certainly a strong rhythm, but he had a feeling that it would be coming to an abrupt halt pretty soon. 'Can't I just stay camouflaged?'

'These skinsuits can't maintain both camouflage and shields indefinitely. We need to conserve energy. We don't know how long this fight will last. And besides, you need to be visible now and again.'

The tempo of the rhythm in Buggy's head increased. 'What do you mean I *need* to be visible now and again? If they see me, they'll come and get me!'

'Let's hope so. This is a difficult situation. We have to take risks. If they think you're vulnerable, it will make them even more vulnerable. But remember, they want to kill me, they probably only want to capture you,' assured Magna. 'Although that may change fairly soon,' she added.

Buggy didn't remember the Samaritan in the bible being used as bait. And "difficult situation" was an understatement. This was a nightmare. 'Well, at least let me start out camouflaged,' he said.

'Fair enough,' agreed Magna. 'Follow me. And if you can't see me, know I'll be nearby. Look to the surface of the sand for my footprints. Avoid the mini whirlwinds, they will hamper visibility and they will whip up the surface, but trust me, today they're our friends. And remember, TAC fight, BIB avoid.' Magna headed for the crater.

When his eyes could no longer pick her out, Buggy went to her footprints. He was still in camouflage mode when he encountered his first Dreddax butcher. It was lying on the ground, dead. It's left arm was missing. A few metres away, that severed left arm was being aimed, by Magna, at other Dreddax butchers. She was squeezing down on its brachial artery, firing molten red missiles that ripped through their targets. Just as Magna's camouflage kicked in, the missiles ran out. She discarded the arm and moved on. Worryingly for Buggy, his skinsuit went back in black. There were no Dreddax butchers close enough to see him. He ran over to the severed arm, found Magna's footprints and followed them down the slope a ways. When one of the dusty whirlwinds began covering her tracks, Buggy took an angry swipe at it. Weirdly, it contracted and avoided his blow. A moment later it slid aside. Buggy cried out in shock. A Dreddax butcher, hidden behind the dust devil, stepped forward and punched him to the ground. A poison barb came shooting through the air towards him. Buggy raised a shield to block it. He wasn't fast enough . . . but the barb didn't hit him. It hovered in the air just inches from his neck.

Magna's camouflage fizzled out. And Buggy immediately understood why the barb hadn't hit its mark. It was sticking in the palm of Magna's hand. She had taken the hit to save him. He was horrified. This would spell the end of them both. A tiny amount of barb poison had been injected into him on Earth. It had knocked him out. 'Magna! The barbs have poison in them! You're going to pass out!'

'No.' Magna shook her head. 'No, I'm not.' Her good eye widened, the black pupil within it flexed. She plucked the barb from her palm, wrapped the tendril around her arm and gave it a powerful tug. The Dreddax butcher jerked forwards. Magna thrust her spear up, through the base of its chin. Three other Dreddax butchers saw the incident. Two headed for Magna. One headed for Buggy. Buggy had no idea what he was going to do when it got to him. Magna was already running towards the first of her two. The poison from the barb hadn't knocked her out. It hadn't even slowed her down. It had done the exact opposite. She tossed her spear high into the air as she ran. Two skinsuit blades, extended from each of her wrists, windmilled down and scythed through the first butcher's shoulders. Both arms fell to the ground, but not before Magna had caught her spear and driven it through the creature's neck. She moved on to the second.

Buggy looked at the bloody mess that Magna had just created. He ran towards it. He could use what he had learnt. The butcher that was after him ran towards the same spot, but Buggy got there first. He grabbed the severed arm, aimed it at the oncoming butcher. Just as Magna had done, he pointed the barbs and squeezed down on the brachial artery. Nothing happened. The Dreddax butcher was just a few feet away. Buggy squeezed again, expecting the it to be cut down with molten red missiles. None were generated. Barbs and tendrils came whizzing through the air. Instinctively, Buggy swung the severed arm, batting the barbs away before they hit him. He swung again in the opposite direction and caught the butcher with a lucky blow on the side of the head. Fresh black blood from the severed arm coated Buggy's palms. At the end of his swing, the arm flew from his grip. But it didn't matter. Magna was already high up on his attacker's shoulders. Her spear burst through the front of its visor and the butcher fell, face down with Magna still perched on its back.

'The arm,' gasped Buggy. 'It didn't work!'

Magna snapped off a barb from her victim and jabbed it into her hand. Her sparkling green eye stared up at him. 'When you've learnt your left from your right, have another go.'

Buggy looked at the arm he'd dropped. It was a right arm. Magna had specifically said the brachial artery in the left arm stored the liquid.

'Now move!' shouted Magna. 'There are more on the way.'

Chapter Thirty-Nine

U sing active camouflage, they'd manoeuvred unseen to the very top of the slope. There was a deep, dark crevice just under the ridge. It provided a perfect hiding place. Scuba crawled in. She pressed her suitcipher to go back in black. Muddy joined her. He could hardly see his hand in front of his face. Scuba shuffled closer. 'You need to place Little Dog over the lip of the slope.'

'Why?'

'Little Dog is a beacon. The Amorphi serpent will recognize it as a landing signal.'

'What! That's goal two? Getting the Amorphi serpent to land on our heads?' Muddy couldn't quite believe it. In the darkness of their little cave, he could just make out the curve of Scuba's white teeth. 'And you're smiling again,' he hissed, finding that even more difficult to believe.

'Do it.'

Despite every fibre in his body telling him not to, Muddy bobbed out from the crevice. He dropped Little Dog over the lip and ducked back to safety.

'Now we wait,' whispered Scuba.

From the other side of the ridge came a sound like a giant ripping a hole in the sky.

'Follow me!' Scuba slipped out of their hiding place and acrobatically swung over the top ridge.

Muddy clambered after her - out of darkness, into light, then into the shadow of an Amorphi serpent. It was directly in front of them, gently writhing like a freakish sea monster. Scuba stared at it. Transfixed. Muddy gave her a gentle nudge. She looked at him, her eyes suddenly moist. 'I am sorry that I was mistaken about Mrs Magner,' she said. 'And I am truly sorry for other things also.' She looked back at the serpent. 'Merge a double shield when I say.'

The serpent edged forwards, massive and menacing. Its mouth began to open. 'Now!' commanded Scuba.

A raging torrent of fire spewed through the air. It thudded into their combined shield. Muddy was barely able to stay upright. He felt his feet slipping back in the sand. It was like holding an umbrella against a gale force wind. Through the heat and the flames, Scuba leaned towards him. 'Goal three is to take Little Dog back to Magna. Goal three is yourn goal.'

'And what about you?'

'Just promise me that you will take Little Dog to Magna.'

Muddy nodded.

'Good,' said Scuba. 'Now, when I say, you must push forward alone into the flames. It will be challenging. You must concentrate on making yourn shield stronger than it has ever been. The flames will eventually cease, but only for a few precious moments. As soon as they do, you must kneel down and dome a shield over yournself, just like you did when we fought the Dreddax on yourn planet. I need you to do this for me. Can you?'

'Yes,' replied Muddy. For her, he could.

Scuba glared at the Amorphi serpent. Thought about everything it had done, everything it would continue to do. She also recalled what she'd seen inside that same monster on the planet Earth. Her heart became heavy. She moved closer to Muddy. 'I remember yourn story. The things you dreamt of as a child. I should not have laughed. Look at you now. You have become an astronaut . . . of sorts. You are helping to slay a dragon . . . of sorts. And . . . with regard to getting the girl, well . . .' She leaned in, pressed her lips to his.

Muddy closed his eyes. Heat raged all around him, but Scuba's kiss was as cool and sweet as the first Earth snowflake that had settled on his lips. His spirits soared, higher than they ever had. And yet, deep down, nestled in the pit of his stomach, was a sense of impending loss – just like that snowflake, so beautiful and unique, he feared that Scuba was about to melt in the heat and disappear forever.

Scuba drew back. 'Of sorts,' she said. 'Now go!'

With renewed strength, Muddy turned alone to face the flames. Step by arduous step, he fought his way forwards. He concentrated on his shield like never before, willing it to stay strong. Flames roared around him, flowing orange to yellow to white to blue, becoming more intense, more ferocious with each step he took. Suddenly the onslaught ended. With nothing resisting his push, Muddy lost his balance and fell to his knees. Obeying Scuba's instructions, he stayed there and domed a shield over himself. He looked for her. She had gone a little way down the slope. The bodies of Dreddax butchers lay scattered around. She had cleared the beginnings of a path back to Buggy and Magna. When she saw that he was ready, Scuba nodded to him and began running back. Muddy figured they would re-combine their shields and make their way back to the base of the crater.

He'd figured wrong.

Scuba didn't slow down. And she hadn't told him to dome his shield for protection. She used him as a springboard and leapt straight into the serpent's cavernous mouth.

Muddy gasped, half in awe, half in horror. He stood and stumbled backwards for a better view. Scuba was regaining her balance. In her hand he could see a folded piece of paper – the page from the bible that Magna had handed to her in the cabin. She unfolded it and took out a small black disc. Muddy recognised the DNA specific transporter, the one that the Dreddax had tried to attach to Scuba to capture her. Muddy was at a loss. Why had Magna given that to her, hidden in a page from the bible? He looked from the disc to Scuba's face. She was frowning at him. She pointed to Little Dog, waved him away. But he couldn't go.

The jaws of the serpent began to move. Its mouth opened and closed rhythmically, teeth clanking with each bite. Scuba was smiling again. At first Muddy was horrified, but he realised that she was safe. She had found the perfect position in the centre of the serpent's mouth, away from the razor-sharp fangs. Still, he motioned for her to come down. Scuba shook her head. She scrunched the page from the bible into a ball, pointed to her eyes then threw it down to him. She stepped towards the serpent's throat and began firing shield pulses deep into the flame mechanism. The entire serpent juddered. Softly at first, but the movement became more violent, more spasmodic with each pulse. Hope surged through Muddy. Scuba was destroying the serpent from the inside. But she didn't have much time. The flames would restart soon. He shouted for her to hurry. Shouted again, louder. Scuba turned around. He thought she was going to respond to his shouts. But she didn't. She took one step sideways, positioned herself beneath a lethal silver fang. She looked at Muddy, mouthed the word *sorry*.

The serpent's jaw crashed shut. Needle sharp metal sliced through Scuba's flesh.

She screamed.

She dipped the disc into her own blood.

She reached up.

She slapped the disc against the roof of the beast's mouth.

Chapter Forty

Muddy shouted her name. But he was shouting at an empty patch of swirling air. Scuba was gone. The Amorphi serpent was gone. A second later, way above him in the outer atmosphere, there was a sudden starburst of light, a sound like distant thunder. Muddy felt numb. His world had changed again. He stared at his closed hand, scared to open it. Slowly, he unfurled his fingers. Slower still, he unfurled the page from the bible that Scuba had thrown down to him. Magna had circled a sentence, *Behold, I give unto you power to tread on serpents and scorpions, and over all the power of the enemy: and nothing shall by any means hurt you.* Muddy stared at the words. One stood out from the rest. *Power.* Scuba had used that power. She'd used it to tread on this serpent, to take it thrashing and crashing into the belly of the main Dreddax ship. She had destroyed the power of the enemy. But the last part ... *and nothing shall by any means hurt you* ... that last part was a lie.

Red lava bullets lit up the area around him. Muddy hardly felt the one that nicked his upper arm. His skinsuit stretched to cover the wound and dull the pain. But no skinsuit could dull the real pain that he was feeling. He should move. But his legs felt as heavy as his heart. Then he remembered his promise. His last promise to Scuba. It was a promise that he had to keep. Scooping up Little Dog, Muddy ran for the centre of the crater.

Chapter Forty-One

Magna looked to the stars. There it was – the explosion she'd been hoping for. She felt a pang of regret, a feeling she hadn't experienced for many years. Then she felt an immense sense of pride in the Quarasian. Thanks to Scuba, impossible odds had become merely insurmountable. Magna turned her camouflage off, allowing the nearest group of Dreddax butchers to see her clearly. She screamed as she ran at them, 'And the great dragon was cast out, that old serpent, called the Devil, and Satan, which deceiveth the whole world. And his minions were cast out with him!'

Buggy could feel Magna's fury as she cut into the butchers. He stayed as close as he dared but was more concerned about being killed by her than by them. Relief washed over him when he saw Muddy striding over. 'Scuba?'

Muddy shook his head.

The fight that remained in Buggy fell away. 'Then it's hopeless,' he said. 'Without Scuba we can't win. Magna's lost her mind.'

The boys looked at her. As though she'd heard Buggy's words, Magna's green eye glared back at them. A ghostly aura surrounded her now. It blurred her movements, distorted her shape. Vicious vapour claws shadowed her hands as she swiped at oncoming Dreddax butchers. Her shouts merged with growls and snarls. In that moment, Muddy and Buggy truly understood what it was to be a Lupella. One was in full-blooded battle before their very eyes - the white wolf spirit engulfing her human form, filling her with devastating speed and power . . . animalistic savagery. Magna was fighting like the dog demon she had become. Dreddax butchers fell like wheat under a farmer's scythe. But her titanic efforts were futile. The Dreddax butchers had realised that the three figures in the middle of the crater were all that was left – and they were converging on them in their hundreds. There would be no capturing. No selling of live trophies. The Dreddax butchers wanted blood. Muddy and Buggy looked at each other. This was the end. They both knew it. They exchanged a silent nod. It carried more than words ever could. A thank you – for the shared experiences, the shared joy, shared sorrow . . . shared stupidity. A goodbye to the finest friendship.

Even Magna gave up. She had cleared a space in the very centre of the crater, but it wasn't enough. She strolled towards the boys, shoulders slumped, hair matted with the black blood of Dreddax and streaked with the red of her own. She looked tired. The white wolf spirit was fading. She was limping. Cuts peppered her face. She was bruised. She was broken. She was weak. She was worn. As she walked, she took in the scene – every last Dreddax butcher closing in from every last angle. Magna nodded to herself, reached for the chain around her neck. She felt for the silver cross and raised it to her mouth. A kiss goodbye, or perhaps preparation for meeting her maker.

Or maybe neither.

The Lupella's green eye sparkled at the boys . . . and she smiled. She flipped the silver cross in her hand, placed the long end onto her lips . . . and blew. There was no sound. At least, no sound audible to human ears. Magna lowered the cross and looked to the east. The boys followed her gaze. They saw nothing . . . then something . . . two white flecks – triangles, growing slowly larger. Something in the distance, moving their way. The white triangles had a base – and the base had . . . eyes! One vivid green and one sparkling blue. With fur as white as snow, a mighty wolf strode to the lip of the crater. It cast a foreboding shadow down the slope. A few Dreddax butchers turned to see what had caused that shadow. And maybe the stories about their failed conquest of this planet replayed in their heads, because they stumbled. The white wolf raised its muzzle to the sky and howled. Any Dreddax butcher that hadn't noticed it already, did so now. At the wolf's howl, the dust devils that had littered the landscape suddenly stopped spinning. Sand and dust fell to the ground with a crisp thud. It marked the beginning of an absolute, eerie silence. The pockets of air that had made those dust devils kept their shape and glowed an ethereal green. Another howl smashed the silence. The green spirals appeared to bow before gently seeping into the ground. The white wolf pawed at the sand. It buried its huge nose just below the surface and snarled. Green mist flowed from its eyes, its mouth, its nostrils, linking and mixing with the substance from the dust devils. The crater shuddered. Patches of sand around its edge began to ripple and swell. Something deep under the ground was stirring. Muddy looked to his right. A gigantic muzzle of bleached white bone broke through the sand and ash, fangs glistening. Ahead of the muzzle, two colossal claws pierced the surface and dug back down to gain purchase. A giant skull followed, then vertebrae . . . ribs. The entire mammoth skeleton of a long-dead alpha wolf heaved itself free of its ancient grave. It shook the sand from its bones. Streams of green funnelled upwards from its resting place, coiling around the carcass, coating the beast with muscle and skin. The exterior of its new translucent body glowed and flowed like the fur of old. One blue eye and one green eye appraised the surroundings with a ravenous scowl. More and more skeletons emerged from their graves. Enormous. Imposing. Each one restored to its former glory by the ghostly green mist.

Muddy looked at Magna. A tear rolled down her cheek, clearing a thin line through the dirt and dried blood on her face. But the tear wasn't for the giant wolves. She was looking past them, towards the cabin. On the lip of the crater, standing beside the white wolf, was another skeleton. This skeleton was different. It was small. It was delicate. It was human shaped. As the green mist gave it form, the resemblance was unmistakable. Even from a distance, Muddy knew he was looking at a younger, two-eyed version of Magna. It was May Yania, Tinta – her twin sister.

The white wolf leapt down the slope. It headed towards Magna, annihilating any Dreddax butchers in its way. Its long, lolloping stride swallowed the distance in no time. It slid to a halt, its muzzle dripping with black Dreddax blood. Lowering itself to its belly, the wolf crawled the last few yards, head bowed. Then it waited. With a whisper from Magna, the wolf stood. It licked her face. Magna returned the greeting, holding the wolf's massive head in her hands and licking along the line of its muzzle, right up to its ear. Magna grabbed the scruff of the white wolf's neck and swung up onto its back. She pointed at two resurrected alphas with her spear, snarled and flicked her head towards the boys. She looked at Muddy and Buggy. 'Stay alive,' she said, simply.

Magna and the white wolf charged away. They cut a direct path back through the Dreddax hordes to the top of the crater. Magna dismounted. She stood still, taking in the sight of her sister's spirit form. Then May Yania, Magna and May Yania, Tinta embraced. Magna tied her cloth to the staff and handed it to her sister. For herself, she generated a skinsuit shield and blade. The two Lupelli and the white wolf moved to the crater's edge. Magna's green eye glowed. She raised her sword and shield to the sky. This was it. The years of running, of hiding, of surviving. The years of unimaginable hardship. Everything she had done. It had all been for this moment. With a wild howl, Magna hurtled down the slope and tore into the Dreddax below.

In the centre of the crater, two glistening green brutes skulked over to Muddy and Buggy.

'There's no way I'm licking one of those,' said Buggy. 'I've got allergies.'

'I think our Dreddax butcher allergy is more serious right now,' said Muddy. 'So, you better pucker up if that's what it takes.'

Around them, the wolf army began its attack. Mayhem reigned. The hulking beasts snatched up Dreddax butchers from the ground, shook them apart, hurled their broken bodies into the air. There would be no quarter. This was revenge. Not the revenge of a single Lupella . . . but the revenge of an entire planet . . . revenge of the dead.

The Dreddax were in disarray. They had seen the explosion in the outer atmosphere. That had unnerved them. The appearance of gargantuan wolf skeletons, brought to life by some incomprehensible force, had sent them into absolute panic. They were fighting back, but mostly as disorganized individuals, trying to save their own skins. Some though, had formed into groups. A functioning team of at least a dozen butchers headed for Muddy and Buggy. Muddy generated a shield with his left arm. Buggy did the same. They took a pace closer together, allowed their shields to merge. Their two wolves automatically peeled away, one guarding each flank.

'We can't just defend. We have to attack,' said Muddy. 'Scuba taught me this trick.' He swiped down the centre of their combined shield. A thin rectangular gap appeared. 'I can set that gap to appear intermittently. You see how we can use it, right? We move forward slowly, we stab through the gap.'

Buggy nodded and generated a blade in his free hand. Muddy did the same. Butterflies filled his stomach. His whole body felt like it was about to turn to jelly and collapse. Scuba wasn't here to protect them. Magna had her hands full. Muddy looked at his friend. Neither of them had ever been through anything like this. But they had been through a lot. And there was no one he'd prefer by his side. 'You ready?' he asked.

'No,' replied Buggy.

'Good. Me neither. Let's go.' They trudged forwards and entered the fray.

The Dreddax butchers hit them hard. Barbs hammered the outside of their combined shield, molten red missiles smashed into it, some from distance, some from point blank range. A snarling muzzle crunched into a Dreddax head on the left flank. The head burst like an orange being crushed underfoot. Muddy turned to Buggy. 'Our turn,' he said. He swiped the centre of their shield to create the gap. The two boys gave a little ground, inviting the Dreddax butchers on to them. Then they dug their feet into the sand and pushed forwards, jabbing and stabbing through the gap. When the gap closed, the boys held firm. Frustrated, the butchers intensified their assault. More molten red missiles slammed into the shield. More barbs rained down. Muddy's arms began to burn. Even with the skinsuit extracting lactic acid, he felt drained. The gap in the shield opened up again. The boys advanced. Muddy counted. The group attacking them was down from twelve to seven. A blur of green to his left – a ferocious claw cut through a

Dreddax neck . . . six. Buggy's blade took another down . . . five. Then the unthinkable happened. Just before the gap in the shield closed, a Dreddax missile ricocheted through. It thudded into Buggy's thigh. He fell. The combined shield collapsed. More molten missiles hissed through the air. One thumped into the base of Buggy's spine. Another shattered Muddy's left wrist. He tried to go on the attack, but his right ankle took a direct hit and he too, fell. He crawled to Buggy's side, domed a single shield over them both. Seeing their vulnerability, the two giant wolves ran in, snapping and snarling at the advancing Dreddax butchers.

Muddy shuffled closer to Buggy. 'You OK?' he asked.

'Feel like I've jumped off a high wall and forgotten to bend my knees,' groaned Buggy. 'You?'

'Same wall, only I landed sideways.'

Beneath the shield, beneath the wolves, the boys had a perfect view of the battle. Magna had organized her army into three rings. Still astride the white wolf, she was leading the outer ring clockwise around the very perimeter of the crater. About eight hundred metres inside that, May Yania, Tinta was riding one of the largest translucent green wolves. She led the second ring in an anticlockwise direction. The final, inner ring of wolves was travelling clockwise. There was no way out for the Dreddax. They were surrounded. Some made it through one ring of wolves, only to be cut down by the next. They had no back up and no escape route. Without their main ship, and without their Amorphi serpent, they were doomed. The rings of wolves began to converge towards the centre of the crater, corralling the remaining butchers, killing their hope, killing them.

Finally, the carousel of carnage slowed. Magna gave the signal for the wolves to split formation and finish off the stragglers. Within seconds they were done. Not a single Dreddax butcher remained alive. Bodies and limbs and visors and armour lay strewn about the crater. Battle worn and bloodied, the alpha wolves idled in the warm sand, their chests heaving. One by one, they raised their mighty heads to the sky. The air vibrated. Harmonising howls throbbed through the crater before overflowing into the surrounding land. As the cacophony faded, so did the brightness in their eyes. The green mist that had given them form began to drain from their giant frames. Just as the dust devils had fallen to the ground to signal the start of battle, the bones of the long dead alpha wolves fell to the ground now, to signal the end.

Muddy and Buggy stared out over a silent, mass grave, littered with sun-bleached skeletons and decapitated Dreddax.

The white wolf stood guard over the only skeleton with a little of its green spirit remaining. May Yania, Tinta. She was lying on the sand, her head in her sister's lap. The twins gazed at the devastation around them. 'I made you a promise, Tinta,' said Magna. 'All those years ago. A promise that is now fulfilled. A promise that has ended in their blood and mine.' Magna untied the cloth from her sister's staff. She placed it on the ground and gently lowered her sister's head onto it. Tinta smiled and reached for her sister's hand. Magna took it. She squeezed it, hard. As the last of the wolf spirit drained away,

Magna leaned forwards and kissed her sister on the forehead. 'Sleep now, little sister. Know that revenge is ours. Sleep in peace.'

Magna stood and patted the broad shoulders of the white wolf. At her feet, the bones of May Yania, Tinta sank through the layers of soft, warm sand to rest with the wolves of the past.

Chapter Forty-Two

The Earth church was silent. Light from an engorged moon oozed through the stained-glass windows. It cast a serene glow across the inner sanctum. Exhausted, Muddy and Buggy lay on the front pews. Their skinsuits had recharged just enough to initiate a little healing following transportation. The white wolf's final, melancholic howl still rang in their ears.

'You really think this planet is the safest one?' asked Muddy. 'Scuba did say that it had somehow slipped off the Amorphi radar.'

'Well, there aren't any Dreddax here now. They're among the corpses we just left behind. And any planet without Dreddax is a good planet. Earth has a big population. Diverse too. You'd be surprised how anonymous you can be in a crowd,' replied Magna.

Muddy watched as the Lupella walked over to a table of candles by the pulpit. She ignited the end of a long, thin firelighter and used it to light two candles. It was a tradition he was familiar with. One candle was for her sister and one candle was for Scuba.

Then she prepared four more.

'Why another four?' asked Muddy.

'Before I tell you . . . ' Magna dabbed the end of the firelighter on the additional four wicks, one by one, 'understand that Scuba was thinking of you. She wanted you both safe. But there shouldn't be any secrets between us.' Magna paused. 'And ye shall know the truth, and the truth shall make you free.' She leaned against the pulpit railings, stared at the tiny flame on the end of the long, thin stick. 'Don't speak. Just listen. As you know, I waited for Scuba in the levels below this building. I needed to reclaim my cloth from her backpack. I decided to wait for her inside the Amorphi serpent because I knew her history with it. I knew she'd feel compelled to inspect it. And, inside the serpent, I saw what she saw.' Magna looked to the floor, composed her thoughts. 'Each segment of the serpent was manned . . . fully manned. Two unthinking, unfeeling occupants had been placed in each section, their brains destroyed by the Dreddax gas worm.' She looked up at the boys . . . *no secrets*. 'Your parents were among them.'

Magna blew out the flame on the firelighter. Her green eye scrutinised the delicate line of smoke that twisted and twirled in the still air. 'When Scuba and I spoke privately and I told her that I had the transporter disc, she said she could use it to force the entire Amorphi serpent to materialise inside the tiny holding cells of the main Dreddax ship and, in doing so, destroy them both. She knew that destroying the serpent was a one-way mission. But it was one that she desperately wanted.' Magna addressed Muddy directly. 'She made me memorize this phrase, "*Kas'ood Quarasian on famik'yun bi depaar*". She told me about Dead Mezko. That's what he said to you. Scuba told me she'd pretended not to understand when you tried to repeat it to her. She asked me to apologise to you on her behalf. That phrase means, "Ask the Quarasian exactly where your family members are before you leave". She didn't want to tell you then, and for good reason. She hoped that the desire to re-join your families would take you away from . . . everything. But you chose to stay. Remember that. *You* chose to stay. It was a brave choice. An unexpected choice. I'm telling you this truth so that you don't destroy yourselves, thinking that you abandoned your families. Your families were already lost.'

'She was going to send us away knowing that?' asked Buggy.

'Your minds would have been defragmented. You'd never have known. You'd have been happy. You'd have been safe. That's all Scuba wanted.'

Muddy said nothing. He didn't want to think about it again. He'd had that awful feeling of loss in the police cells. He'd had it again on Magna's planet, when the serpent's fangs had plunged into Scuba. He looked up at Magna. 'What are you going to do now?'

'Mourn my sister. Recover.'

Magna walked past the two boys and touched them lightly on the forehead. 'Because thou shalt forget thy misery, and remember it as waters that pass away. And thine age shall be clearer than the noonday: thou shalt shine forth, thou shalt be as the morning. And thou shalt be secure, because there is hope; yea, thou shalt dig about thee, and thou shalt take thy rest in safety. Also thou shalt lie down, and none shall make thee afraid.' She sat on the altar steps, next to the candle that she'd lit for her sister. That's where she'd also placed Little Dog. Magna removed the toy's collar. She began crushing the sparkling lights one by one. 'But the eyes of the wicked shall fail, and they shall not escape, and their hope shall be as the giving up of the ghost.'

'And what will *we* do now?' asked Buggy.

'Mourn your parents. Recover.' Magna caressed the cross that was back around her neck. 'You will also mourn Scuba and forgive her. She died so that you may live. Thanks to her you have a new life, here on Earth. And we will start it as we mean to go on. With the truth. Feel free to speak your minds.'

And so, they sat, ready to speak their minds – two lost boys and the last of the Lupelli. And not one of them spoke a single word.

Buggy was the first to fall asleep.

Watching over them, high up in the wooden church rafters, hidden among the gargoyles and the carvings, was an Angel. She frowned. Her first trip in an Amorphi serpent had been a lot more eventful than she'd expected. She'd been lucky to escape. A movement disturbed her thoughts – something wriggling and jiggling in her damaged fist. She'd forgotten it was there. She stared at it. Frowned again under the weight of heavy decisions. Angel sighed and crushed the tracknid between her small fingers, letting the tiny pieces flip and sway to the church floor. She smoothed the hair of the unconscious girl lying in her lap. The girl's worst wound, the unholy gash on her thigh, was still raw and drooling, but her skinsuit seemed to be working away to fix it. The black material was slowly reforming, closing the rips and repairing the body beneath.

Angel leaned towards the girl's ear and whispered, 'Here's to a fascinating future . . . Crazy 'un.'

Books by this author (so far!):

Shadow Skin

Scratch Planet

About The Author

Well, I'm still just a guy who sticks words on a page hoping that they magically enter your brain and make the real world fade away, for a while at least. Hmmmm . . . *scratchgas* anyone? If you've read my previous book, Shadow Skin, you'll know that I love using the streets, buildings and landmarks of London as settings. The eagle-eyed among you will have noticed that London features in Scratch Planet too! Even though it's a sci-fi space adventure! How did that happen! It wasn't my fault. I blame Scuba. She rolled the dice with that PIP and landed on London. On the plus side, if you do go on a trip to the capital of England, you get to see the sights from two books instead of just one! Bargain.

Thanks so much for picking up Scratch Planet and having a read! I hope you enjoyed it. I'd love to hear who your favourite characters were and whatnot! So, feel free to leave a little review (minus spoilers, of course!). You can also follow my instagram account for book related stuff and random bits and bobs:
davidwatersauthor_ish

Take care and stay safe.

Oh, I forgot to say, both mineself and Angel wish you a *fascinating* future!

Printed in Great Britain
by Amazon

86320319R00171